MW01095039

WHISTLE AT NIGHT
AND
THEY WILL
COME

Also By Alex Soop

Midnight Storm Moonless Sky
Indigenous Horror Stories, Volume 1

INDIGENOUS HORROR STORIES VOLUME 2

WHISTLE AT NIGHT AND THEY WILL COME

ALEX SOOP

FEATURING CARY THOMAS CODY

FOREWORD BY EUGENE BRAVE ROCK

DURVILE &
UpRoute Books

Calgary, Alberta, Canada

DURVILE.COM

**DURVILE &
UpRoute Books**

UpRoute Imprint of Durvile Publications Ltd.
Calgary, Alberta, Canada
www.durvile.com

Copyright © 2023 Alex Soop

Library and Archives Cataloging in Publications Data

WHISTLE AT NIGHT AND THEY WILL COME
INDIGENOUS HORROR STORIES, VOLUME II

Soop, Alex; Author

1. First Nations | 2. Blackfoot | 3. Indigenous | 4. Supernatural | 5. Paranormal

The UpRoute "Spirit of Nature" Series
A "Tales of the Dark" Title

Series Editors, Raymond Yakeleya and Lorene Shyba
Issued in print and electronic formats
ISBN: 978-1-990735-30-1 (pbk); 978-1-990735-32-5 (e-pub)
978-1-990735-31-8 (audiobook)

Front cover design, Austin Andrews | Book design, Lorene Shyba.
Photos of Alex Soop, back cover and throughout, Dima Gulpa.
Photo of Cary Thomas Cody, Mikey Hevr.
Illustrations by Alex Soop generated in part by AI.

Durvile Publications recognizes the land upon which our studios are located.
We extend gratitude to the Indigenous Peoples of Southern Alberta, which include the
Siksika, Piikani, and Kainai of the Niisitapi Blackfoot Confederacy; the Dene Tsuut'ina;
the Chiniki, Bearspaw, and Wesley Stoney Nakoda First Nations.
We also acknowledge the Region 3 Métis Nation of Alberta.

Durvile Publications acknowledges financial support for book development and production
from the Government of Canada through Canadian Heritage, Canada Book Fund
and the Government of Alberta, Alberta Media Fund.

Printed and bound in Canada. First Printing. 2023.
All rights reserved. Contact Durvile Publications Ltd. for details.

This book contains violence and
supernatural elements including ghosts, demons, and other
paranormal entities that may be frightening to some readers.

For Karly and Barry "Pops"

ACKNOWLEDGEMENTS

I am deeply honoured to have Eugene Brave Rock and Cary Thomas Cody join me as storytellers and supporters in "Whistle at Night." Working with you both has been a tremendous privilege, and I hope we can collaborate again in the future.

To the love of my life, Mary-Grace Pableo, your love and unwavering support since the beginning of our journey together mean the world to me. You are my rock. I also want to acknowledge my mother, Crystal Many Fingers, and my sister Patricia Soop, who have been my steadfast pillars of support. Sadly, we lost my stepfather, Barry (Pops), this year. He was a true father figure in my life, and may he rest in peace.

A heartfelt thank you goes out to my publisher and editors, Lorene Shyba and Raymond Yakeleya at Durvile & UpRoute Books, for their tireless dedication to perfecting my manuscripts. Your support and the opportunities you've given me will never be forgotten.

I express my heartfelt gratitude to the Creator for the gift of life and for surrounding me with wonderful people who have been a source of encouragement. I'm grateful to the many friends and family members who have read my earlier works and encouraged me to keep going. To my very first fans, you hold a special place in my heart. Thank you to everyone who has ever shared kind words about my writing. Your support means the world to me.

CONTENTS

EUGENE BRAVE ROCK

EUGENE BRAVE ROCK

OUR STORIES AND
THE SUPERNATURAL

I AM WRITING this foreword to support Alex's talent and promote Indigenous storytelling. Like Alex, I am from the Blood Reserve, Kainai Nation, which is part of the Blackfoot Confederacy of Southern Alberta. I was raised by my grandmother, Florence Brave Rock, and spent time around the Elders with their storytelling, language, and respect for the Creator. Among their stories were tales of the Creator and the trickster, Napi. The Elders taught that each of us embodies Napi within.

I am working hard to preserve the Niisitapi Blackfoot language so we can educate our People, and a big part of that is the telling of stories. In addition to that, I am an actor and a stuntman and I feel that being an actor is the oldest way of expressing our traditions by sharing and connecting with others. I have a big platform to share our culture as Native American and I am very grateful and proud to have that connection and influence as a way of celebrating our land.

Indigenous stories and the supernatural go hand in hand. Our Indigenous stories are based around the supernatural. I've heard stories from Elders that are unimaginable; like superhero movies where you walk without obstacles. In Alex's writing, he shows that various tribes have their own unique mythologies. Common among them is they have big fear factors, but also important lessons to be learned.

In English, our stories are known as myth, fairytale, or legend. In our language, they are truth. I had the privilege lately of listening to a 94-year-old Elder telling a story in our language and it took me to a place where I could feel the temperature and the dampness of the cave, and the tastes and textures in the story. That's how powerful it was ... and is.

There are comparisons between Alex as a writer and me as an actor. We are both living the stories and making decision on the fly so we can go in any direction at any time. In his writing style I have seen Alex pick and choose the foreshadowing and consequences in his stories and for me, as an actor, the stories of the Elders have empowered me to become who I am and to show that we are still here and to be proud of who we are.

One of these days I can see myself working with Alex to make a short or feature film out of one of his stories. In Indigenous filmmaking, there are writers' rooms opening up so that's where I see Alex going. Things are just going to get better, and better, and better. We are in an amazing time and an amazing space and I don't think our meeting was coincidence. I've heard Alex say that one of his proudest moments was watching my performance in *Wonderwoman* and he said to me that he thought, "Hey, that's our language he's speaking... in Hollywood!" By bringing a demigod, 'The Chief', back to life in that movie, I opened up our culture to the world, and I am proud that Alex found this meaningful.

My advice for Indigenous youth who want to pursue being creative in life is to connect with your inner selves to find what makes you happy and what makes you sad. You can learn your lessons and take them as blessings and keep your story going. My journey so far has taken me a lot of different places and I find this travel is creating who I am becoming to be. So, my advice is to live, learn, and travel.

In my life, when I was furthest from home is when I found out the most about myself as Niisitapi. There were times when all I had were my prayers. Experience is wisdom, so get out there and get it. I'm from Standoff, Alberta. If I can do it, anybody can.

—*Eugene Brave Rock, 2023*

MY FIRST ENCOUNTER
WITH THE PARANORMAL

W HEN MY FIRST BOOK, *Midnight Storm Moonless Sky*, came out, I answered readers' questions many times about how I came to be interested in horror and the paranormal. For everyone still wondering, perhaps those who didn't meet me in person or on Facebook, here is the backstory to my fascination.

I went through most of elementary and junior high school off the reserve. So, one year after graduating from grade 9, I decided to take the whole summer and go visit my grandparents on the Blood Reserve. I immediately made new friends and became close again with old friends I hadn't seen much since my early childhood days.

Where my grandparents lived was near one of the reserve's two old residential schools, St. Paul's. This old school, built in 1924, had been renovated and now sat as an affordable apartment complex for people on the reserve. Some of my new friends lived in that complex, which they still called St. Paul's.

One night we all decided to have a few drinks and light a bonfire near the forest that was adjacent to the complex. That summer had been very rainy, but on this night, it was nice and warm out—a perfect time to gather and visit while sitting around a bonfire with old and new friends. Someone brought their battery-powered boombox, and some carried a beer or two each under their jackets. It wasn't long into the night when things got loud. That's what happens at parties involving a squad of teenagers. Before long, to no surprise, one of the apartment building's concerned and angry residents called the police.

I was the first to notice their arrival, as I hadn't bothered to indulge too much in the drink. "Guys, look!" I screamed out loud enough to overpower the booming music. "Shit, it's the cops," belted out one of the girls, Brittany or Paige, I believe. Someone shut off the boombox and all that could be heard was the crackling fire and some distant chirps of the nocturnal insects.

We all did our part to put out the fire using whatever was at our disposal—mostly kicking rocks and dirt from prairie earth that was mounded up around us. In less than two minutes, the fire was down to embers, but two of the guys decided to douse it some more.

"Alright, girls," said Jack, followed by his brother Melvin and our buddy Cam. They stepped up to the fire and began discharging their night's worth of fire water and beer. The three girls laughed and jeered, and I did too.

Then it was time to run. The bright LED police lights carved through the thick foliage, giving us a heads up to get the heck out of there. We split up, heading our own ways. I took off to where I knew the cops would have the most trouble reaching me.

I bolted through the dense forest, ducking overhangs of branches and thick vegetation. I grew up in this area so I knew I was in the safe zone when I reached the barbed wire which sliced through the forest. I ducked low as I heard an unfamiliar voice not even forty feet away. A bright flashlight beamed out in my direction, forcing me to my knees, and then to my stomach. I belly-crawled under the barbed wire, tearing my shirt in the process. At least I was safe and away from the handcuffs that were probably awaiting me. Having a fire in the middle of the trees and, of course, underage drinking, were both big no-nos.

There was an old gravel road that led to a possible escape up and over the disused train tracks, but I had a feeling there would be cops hiding there, waiting. So, I scrambled along the ditch instead, which was covered with enough waist-high grass for me to duck down and take cover. Under the pale crescent moon, there was barely light enough for me to see my hands right in front of my face and the dark jumble of trees off to my right. I side-eyed the blackness and it frightened me so I stopped; the only sound was my nervous breathing. Even the bug chirps hushed. I felt as though there were unseen eyes staring down at me—and not of the police or my friends. Who could be there?

A shiver dove through me. I had to get back to my friends. I knew that over where the trees ended, there was a small, man-made dirt road which skirted the forest and ended up at an old baseball diamond. I broke into a dash, my footfalls muffled by the soft ground. In no time I was able to reach the baseball field. I crossed it and headed towards the disused gym building, which sat directly behind the St. Paul's apartment complex. I thought some of the squad might be hiding in or around the gym.

I looked both ways. Clear. It was now or never. I stormed across the gravel road, which divided the apartment grounds from the old gym area, and headed for the dark awning of the gym entrance. I took another glance. Still no police. So, I skulked back towards my home, thinking that everyone else had taken off for good.

Then I saw him; my good buddy Cameron who, like me, had split off from the others. He stood stock-still, near the back of the gym, close to the entrance to the boiler room.

"Yo, Cam," I whispered harshly, stepping closer to him.

He remained quiet, putting his index finger near his face to shush me. "Quiet, bro. Listen. Can you hear that?"

I held my breath and listened intently. Then, when I heard it, my arms popped up in gooseflesh, the tiny hairs on my neck and forearms electrifying and standing on end.

A whimper ... just the slightest whimper of a little girl. It came from somewhere in that dark and dirty boiler-room in the cellar. Due to the rainy summer, I knew for a fact that the boiler room was flooded with at least a foot of water.

"What the heck is that?" I asked. But before Cam answered, the bright lights of an incoming vehicle hit us. We were busted like two deer caught in the headlights—police headlights.

I snatched Cameron by the shirt sleeve, and we dashed into another cluster of tightly packed trees, leaving the police and crying girl behind.

Of course, I made it safely home that night. But I couldn't catch a wink of sleep. I could only lie there under my blankets, wondering: "Who was that crying in that old abandoned boiler room?"

• • • •

When I was a kid, my grandmother and other Blackfoot Elders warned us kids about things that might harm us, including the taboos of whistling at night. When I asked them why whistling is taboo, I remember being told, "They will come." I was afraid to ask who 'they' might be, but to this day, I suspect they meant the 'spirits'.

There are other First Nations Peoples who warn against

whistling in the night too. The Inuit, for example, hold a belief that if you whistle at the sky during the Northern Lights the aurora borealis might descend to size you. The Ktunaxa Nation of British Columbia have concerns about whistling at night too saying that, "Something's going to get you because they'll know you're there."

The taboo of whistling at night played a big role in instilling fear that served as inspiration for my stories in this book. Just like Eugene Brave Rock says in his foreword, the Elders sharing their stories hold tremendous power. I trust that these stories will indeed evoke a sense of fright in you, or at least of spirits awakening.

—*Alex Soop, 2023*

PART I
SHORT STORIES
BY
ALEX SOOP

PHOTO: DIMA GULPA

~ ONE ~

IT COMES AT NIGHT

"I WIN AGAIN," Mark crowed with bravado, slamming his hand of cards down onto the glass table, causing the coffee cups resting there to clatter and vibrate. "Full house, baby!"

"Damn it man, ya got me again," Tommy groaned. "Where the deuce did you learn to play poker so good anyhow?"

Mark gathered the table full of poker chips as if he were embracing a phantom bear, his shoulders lifting in a shrug. "My great-gramma, dude."

"Wow. You have one cool gramma," Tommy sighed.

"Great-gramma. And yeah, she learned to play during her stint in the army air corps, way back in her day. After getting damaged airplanes back up into the sky, she had nothing to do but play cards, so she'd play with her brothers and sisters in arms, you know, while the fighter planes and bombers were off on missions."

"Air Force too, huh? Damn man, can she get any cooler than that?" Tommy said before taking a long swig of his warm soda, emptying the cup.

9

"Army Air Corps," Mark corrected. "Hey, what time is it? It's getting late." He glanced out the boxy window where a blur of blue-black darkness was visible.

Tommy said, glancing at his watch "Just past nine now."

"Oh shit," Mark shouted. I promised great-gramma I'd be home at nine. Look I better be hittin' the road—like twenty minutes ago. Can we put this game on hold until tomorrow?"

Tommy stretched his arms and yawned, his body feeling the oncoming touch of grogginess. "Yeah, no worries. Just leave the chips where they are. No one ever comes down here for anything but to do laundry, anyways."

"Alright, thanks brotha. I'll for sure be back tomorrow. Let's say sometime after lunchtime?" Mark stood up and started gathering up his coat and backpack from a heap on the floor. Tommy joined him.

"Sounds good," said Tommy. "Can ya bring over some of your great-gramma's frybread? I like that extra secret ingredient she adds to it."

"Yeah, of course," replied Mark. "Walk me upstairs?"

"After you," said Tommy with a hand gesture and bow.

Tommy started following Mark up the steep, linoleum-covered stairwell. Before hitting the light switch, he felt a shudder, like a brief chill coursing through him. Tommy took a probing look down the steep stairwell and exhaled deeply before flicking the light switch, causing the basement to once again become a black abyss. It stopped him in his tracks.

A memory flashed of the taunting laughter of his older cousins, cruel jesters in his personal nightmare. Six years old and bullied, they had imprisoned him here, twisting out the light bulbs like a cruel punchline. No matter how many switches he'd flipped, the basement remained in darkness, a cave of his childhood horrors. And then, the sound. That ghastly, serpentine slither, a monstrous creature navigating the concrete expanse. It slunk and paused, a beast at the threshold, its energy radiating upwards, step by linoleum-covered step. Tommy's mind had teetered on the edge of madness, terror flooding his senses.

His mother recalled that his muffled shriek from the basement stairwell was enough to make her own hairs stand on end. The two cousins, Darwin and Darnell, were never welcome at his house again after that incident.

"You coming or what, Geronimo?" shouted Mark from the top of the stairs. Mark had given Tommy the nickname, Geronimo as kids and couldn't remember the exact reason why.

Tommy whipped his head around and faced Mark, snapping back from his momentary daydream. "Oh, yeah. Sorry I was just thinking about—"

"—about that time those pricks locked you down here. Yeah, bro, so not cool. Your two asshole cousins? They're good-for-nothing bullies."

"Yeah, but that idiot therapist told me it was just my imagination. Geeze. No one ever really believes kids when we see a clown smiling under the bed; or the boogeyman peeking out from the closet. Do they. Or the shadow man wandering by the mirror. Right? "

Tommy turned and said to Mark, "Come on let's get you going. Don't wanna keep your grams waiting too long now."

Mark replied, "Indeed brotha, indeed."

• • • •

The sound of Mark's bike tires rolling through the loose gravel bounced through the stagnant night air. He dearly wished he had asked Tommy for a flashlight, or better yet, wished he hadn't dropped his own on the way to Tommy's.

The desert flats all around him were dark like an unmoving ocean at night. Only the faint glimmer of the fading twilight danced in the far distance above the tops of the large mesas, making them look like interval sets of enormous teeth. The long strip of narrow gravel road before him glowed dimly extending through the surrounding dark of the cold desert.

He had taken this route many times, and it wouldn't be so scary if it wasn't for the danger of the odd roaming rattle snake and coyote packs. But at least the coyotes easily proclaimed themselves with their constant yelps and whines. Coyotes weren't sneaky and cunning like wolves at least. There were barely any wolves around these parts. And at least he wasn't on foot.

Mark's house was only a few miles from Tommy's, an easy ride with his brand-new mountain bike he had received for his birthday from his favourite uncle. The ride was smooth going over the tops of the rough and loose gravel Rez roads. The 18-speed gears made it all the better when he had to ride up and down through the dips.

A chill picked up. It wasn't a wind, or even a breeze. It bit at the exposed skin on Mark's arms and neck like he had ridden right through an invisible barrier of frost. Desert nights were known to be cold, but this was different. It had a smothering feel to it.

His roaming thoughts stopped suddenly when he saw a glimmer. No, two glimmers. Eyes. Canine eyes, not even fifty feet ahead of him, standing directly before him on this dirt road path.

Mark squeezed the break lever placed in front of his knuckles and the bike immediately came to a long skidding stop on the gravel road.

"Nice doggie," he whispered hoping, just hoping, that the hound was one of the reservation's many night-roaming mutts.

And then the worst happened. The patter of paws, light but steady, accompanied by a deep snarl intruded upon the night's silence, the gravel crunching beneath the animal's relentless advance. Mark fumbled to drop his pack so that he could grab a weapon—any kind of a weapon. And he had just the thing. His faithful pocketknife, the blade just long enough to do some damage and maybe give him a head start on making it home alive and unscathed. The backpack slithered free from his grip. Cold sweat pierced his nerves, his pulse a wild drumbeat that seemed poised to explode from his chest. Instinct screamed at him to crumple to the ground, arms raised in a futile defence, like a limbless ventriloquist dummy.

A hoarse burst of air rushed from the pit of his lungs and he whistled through his lips as he hit the ground. Luckily, his backpack took the brunt of the fall. He tried to roll onto his side and anticipate which side the big canine would attack from.

But no mauling happened. Mark whipped his head back and forth, his eyes x-raying the darkness. His ears, on full radar mode, scanned for sounds, but there was nothing. Only absolute silence; the sound of a death which was being put on hold—for now.

As if the danger was still inevitable, and it was, Mark forced himself to his feet. The crunch of gravel beneath his feet was his worst enemy as it gave his position away.

Mark made an attempt to climb back onto his bike but he felt a stare. He snapped his head to the side, his eyes, which were now accustomed to the dark, pinpointed the figure of the wilderness-born canine. But at that moment something had him feeling okay — the size of the animal made it clear it was not a wolf.

"You stupid, dumbass," Mark said to himself. "Stop over-reacting." He hunched low and patted his kneecaps, whistling at the dog. He thought whistling would be the friendliest way to summon a dog, whether it is your own or belongs to someone else. But the animal did not move toward him. Although he could not see its retreating figure, Mark could hear the soft sounds of paws dashing in the opposite direction. He whistled again.

"Fine, suit yourself," Mark said with a half titter, still feeling the tremor of cold slapping his body. He removed his backpack and unzipped it. "Ah yes. I knew this would come in handy." He rummaged through his bag for his tightly packed windbreaker jacket. He threw on the jacket, zipped up the bag and sped down the gravel road.

A wet drop. Followed by another. In mere minutes the drizzle of rain had turned into a steady downpour. Mark wasn't deterred though. He loved rain, and Arizona didn't see a whole lot of it, especially during the summer months.

He upped his pedalling pace, and raced through the rain as it pelted him hard in the face. He knew which road to take by the lone mesa silhouette in the far distance, standing tall against the backdrop of storm clouds.

In due time he arrived home. His windbreaker was soaked. He hopped off his bike and leaned it against the bare concrete foundation wall of his garage.

"Hello ... Gramma ... I'm home. Sorry I'm late, but we lost track of time because I was beating Tommy at cards." He stood motionless in the porch vestibule and listened. Nothing. He kicked off his muddy shoes and removed his wet socks, then tiptoed his way up the carpet-covered steps. If great-gramma was already sleeping, then he preferred to not wake her.

"There you are," said great-gramma Josephine and she slowly appeared in the upper porch area through the darkened hallway arch.

Gramma Josephine's sudden appearance sent Mark's

heart into a frenzied gallop. Nearly toppling back down stairs, he flailed and clutched at the wooden banister. "Holy, heck gramma. You scared the bajesus out of me."

"Now, now. What did I tell you about that blasphemy in my house?" teased Josephine.

"Umm..." He vaguely tried to remember when his great-grandmother had scolded him about blasphemy. He couldn't recall. She wasn't really the churchgoing type. "Not to use it?" he blurted out.

"That's right. Now come, give me a hug. I've missed you."

He pulled himself up to the landing and entered his grandmother's embrace. "How about some soup and poker after?" Mark suggested, gingerly pulling away from her grip, his eyes scanning her face for approval.

Josephine let go of her tight embrace on Mark and padded across the kitchen and into the small dining room. "Sure, soup, then cards," she said. Even at the ripe old age of eighty, Gramma Josephine moved like a fox on the run and the soup was heated to perfection in no time at all

"Okay, just let me go get changed out of these soaking wet clothes. It's pouring out there." Before Josephine could reply, he was already jetting down to the basement where his room was situated.

Gramma Josephine had moved in with Mark and his family not long after great-grandpa went to be with Creator. Mark's father had detested the idea at first, but his mother put her foot down, and hard. Mark's father had no choice but to give in—and even grew to become fond of great-gramma, often sitting with her to hear of her life's exploits. Mark had been close with family Elders since his childhood days, so he was excited at the news of his great-grandmother moving in.

Mark was enrolled at a local junior high school in the town of Ash Fork. It was there where he told his good friend, Lance, the good news of his gramma moving in. "Moving in? With you? Good luck with that bud," Lance had said with a scoff. Mark always wondered why so many of his non-Indigenous friends had viewed their grandparents as nuisances. Why? He would never know—and didn't really care to know.

On his way back up to join his great-gramma, Mark went outside to stand beneath the small porch awning. He gazed at the falling rain in awe. It reminded him of the time he went to Louisiana for a school trip. A small, swift stream had already formed and was coursing by the illuminated concrete porch stoop. He imagined that it was the mighty Mississippi river after a fresh Louisiana rainfall.

"Are you coming back in, or what?" hollered Josephine.

Mark jumped at his gramma's creep-up, and nearly went careening off the porch into the small stream "Holy. That's twice now, gramma," he snickered uncomfortably. "How'd you get down here so fast and quiet?"

"Oh, your gramma still has it in her. You'd be surprised, my dear boy. Now come on, there's soup then let's get to our game already."

"After you," said Mark holding the screen door open.

• • • •

Poker lasted deep into the night, past the stroke of midnight—Texas hold'em and five card stud. The storm showed no sign of relenting, and the rain was falling even harder, drumming an eerie beat against the shell of the house. Bold thunder was followed by brash streaks of lightning that lit up the water-teeming, skies and illuminated the living room like a camera flash.

"Wow," laughed Mark, "That one was huge." He glanced up at his gramma from his hand of cards. She was smiling like he had never seen her do before. She was smiling and staring right through him so hard that he had to turn his head around to see if there was anything behind him. "What is it?" he asked.

"Ready to throw down your hand?" Josephine asked bluntly.

"Alright, then. Here I have a—whoa. What the heck was that?" He stopped and placed his cards face down and slid out of his chair to take a look at the blackness settled beyond the living room window.

"What is it?" asked Josephine, staring hard at her hand of cards, although her attention was far away.

"I thought I saw a form, like a person walking by the living room window," Mark said as he glided across the slippery dining room floor towards the faintly lit living room.

"Are you expecting anyone?" asked Josephine, eyes now watching her great grandson.

"Not in this weather. And definitely not this late, no way no how," answered Mark.

"Could have just been a Rez mutt. You know how they like to roam around in packs looking for scraps of food," conjectured Josephine.

"Naw, too big for that. It was definitely person-sized." Mark cautiously paced into the living room and slowly slid down the dimmer light switch. The living room gradually slipped into darkness like a sunset disappearing beyond a mountainous horizon.

Josephine placed her own cards down and pivoted her body in her chair. "What are you doing, my boy?" she asked.

Mark put his hand in the air in a signal to quiet Josephine. "Do we have any flashlights kicking around?" he asked in a loud whisper.

"Try the junk drawer."

Mark slowly backed out of the living room until his sock feet slid out from under him on the waxed kitchen linoleum. He regained his footing and dashed for the kitchen island counter. With full force, he pulled out the junk drawer and immediately got to work combing through the drawer full of odds and ends.

"There's nothing in here—wait I know." He closed the drawer with a slam and slid across the kitchen. "Where mom usually hides them in case of emergencies." He opened and reached for the top shelf of the old, handcrafted cupboard. He groped around for a few seconds before retracting his hands, two small, silver flashlights tightly in his grasp.

Josephine, now peering from behind him, observed curiously. "Okay, you've found them. Now what?"

"I know I saw something. I'm gonna go to the window and just have me a quick look with these. If there's anyone out there sneaking around, then I'm gonna catch them by surprise." There was something out there, he was sure of it.

Mark wasted no time. Again he dashed across the large living room floor, his hurried foot stomps muffled by the thickness of the shag carpet. He took a knee in front of the outward protruding, convex-shaped windowsill and peered out into the darkness.

Meanwhile, Josephine's movements echoed softly through the house. "You want something to drink?" Her voice floated in from the distance, a reminder of the mundane world beyond Mark's anxious vigil.

Mark crouched in the darkness of the living room clutching the powered-down flashlights in either hand. He squinted his eyes to see if he could catch any more movement in the dark stillness of the night.

A sudden movement. Like a person dashing for cover behind the trimmed hedges.

"There." Mark flicked the flashlights on with the click of rubber buttons. The flashlights' bright LED beams swept across the front yard like an ocean wave, lighting the outside with the intensity of a blue rayed sun.

"Well, see anything, my boy?" asked Josephine with no real hints of concern in her voice.

Mark remained calm and unspeaking as he examined the front yard with the two flashlights. He saw it again. For sure this time as his eyes caught the obvious movement of a body moving behind the planted hedgerows. He kept the flashlight beams centred on the movement, following it until the person seemed to dash for the front porch.

"Whoever it is, they're now at the porch step. Maybe it's Tommy. He likes to play games." Mark got to his feet and calmly strolled for the porch, leaving the powered-up flashlights resting on the windowsill.

Josephine watched Mark with probing eyes from behind the dining room table.

"I'll be right back, then we can get back to our game. Okay, Gramma?"

Josephine only nodded and continued taking small sips from her steaming cup of tea.

Mark descended the slippery stairs, two steps at a time until he hopped the final three and landed with a loud bang which rattled the light fixtures.

"I heard that," yelled Josephine from up the stairs.

"Sorry Gramma," said Mark, wincing. He flicked on the front porch light, but to no avail. "Shit, I bet I broke the switch again. Ah well, I'll fix it tomorrow." He swiped at the front door's almost transparent window blind for a better look but saw nothing.

He was about to reach for the doorknob when a sense of danger flooded his senses. He stopped immediately, pulling his hand to his side. From the dim light of the upper kitchen shedding down the stairwell, he knew it wasn't Tommy standing at the door.

The silhouette was shorter and stockier than Tommy, with what looked like a head of rain-drenched, dishevelled hair. The figure raised its arms in the air and brought them down on the door. Hard.

BANG BANG BANG! The forceful pounding on the steel door reverberated through the air like a thunderous drumbeat. It was soon accompanied by chilling screams, their terror muffled by the door's formidable thickness, almost lost amidst the raging storm outside. Mark's heart jolted as he involuntarily flinched, his body tensing with alarm. He hastily retreated, his steps quick and unsteady, until the balls of his feet made contact with the base of the first step. He fell onto his elbows, ignoring the burning sense ripping through his arms.

"Well, who do we have?" said Josephine, standing at the top landing.

"No one, Gramma."

"Didn't sound like no one to me. Was that a crack on the door I just heard?"

He couldn't lie twice to his dear great-gramma. He twisted his head and spoke sideways. "Someone's out there, Gramma. But I don't know who it is—and I think they want to come in."

Seeing the fear playing through her grandson's face, Josephine placed her mug of tea on the floor and began her downward climb. Mark watched as his gramma disregarded the hand railing—which she had always needed for the last ten years or so. Plastered on her wrinkled face was a true expression of a lady warrior. There was something about that face, something he'd never seen. Ever.

"What you gonna do, Gramma?" he asked politely, pushing himself to his feet. He remained still, watching with utter curiosity as his Gramma reached the main floor landing and moved towards the closed door.

"Let's have a look now, shall we?" she said, reaching out to unlock the door.

But then Mark pounced, landing his hands on his grandmother's forearms before she had a chance to go for the doorknob. "Wait," he cried out. "Let's have a better look." He then pulled out one of the flashlights from his pocket and snapped the power on, moving to the side window and aiming the LCD beam on the intruder standing behind the closed door.

His mouth dropped open at the sight. A gasping whimper croaked from his mouth as he dropped the flashlight and lurched backwards.

"What is it?" questioned Josephine.

Mark's gaze extended beyond her, a vacant stare gradually consuming his features as he muttered, his voice a symphony of terror. "She has—its you, Gramma. But how can that b—"

"What the hell are you talking about?" she snapped, whipping her head abruptly as she swiped at the curtain to peer outside. Just as she moved the white sheer, a burst of lightning ignited the entire landscape like a split-second nuclear holocaust. For that flash of time, a woman standing outside was as clear as day, a deadly looking knife in her shaking hands that gleamed to match the look on her face.

As the thunder boomed out Mark cried, "See, it's you, Gramma. But how ... can that be?"

Josephine remained silent, caught in a trance, locked in a confrontation with the unfathomable. She remained motionless, staring hard at the impossible manifestation that was herself, standing on the outside, straining to get into the house and do god knows what to Mark and herself.

"Gramma," Mark's voice quavered as he hesitated, his

feet inching towards the door. "We need to call the cops or something, right now—"

"But why would you want do that?" Josephine hissed, her voice transforming, growing strange. Then the inconceivable unfolded into the impossible. Gramma's body expanded, her hunched form stretching, contorting into the proportions of a robust grown man. Slowly, inexorably, her features flickered, like a malfunctioning projection, shifting from the benign familiarity of a cherished grandmother to the visage of a demon from the abyss. Her braids remained, an eerie constant in her transformation, but her face twisted into a grotesque mask. The wrinkles, once familiar, morphed into monstrous snarls as her mouth contorted around rows of corroded, razor-like teeth.

"Now you shall die," she roared but as she readied herself to pounce like a feral rat, an abrupt sound of smashing glass interrupted the moment. The demonic entity's scream erupted from her—a wail like the howl of a wolf ensnared in a bear trap.

"Run!" yelled the real Josephine through the howls and heavy sounds of rain. Her fingers scrambled, seeking the doorknob, an urgency that ignored the bite of jagged glass still lurking in the window frame, drawing crimson lines across her bare arm.

Mark was ready to bound up the stairs when he was struck by a sudden notion. He dared not let his great-grandmother fight off the ungodly creature alone. Heart hammering against his eardrums, he took his one and only chance, his fingers wrapping around the largest shard of glass. He thrust it towards the creature's exposed ribcage, a gamble driven by raw instinct. A howl rung through the air.

"I told you to run, boy," hollered Josephine, her body now standing in the open doorway. She brought a shotgun up and shot from the hip. Mark ducked down low. The blast reverberated through the house as the monstrosity crumpled to the ground, squirming in its own pooling blood.

Mark couldn't believe his eyes, watching in horror just as Josephine brushed past him, her hand hooking his elbow and yanking him with her. "Come on. It won't stay dead." Mark turned to face her. "What do you mean? It's been stabbed two times and shot point-blank with a shotgun."

They reached the top of the stairs safely, Josephine taking up a defensive position, aiming the double-barrelled shotgun at the creature as it began to slowly stir.

"I told you, my boy. Now go, get on the phone and call Police Chief Todacheenie."

Mark did as he was told, dashing across the kitchen to grab the cordless phone. He was less than a minute, returning while put on hold by the local constable. "Here, Gramma," he said handing her the phone. "They put us on hold while—"

He stopped speaking, his attention given to the emptiness of the porch, the door wide open and thunder roaring off into the horizon.

"Where did it go?" he asked.

Gramma Josephine didn't bother turning to face him, her eyes steady on the gleaming barrels still pointing at the specks of blood on the porch floor. "It's gone," she said boldly. "But it ain't dead. Not tonight."

"Gramma," Mark said, tugging on the loose end of Josephine's soaking wet shawl. "Was that—"

"Yes, it was, my dear. Yes, it was." She at last turned her head, her lady warrior eyes swimming in dismay.

Mark felt his legs go weak as he fell to his knees. He knew better than to speak the creature's real name. But he thought it. Over and over, like a grotesque song on repeat. Skinwalker.

~ TWO ~

RISING SUN

I AM JUST ABOUT TO GET on my phone and grill my brother, when he unexpectedly calls at the very moment my fingers grasp the screaming smartphone resting in my cup holder. I shudder as my mind is lost in a roll of angered thoughts. "Speak of the fuckin' devil," I say under my breath. I hit the answer button on my flashing phone. "Yo, dude," then, without waiting for him to answer, "Your buddy lied to me man. That son of a bitch, he—"

"Hey man, what's up?" answers my brother's buddy Darrel, unmoved it seems, by the string of cuss words I had directed against him. I'm briefly caught off guard by Darrel's unexpected call from my brother's phone, but ultimately, Darrel is the guy I need to talk to anyway.

"Hey," I reply in a calm, slightly sheepish manner. "I uhh—I think I'm lost, dude."

"Did you bring an old map like I told you? Like old, old?" he asks, his voice coming out all aged and crackly like we are corresponding through old World War II style comms radios.

"I'm talking, like, 1970's to the early '80's old, man. The kind of stuff before personal computers and Google maps were even dreamed of—"

"Yeah, I managed to get my hands on an old map. But what's that gonna do, though? I've got a state-of-the-art GPS installed in my car."

"That won't do, man. Not at all," Darrel asserts. "This place is old, like, the government not putting it in their electronic database anymore old. And I'm pretty sure there's other reasonings behind it too. So, what I want you to do is pull over right now, break out the old map and pinpoint that part of New Mexico, exactly where you should be right about now. Call us back when you do it, cool?"

I'm skeptical but I sigh and say, "Okay, fine. Call you back in a minute or so." I tap the hang up button and flicker my headlights to make sure they're still on the bright beams. They are indeed, but the illumination only spreads through the flat and endless desert terrain like I was holding a cheap flashlight while riding a bicycle in the prairie flats at night. After a few miles of wasteland cruising, I am able to safely take a sharp right into a small roadside turnout. I pick up the old map, water-stained and musty from years of neglect, and identify my exact location, remembering the last destination my trusty GPS read to me.

I find it. The old road is nothing but an old squiggly line next to the main road markers.

I glance up and take in the desert dust, still lingering like frail ghosts. The dust enshrouds my headlight illumination like a gas attack as I sit and scroll through my recent cellphone calls. Darrel finally picks up after four rings. "Yo," he says in a way that further irritates my shabby mood.

"Okay, gimme the details," I demand.

The line goes dead silent like he has hung up on me, until I hear the crunchy rattling of stiff papers. "Okay, I found it," he says, his breath ragged like he is just as excited as me. "What's your location right now?"

"I am on the 380 about halfway between the towns of San Antonio and Bingham. I—"

"Perfect. Look for an old sign marker that says, 'Rising Sun Hotel.' It'll be the only one standing in the area by a longshot. Once you come across it, take a turn going northbound. You'll travel about ten miles through almost nothing but plain old desert, and then you'll see it. Right there, and boom, you're there. Won't be hard to miss, man. If you get lost, just call us back. Hope you see her." He hangs up before I can either thank him or scold him.

My destination in mind is just where Buddy said it would be. I take the only gravel turnoff past a dilapidated road sign marker half buried in sand and weathered to near nothing that reads, 'Rising Sun Hotel,' in old, non-reflective letters that are nearly falling off the antique sign. The bumpy drive runs through an ancient road filled with potholes and small debris from years of desert windstorms and neglect. At last, I see it looming beyond the range of my headlights—a tall, neon sign brightly lit, its radiance spraying over a small hamlet of buildings. I pull into the gas bar and general store first. No dice.

"Must close early," I say to myself, slowing my speed as I coast past the gas pumps that look like they haven't been used in years, crimson rust draped over the metal like a person with a bad skin disease.

The hotel is the next building over. Three-tiered with something like minarets on the roof. Some of the chamber doors line the outer perimeter like an old-style jailhouse.

At least I'm not the only patron at this old hotel that lies smack in the middle of nowhere. There are four more vehicles: an SUV, a jacked-up pickup, and two older model sports cars that still look as though they're able to do damage in a street race. Beyond the four vehicle is an arrangement of about twenty motorcycles lined up in perfect order.

A darkened area of the lot is a more suitable place to park, out of the limelight and therefore less susceptible to being broken into. Bikers usually mean crime sprees. I pull in behind a dumpster, endowed with the same bouquet of rust.

I shut off my engine and wait, taking a second to gather myself before entering this strange property. By the sounds of the lively music pouring out from the open windows of the hotel's attached bar, there are a plenty more patrons inside than the four cars and motorcycles declare.

I skip the bar's rough-looking, bouncer-free entrance and head inside through the motel's lobby entrance doors. Couldn't be more of an eerie omen, I think to myself as Hotel California plays through an old radio located in the waiting area.

"Good evening, sir," says a polite gentleman standing behind the reception desk as his eyes scan a fat 1990's computer monitor. "Late night, isn't it?" A British accent. Way out here in the middle of the American wasteland.

"Uhh, yeah. It is. But I'm supposed to be meeting someone here."

The well-mannered counter clerk lifts his regard from the old-fashioned screen the size of an old tube television, and eyes me carefully. "I assume that you're not from around here. Am I quite right about that?" he asks in a cheery way.

"You can tell?"

"Well actually, nobody who steps through those doors is from around here. But hey, that's why I found it all the better to open this motel. Looking to check into a room for the night?" he asks, as he steps away from the computer screen and waddles alongside his side of the desk, organizing scattered papers and shooing away dust build up with his baggy blazer sleeve.

I don't have to think for a moment. Even after meeting up with my special someone, I wasn't planning on driving the four-hour journey all the way back home in the middle of the night. "Yes, please."

The motel owner takes up position back behind the computer and waits patiently for me to approach. I rummage through my jean's back pocket and pull out my wallet.

"How much for one night?"

"Fifty-two dollars exactly," he says.

"Wow. Cheap."

"The cheapest," he asserts, winking at me. "I opened up this place with strong intentions of keeping the weary traveller happy."

And that I am, with this price.

"And indeed, you have," I say.

"As well, sir, if you are not tired just yet, you are more than welcome to treat yourself to a nightcap in the open-late, ye olde saloon," says the clerk as he hands me the keys, his devilish smile not waning once throughout our brief engagement.

The guestroom locks are old fashioned. A key is the only way into my room rather than the modern, magnetized card reader. I shove the heavy door open with the tip of my shoes, and I am slammed with the reek of ripened mustiness and stout chlorine bleach. When I hit the lights, I see that the appearance of the room is much better than the smell of the place. A fairly comfy-looking, queen-sized bed lies in the centre of a beige carpet. The walls are covered in a 1970s era floral design wallpaper, a tangle of green vines overlapping fancy flowers. Two faux plants rest in corners of the room and the classic touch tone phone, tube television, and pull-cord lamplight complete the decor. A small, two-tiered nightstand is posted by the bedside, an old Holy Bible resting in place.

The plan is to meet Annalise in the bar at exactly a minute past midnight. I settle into my room and shower. Shortly before midnight and all freshened up, I make my way downstairs and follow the sounds of the drifting music, along with the spicy aromas of southwest cuisine. The saloon is lively but not packed. Garth Brooks is playing on the jukebox as a pair of couples two-step on the dance floor, the men in cowboy hats and women in striped button up blouses. A few round tables are hosting patrons, each one deep in drunken conversation. I step to the bar, lit up by only two neon lights, one in the middle of the bar top and one near the ceiling, atop the mirrors edge.

"What'll you be havin'?" asks the barkeep as he struts toward me.

"A beer if you have—"

"—MGD? You look like a cold filtered kinda guy," he says brightly, his voice carrying a distinct Southern inflection.

I smile and nod at him, feeling somewhat impressed by his capability to read his customers. But I guess that should be a given. "Yes, please."

He lifts open an old-fashioned cooler and snatches out an ice-cold Miller Draft, hand cracks it and hands it to me. "First one's on the house, my friend. Management guidelines." He tosses his hand towel over his shoulder and leans in, almost whispering. "Waitin' on someone, are we?"

I knock back a refreshing shot, letting the suds trickle down my desert-dry throat. "Yeah," I breathe out. "She's supposed to meet me here,"—I glance at the wall mounted clock— "in about five minutes, or so."

"Oooh la la, a special lady, huh?" he says friskily. "Well, she oughta be here soon then. It ain't too often I see a man stood up in my bar. Good luck brother." He nods at me with a mischievous smile and disappears behind a makeshift curtain leading to an off-limits back room.

She was late. Either that or she had decided to stand me up. I waited until a quarter past the stroke of midnight, nursing my one beer while I waited impatiently.

Now past 12:45 a.m., I am six beers, two shots of whiskey and one tequila deep into the night. My buzz is helping defuse the feelings of resentment and abandonment, but we all know that numbing sensation never lasts long.

"Hey, darlin," says one of the saloon's few remaining patrons. A pretty woman in her early thirties with skin-tight jeans and a halter top revealing a silvery piercing in her navel. Her chiselled body looks as though it was constructed in a laboratory. Her blonde hair is twisted into locks, the old style of the 90s; maybe even the 80s. Nothing too peculiar as I am sitting inside an even more unusual bar. "She stood you up, didn't she?"

"Could be," I hiss in a low baritone, keeping my eyes forward and polishing off the rest of my beer in frustration. "It isn't like her though." I say. "Not like her at all. She's never done this. Ever."

"Well, it's like that now, darlin," she says pitilessly, one of her frisky hands landing on my forearm as she chomps on bubble gum in an enticing, yet annoying manner.

I ignore her attempt to seduce me, eyeing my wristwatch. "Well, it's getting late. I should probably turn in. It's a long drive back to where I'm from." I face the bar's expansive mirror, an assortment of half-gone spirits lining the shelving, and wave at the bartender. "Goodnight there, barkeep," I say, standing up and heading for the exit. "Thanks for the cut-rate drinks. I really appreciate it."

"You betcha, my friend. Real sorry she didn't show," he says as he slings the same hand towel over his shoulder and begins stowing away bottles of spirits. I nod politely and vacate the drinking chamber as fast as possible before the loitering seductress has a chance to give it another go.

The television programming is just as lacklustre as the screen it's being broadcast on. Dull colours flicker, with occasional blips of static interrupting as I drunkenly goggle an old sitcom on low volume, the background laughter sounding like echoes of water splashing against a wall. As infomercials take over and my eyelids finally begin to feel heavy, I hear knocks sounding like birds pecking at the door. I am jerked to consciousness and a jolt runs through my body, putting my nerves on edge.

Adrenaline spike.

I had already settled my mind on the fact that Annalise wasn't coming. Any visitor, especially at 2:00 a.m., is entirely unexpected.

"That stupid seductress found my room, dammit," I whisper harshly, rolling off the bed and onto my feet. I creep to the door and peek through the dirt-smeared peephole. There stands Annalise. She stands impatiently, her head of lavish hair swinging from side to side like she is looking for someone who may have been shadowing her.

With excited, fumbling hands, I unlock the chain and deadbolt, and yank the sturdy door open. "Come in, come in," I tell her, grasping at my beloved girlfriend's hand, and tugging her safely inside my cheap hotel room.

Annalise regards me with a tantalizing stare—the very gaze that I had fallen in love with over three years ago. "Hey," she says ever so sweetly, like a bird chirping for its first time, a delicate smile gracing her rosy lips.

No more hesitation, my arms fling around her as I squeeze tightly. "Oh god, I've missed you so much."

She breathes into my shoulder, her breath like cool ice. "Me too. Oh my god, like so much, you'll never know, baby." Our quiet, heartfelt embrace lasts a few more seconds. I wish it could last forever. She breathes out a complaining exhale and whispers, "I love you." And the last words like a dagger pierce to my heart. "I can't stay long."

I push out the dagger. "I love you too," I affirm, tilting my head back until I'm once again gazing into her tender brown eyes. Without saying more, I seize her hand and lead her out of the cramped coatroom foyer, guiding her further into the compact room. I sweep aside my jacket and small overnight bag from the bed, and we settle down, allowing seconds to stretch into minutes as we engage in a soul-reaching gaze, locking eyes.

It feels like an eternity since I last had the chance to lose myself in our love for each other, those eyes of hers resembling sweet, caramel-brown candies, decorated with lush eyelashes.

It isn't long before the stares turn to touches. And the touches turn to all-out caressing and kisses to each other's naked bodies.

I was always told that 3 a.m. is the witching hour. For the past few nights, I had awoken to the dreary still of the night, the dim red illumination of my alarm clock pulsing to the shadows of the darkness. This night is different of course. I rouse, feeling somewhat rested and truly relaxed, my arms snuggly strung around Annalise as she sleeps peacefully.

There is someone—or something else—in the room with us. A silhouette is standing tall and upright against the closed blinds, the perky red and green luminosity of the outdated neon sign pulsating at its back.

For heart-thrashing minutes I lie on my side, my peripherals trained on the statue-still intruder. All I see is arms at its side, no twitching of a finger. No weapons, perhaps. Finally, the adrenaline and dreadful delay are too much. I loosen my hold around my beloved and spring myself off the bed, fists clenched and at the ready.

"Alright mother—"

Emptiness.

Where the shadow of a person once stood has now transformed into emptiness, the only silhouettes being the crossbar outlines draped across the carpet caused by the neon lighting beyond the window blinds.

A faint rustling of bed sheets and a creaking of the mattress, is followed by, "What are you doing, babe?"

Muscles still tensed up, I shift to face Annalise, her exquisite features with their almond-eyed allure illuminated by the alternating hues of red and green dancing across her face. As our eyes meet, her awakened charm eases my surge of anxiety. "I just—I thought I heard someone. You know how it is with these spooky, old-timey motels?"

She chirps out an apprehensive giggle and pats the empty space next to her. "Come. I'm so tired. I need you to keep me warm."

Before taking back to the bed, I take another glance around the room. Then peek out the blinds. The lot outside is as empty as a graveyard—or abandoned motel. Not wanting to alarm my love, I pluck together my threads of courage and join her. She wasn't lying. Her body is cold like we were asleep in an overly air-conditioned room. Yet, the cheap room is void of any such luxury. In no time I am fast asleep, her cold physique cooling down my sprinting heart.

The morning desert sun always hurts my eyes. This time, the burning red ball seems to be magnified, its searing heat burning through the walls and staying affixed inside the stuffy motel room. I open my eyes fully, thoughts of cool water streaming into my head. Rolling onto my side, I pat the empty spot next to me.

I am up and awake like a jolt of coffee. "Annalise?" I half scream, my voice echoing coldly off the enclosing walls.

Once again, she is gone, perhaps sneaking out in the middle of the night. The dagger has returned, driving into my heart.

Every vehicle is gone. My car is nestled behind the lone rusting dumpster. Before heading to my ride, I take a last look around the deserted hotel parking lot. Tumbleweeds roll across the sand-speckled lot, pushed by a westerly wind. Eyes.

Devilish eyes. Staring at me unkindly from somewhere beyond the array of darkened windows lining the three-tiers facing the parking lot. The feeling is too much, enough so that my stomach begins to churn. I steal my gaze from the emptiness and dash for my car, getting in and starting it up. I am out of the parking lot in a haste, flooring past the vacant general store with a cloud of billowing dust in my wake.

Speeding down the sandy, two-lane road, my eyes are still glued to the rear-view mirror, my heart slowing in pace for every retreating foot I am away from the creepy motel.

DING!

I jump at the sudden outcry of my smartphone, my white-knuckled grip on the steering wheel coming loose as I nearly swerve into the sandy shoulder of the narrow gravel highway.

"Holy shit!" I scream, loud enough that my voice hurts my own ears. I take a glance at my phone nestled in my cup holder. Clive. My eccentric little brother texting to see how I'm doing. Perhaps to see if I'm still alive.

The speed I am travelling would be more than enough to get me pulled over, but I keep on until I see the looming, fragmented sign with the hotel's name scrawled across it in broken lettering. I barely slow down, letting my low-profile tires pay the price as I screech onto the main highway.

Now's the time to slow my speed. I take the first roadside turnout, letting my overworked car coast to a halt, the reek of burnt rubber still evident. I opt to call my brother rather than to text him of my good news.

"Hey," Clive answers after two rings. "Well? Did you see

her?" His husky, teenage voice is painted in an overabundance of enthusiasm.

"I did," I answer nonchalantly.

"Awesome. So, you on your way back now?"

"I am."

"Cool. Will you be back in time for the wake?"

"I should be. If I drive a little over the limit."

A pause. Followed by my brother's voice turning low and empathetic. "I'm really glad you got to see her one last time before we bury her and she crosses over through the gates of Heaven."

"Me too, little brother. Me too." I hang up and casually pull back onto the highway, punching the accelerator until my car is freewheeling just past the posted speed limit.

⌇ THREE ⌇

HIDE-AND-GO-SEEK

It wasn't supposed to end the way it did.
Life. It wasn't supposed to end like that. But it did.
Kids. What can we really say? They have their imagina-
tions—something we seem to lose as soon as we hit that
tender age where sex becomes the only thing on the mind.
But I'll never get to that age now, will I?

THE ABRUPT JANGLE of the house phone makes me jump; tearing me away from the gripping clutches of the book of dark tales I hold tightly gripped in my hands. The story I am immersed in is a tale of two horrors, woven with strands of malevolence that grips a poor soul. The unfortunate protagonist is a mere teenager, just two years my senior.

"Holy effin' shit," I say through a tight grin, my spirit dropping just like the book I had in my hands, the thump on my leg giving me another jolt as I sit like a toddler aboard my grandparents' brand-new sofa. "Who the hell's calling me at this damn moment?" I glance at the clock and then wriggle from my comfy, balled-up posture and push aside my lucky blanket, eager to see who is calling me on this Friday night. Stepmom and dad are away at bingo for at least another three hours. I may be only 12, but I would still prefer to have a social life of some sort.

The caller ID announces back to me: R. Rain Family. I know exactly who it is. Brady. My new best friend, slash cousin in-law. Also, my best new hockey and football team-mate. Chance just had it that we are the exact same age too. A lucky draw of cards when I thought I would be a new and unwanted nuisance in a new land. Cree land. My new location has come as a result of my dad winning custody of me in the divorce.

"Brooo," I belt into the phone receiver, waiting in guaranteed anticipation for my new cousin to give me some good news.

"Sleepover," Brady asserts, his tone carrying a command that I'm reluctantly at ease with. "My dad said we can come pick you up if you want. There's lots of food left over, too. Indian tacos, bro."

My mouth goes into an automatic surge of watering, my taste buds already detecting the secret spice my aunty Lorna adds to her taco seasoning. Aunt Lorna also isn't from this part of the world. She's Navajo. The originators of the famous Indian Taco.

"Hell yeah, bro. You know I'm always down for that," I say in a childish voice that sounds more ecstatic than it should be.

"Want us to come get you?" Brady asks.

Cordless phone in hand, I glide over the linoleum floor to the kitchen's enormous picture window. It's a window to the world of the night, looking out to the sprawling expanse of Brady's family abode, nestled amidst the fields where the horses graze. It's just a stone's throw away, less than a mile, or so. The only big house in sight for miles on end surrounded by area's the thick foliage. The house stands out beneath the blanket of night like a mirage in the desert. One flickering lamppost dimly lights up the twisting driveway, while the numerous windows projecting inside lighting gives off that spaceship feel to Brady's massive, country-style dwelling. A dash across the hilly, horse trampled grassland seems like nothing to me. Three minutes tops if I can keep my championship 150-metre dash momentum up. But I suddenly heed Kokum Nadine's warning. Never to cross that stretch of land, or to be playing outside, at night. And alone at that. Age-old mythical warnings stemming from the Mosoms and Kokums of long ago.

I disregard Kokum Nadine's warning. "No, man," I tell Brady. "I can walk. Save the gas." I say, a slight tremor of fear caressing me as I seem to notice a darkness darker than the black surrounding my usual prairie home floats in. I wouldn't mind being picked up but at the same time I don't want to look like a wimp to my new family.

• • • •

With flashlight in one hand and an overnight backpack in the other, I gently shut the worn wooden door, like I was a teenager sneaking off to a late-night party. I flick on my flashlight, illuminating the grassy path in an encouraging LED glow. I allow the beam to settle as far as it can go, over the main yard fence and past the two empty barns cradling the gravel road leading to a treed-off nowhere. Another shudder of apprehension strikes me as I try to focus on the tree engulfed, unseen areas not ignited by the flashlight. Twisted shadows of the barns seems to dance like ominous demons as I scan the wide-open nothingness. There is really nothing to dread around here except for the odd roaming coyote or badger.

I exhale heavily and continue my trip to Brady's big reserve homestead. My breath clouds the flashlight beam. My legs carry me swiftly and one look upon his lit-up house, I already feel at ease, knowing I will soon be out of this autumn chill, scarfing down an off-the-burner, southwest style Indian taco.

"You got this, Matt," I say to myself, illuminating my projected path down the darkness enclosed, horse trampled grassland. As I dash across the open field, I wish to Creator that the horses were present, rather than be away with Mosom and Aunt Geena, up north for the rodeo finals, some three reserves away. There's something about the terrain's emptiness—nothing but land that is thoroughly unfamiliar to my 12-year-old Blackfoot knowledge. The land where the Great Plains ends, and the endless bush begins, stretching north until the arctic tundra takes over.

I know—I hope—it's only my preteen imagination, but I feel the conjuring of, what is that? A presence judging my every move from somewhere beyond the black and green spread of birches and poplars, their autumn-coloured leaves masked by the blanket of night. I give it no further thought and finish my run, huffing and puffing until my feet steal away from the damp grasses and touch the Rain family's gravel-laden driveway.

"I made it," I whisper to myself, realizing that I have to let my lungs catch up to my forced breaths.

"Fuckin' rights you made it," says Brady. He leaps over the porch railing and rushes over to me. "Took you long enough, man." I can only see his breath in the dim light of the flickering lamppost, his face shadowed by the fall of night. "You good? Seen you from upstairs hauling ass like the wolfman himself was chasing you."

I hold back a shiver and start walking toward the comforting aura of amber light warming his porch. "Let's go inside. It's friggin' cold as balls out here," I say, not bothering again to face the expanse of black between his house and mine across the way.

"Okay, bro. Lets." He says, ever so calmly. "Let's eat."

• • • •

Mission accomplished. I am full. A little too full for my own comfort. My stomach starts to scream at me not to let any more food pass through my mouth. Now I have nothing to do but let the time pass as the uncomfortable feeling caused by my overeating diminishes like a snail and turtle race.

I take a comfy position on Brady's family-sized leather couch, just off to the side of where his little sister, Nadia, watches an old *Transformers* cartoon at low volume.

"I can barely hear it. How can you watch this at such a low volume?" I say to Nadia.

She barely bats an eye, slightly twisting her head as she slurps on a can of Coke. "Meh," she replies, "I got used to it. It's how I always have to watch it anyways at Mosom and Kokum's. You know, with them being so naggy about TV."

I nod my head in agreement. I am more than aware of how my step-grandparents aren't too fond of TV, themselves settling for an old black and white over the new age colour HDTV's. Even the location of their only television is awkward, placed in a back room near the main floor's laundry room and secondary washroom. Feeling at ease on my stomach I sit back and watch the old cartoon with Nadia, my eyelids becoming heavy after only a few minutes of observing the almost-muted robots change disguises into some fancy automobile of their era.

The trance of a deep, dreamless sleep wanes, and all I can initially make out is a blurry image of Brady's face up close. "Psst, bro," he speaks softly, "come on, lets go." He takes a step back and summons me with a whipping motion of his head. "My older sister has a fun night planned for us. You don't get to go to sleep yet, you dummy."

My mind rapidly snaps to attention, immediately deciphering fifteen-year-old Laura, Brady's older sister. Beautiful Laura, my heart always thumps with extra zeal when she's around. I know it is wrong to crush on her—her being my step-cousin and all—but my teenage mind and soul just can't help it. Maybe when I'm older this feeling will withdraw. Just maybe.

I am full alert when I stand up, rubbing the sleep from my eyes. "What's the fun she's got planned?" I eagerly ask.

"She said she would let us borrow her PlayStation 2 for the night. But first, she wants to play a game of hide-and-go-seek. You cool with that?" he asks with an unexpectedly polite tone, even coming from him.

Hide and seek is my all-time favourite childhood game since way back when, a piece of it forever living within the pit of my adolescent heart. It's the perfect game to play when there are so many places to hide in such a big house as Brady's.

"Heck yeah, I'm cool with that, brother. But you and I aren't the seekers. Let's make..." I pause for a moment, considering who I'd prefer to be looking for us. "Ahh yeah, okay. Let's have Laura be the seeker, since it was her idea to play in the first place," I say with a naturalized grin.

Brady nods and puckers his lips. "Yeah, okay. I'm cool with that." He begins strolling out of the living room. "I'll go tell her. Pretty sure she'll be up for it anyway. Get your coat on, bro. We're gonna play outside for the first few rounds. While my mom and dad are in town gettin' groceries."

A forced gulp halts in my throat, a deep breath pushing past so that I don't drown on my own saliva. "Yeah okay," I say, trying to hide the uneasiness in my voice, "sounds awesome."

• • • •

The weather grew cold over the hour or so we spent inside the comforting warmth of Brady's house. Ominous clouds skate across the skies, blotting out the moon. Someone turned off the porch light.

"Well, there goes any source of light besides that useless old lamppost. Even better for us," Brady jokes as he jogs up beside me. His gaze stares out at the expanse of dead-black space. He slams a hard pat to my back and says, "Ready to play?"

A shiver runs through me. But yet, my jacket is so warm. I can't help but stare in sheer admiration from my cramped-up position beneath the neglected horse trailer wheel well. Laura faces the dark corner of the open-air carport and counts down from thirty. "Five... four... three... two..." she pauses, and I can hear her take a deep breath. That sweet breath. "And one," she says louder than the rest of the preceding numbers. "Ready or not, here I come."

She spins to face the overlooking direction and takes a look around, her eyes scanning right past mine and into the endless black beyond the homestead grounds.

I grin with intensity as though she has already caught me, my mind debating if I would rather find another place to hide, or just stay put and be the first one to be found. And it was me who confidently told my Cree cousins that the Blackfoot are never found when in hiding. My wish is granted as she exits the carport, takes a hard left, ascends the steps to the veranda porch and disappears around the corner.

Now is my chance. I wriggle and slide my skinny frame from under the sloped trailer, pausing to listen amidst a cloud of gravel dust choking me. I peer through the dim illumination cast upon me. Powering through a cough, I get to my feet, look to my left and right, and settle for the tool shed on the far end of the freshly mowed lawn. There's something about the opposite end of the yard, nothing beyond the three-tier fence but obscure twists and incessant shadows of trees. The prospect seems strangely unwelcoming.

I shiver again, quickening my steps to a ninja pace, ducking low and moving smoothly. I reach the shed without giving away my whereabouts. I dart across the damp grass. I make it there just in time as I hear Laura's footfalls rounding the corner of the wooden porch, her beautiful face coming into the dim lamp light mere moments before I delicately close the shed door with the tip of my finger. She doesn't hear the squeal of the rusted-out hinges, her own footsteps loud are enough to drown them out. Luck is on my side.

My muscles are wound tight. Too tight. But why? It's only a game of hide and seek, after all. I take a step back until my shoulder blade brushes something hanging freely. I whip around, my hands shooting outward until they strike something rigid and icy. It's steel.

"Oh my god," I whisper, addressing the obscured darkness in front of me. "Just Uncle Rob's old pitchfork." But then my cold fingers clamp down on my mouth to stifle a scream, as my mind replays scenes from the horror movie Brady had made me sit through just last weekend. The pitchfork—the preferred weapon of choice for killers preying on unfortunate souls caught unprepared in some forbidden farm or abandoned ranch. A ranch, much like the one belonging to Brady's dad, Uncle Rob.

"This is my spot to hide," says the voice in the shed with me. But who's voice is it?

I perform a dizzying spin and face the darkness, spanning twice the breadth of my arms appearing more like a limitless cosmos devoid of stars to my vision.

"Who the hell said that... Who's lurking here?" I demand in a voice that probably sounds like a lost kid at the carnival of horrors.

"Mine," he, or it, growls back at me. "And you shouldn't be here!"

Fuck it. I am already to burst from the shed and give up. Be the loser of the game. But I am too late. I have been beat. I've been outwitted, bested by a reassuring voice just as my shoulder slams into the shed door, and I hurtle forth, my face meeting the cool, damp grass with a thud.

"What the heck are you kids doing out here in the middle of the dark?" Pans my new aunt, Lorna, Brady's mom.

Body grounded, I lift my face and strain my neck until it hurts my spine, then twist my torso until I'm on my back and kick-pushing the grass in a deadly effort to get as far away from the tool shed as possible. In the lamppost's dingy glow the wooden shack is once again reduced to a humble, compact structure, housing hand tools. The darker-than-night, open entry is like a doorway to another dimension, where eternal blackness is bestowed upon all who enter.

"Mom," wails little sister Nadia, followed by Brady emerging from his hiding place just a few feet to the left of her. "We're sorry. We were just—"

"Get in the house. Right Now!" Lorna's scream pierces the night, her fury palpable.

I know we are in trouble.

But at least I am now safe.

• • • •

I take a seat beside the kitchen's picture window, feeling a sense of invincibility now that I am surrounded by reassuring light, five other living souls, and a pane of glass that would take a bullet to break through.

My thoughts remain distracted, unable to detach from the enigma that reached out to me in the tool shed. Was it a real voice, or just (hopefully) a concoction of a voice brought on by a 12-year-old mind, too tainted by an overindulging of horror movies my off-reserve friends wouldn't be allowed to watch until they were at least 14.

"And you," says Lorna, her stern voice directed at me. "You're Blackfoot. I know all about your people's traditions and folklore. You of all people should know better than to be out there in the middle of the night playing hide and go seek. What the hell, man?" She is not all wrong. I should have known better. I already knew better.

I clear my throat and am ready to respond when my sight is taken—stolen—by a swift speck of movement in the front yard barely lit up by the gloomy nighttime lamppost. "Look," I belt out. "There's someone still out there."

Eyes settled coldly on mine; Aunt Lorna barely directs her head toward the window when the doorbell chimes.

"Oh nice," says Uncle Rob. "Jimmy's here." He passes by me and—acting as though the air is cool—he places a hand on Lorna's shoulder. "Babe, he's here. We still on for some cards?"

• • • •

Beneath a lone dangling bulb, Aunt Lorna stares at me framed by the smiling faces of Uncle Rob and his best friend, Jimmy. On the couch, I sit like a lost boy awaiting my fate to be sent back home, or to be let to stay the night.

"She'll be okay, bro," interrupts Brady, slapping a hand to my kneecap. "That's just how she was brought up. You know how those southern Indians are?"

And that I did, having a few of my in-law aunts and uncles from all over the USA and eastern Canada. It was a thing for my family not to marry on-reserve men and women. Too many relations and distant cousins.

I exhale deeply, letting my gaze drop from Lorna's death stare. "What's the plan now?" I ask Brady.

"Oh, we ain't done, bro," he says with a smile. "Come, let's go downstairs."

Without question I follow my newfound cousin and enter the depths of the Rain family basement.

I knew this basement already. Having spent many a sleepover in the "dungeon", as we called it, I can fathom the sense of eeriness and dampness that never seems to leave this basement.

"Sorry about that, new cousin," says Laura, standing tall in the middle of the barely lit family room with her hands resting on Nadia's shoulders. "My mom can be a real... meanie," she says with a flash of her beautiful smile. I am immediately brought back from the hurt of Aunt Lorna's scolding. "You still wanna play, or not? If not than that's—"

"No way. Of course I'm still down to play," I cut her off. "Who's the seeker?"

"I am, of course," she says. "I never had the chance to find any of you earlier, anyways. Okay, go hide. I'll stay over here and count down from thirty."

I wait and watch as Nadia and Brody sprint their own ways, skirting furniture and the mounds of Nadia's toys strewn about the thickly carpeted floor. Laura is at twenty-five when I finally decide it is time for me to find my own place of solitude to wait while she seeks us in the halfway darkness lit up by only one table lamp.

Rob Rain had a say in the layout of his own basement. It was like he never had the urge to let the age-old game of hide and go seek slip his mind. The massive basement was littered with areas to hide and never be found. There was a crawl space that had especially taken in my interests when Brady first showed me it. Perfect. In the dark, the expanse of dirt-riddled ground would seem to span on forever.

That is my spot of choice.

A bad choice.

Suppressing a series of coughs, I maneuver silently to the spot Brady had shown me, the mental map our young minds had meticulously charted permitting me to navigate the space in the dark. Now all I can do is lie in wait as I hope to be the last one found by Laura.

Time drags on, earth's chill seeping into my body as I recline, yearning finally to be discovered.

I am ready to crawl out, quit, and go upstairs to go and enjoy another Indian taco when I feel the air temperature drop like a rock in a pond. Within the darkness I could sense my own breath coming out in pitiful wafts. "Okay, you got this," I whisper to myself as I eagerly scramble for the exit.

But then he intervenes, a formidable presence slithering across and blocking off the only exit from the crawlspace. My agitated movements stall abruptly. I can't see his face as the words speak from a mouth that shifts and expands, jaws much too broad to be of human origin. "I warned you once," it roars, "This is my spot to hide."

My last sight is a sudden and deadly movement like an attacking cobra, as the being slithers toward me, and I am met with the stench of a rotting animal corpse—and what is this—a face so twisted and distorted I know this creature is no human being. Not a creature from this world at least.

Life. It wasn't supposed to end like that.

PART II
FEATURE SECTION
"SNAPPING TURTLE" BY
CARY THOMAS CODY

PHOTO: MIKEY HEVR

～ FOUR ～

SNAPPING TURTLE

BY

CARY THOMAS CODY

DUST PARTICLES fill the air as beams of sunlight force their way through the trees. Two men are shovelling dirt in the woods on a hot autumn afternoon as the sun is chasing the horizon.

Crunch

The shovels stab the earth moving it little by little.

"Do you *really* think there is anything in this grave worth all this work?" Says one man panting in exhaustion while inspecting blisters on his fingers.

Crunch

"Well, Lucy said her dad used to take her and her brother out here all the time as kids to lay flowers on the graves. We all know who her Great Great Grandfather was." The second man retorts.

"Well, let's hope the legends are true."

Crunch

"What do you think we'll find? Gold? Silver?"

Crunch

"Also, why are we wearing these stupid masks?" The first man rips off a black ski mask drenched in sweat and sighs in relief.

"Because we don't want anyone to know who we are, and there might be trail cams out here, idiot! Who knows, dude. Whatever we find will be more than what we have right now." He looks up to see the first man glistening in sweat and drinking water.

"To hell with it." The second man rips off his balaclava.

Thud

"Here we go."

The two men dig around the grave for the next half hour racing the impending sunset.

Lee and Quentin Swift Feet are two Kiowa brothers grave robbing on abandoned Indian land in southwest Oklahoma. They are locally known delinquents nicknamed "The Swift Brothers."

The Swift Brothers were raised by their uncle for the past few years of their lives since their mother died— although the term 'raised' is used loosely. Lee, the elder of the two, was the school bully. Presently, he pulls his brother into his get-rich-quick schemes. This time, it's grave-robbing from an abandoned family cemetery on reservation land, where urban legends suggest that the old Kiowa man, Snapping Turtle, was "buried with his riches" in the 1800s.

Taking it upon himself, Lee convinces his brother Quentin to join him out here on a scorching ninety-two-degree day to dig it up and see for himself.

"On three we'll lift."

One! Two! Three!

The brothers lift the toe pincher coffin out of the earth in unison and both fall on their rears.

"*Finally.*" Quentin says drenched in sweat.

There is something about the atmosphere out in the woods that seems uncanny. While digging, neither of them notice how the woods have fallen into an unnatural silence. It is as if the trees are alive and watching the two boys make the biggest mistake of their lives. The cicada, birds, and crickets sit dormant. The silence is deafening as the sun finally makes it past the horizon.

The boys sit in exhaustion in a circular set of graves all marked haphazardly with stones or tattered wooden crosses marking the family graves on the Native family's land.

Lee points with his lips and says, "Here, grab that crowbar." The younger brother reaches into the canvas duffel bag they brought and grabs the steel bar. He then pulls out an electric lantern to ward off the incoming darkness.

"Okay, go ahead." Lee says, expecting his brother to finish the job.

"Hellllll nah dude. Not a chance, Buck-o. You got us into this. This is *your* thing, you gotta be the one to do the actual illegal part and uhh... crack open this dead guy's coffin." Quentin responds.

Lee reluctantly grabs the crowbar and starts to force it into the casket. "I'm pretty sure everything we did here was illegal, which means you are still my accomplice dummy. But sure, whatever Quen. The cut is 60/40 now since you're making me do this."

Quentin chants "Lee! Lee! Lee! Lee!"

Crack

Lee pops the top of the coffin off and the brothers both back up and wave the dust out of their faces, coughing. As the dust settles, they look inside, realizing it contains no human remains.

"What the fuck?" Lee says. He reaches in and moves around some clothes. It was a corpse-less suit. Not only that, somehow there was a snapping turtle shell on top of the would-be chest of the missing dead guy. Puzzled, Lee keeps digging and finds a suede leather pouch and nothing else in the casket. He opens the pouch to see what's in it and gives his younger brother a disappointed head shake.

Quentin says, "You're telling me we spent all day digging this grave and it's empt—"

"Shh... did you hear that?" Lee whispers. "I swear I heard leaves crunching, like someone is out there. Hello?..."

No answer.

"It's probably just a deer, bro." Quentin says.

Lee grabs the leather pouch and says, "Alright, but we might as well cut our losses and get the hell out of here."

The two brothers toss the casket back into the grave and disregard shovelling the dirt back into the hole. They gather their things and hastily start the trek back to their truck. It isn't long before they realize they were in fact not alone in these woods. Or rather, they feel that familiar sensation of being watched and followed. Every few steps they take, they swear they faintly hear someone in the foliage and small twigs breaking behind them, but the steps stop when they do. Quentin's assumption of it being a deer is proving incorrect. Due to the densely grown forest and the sky darkening by the second, anyone might be hiding behind trees and stalking them.

The brothers stop and listen. The woods are still silent.... Watching them.

Nothing

"Psst... I don't like this. On the count of three, let's make a full-on sprint for the truck." Lee whispers. Quentin, with the lantern in hand nods his head. Lee mouths "one, two, three!" and the Swift brothers are true to their name and high tail it through the forest.

They make it to the truck, not hesitating for a second as they throw everything in the back seat and start the engine of the extended cab of a '09 F150 to head straight back to town. Lee and Quentin have similar horrified looks on their faces as they race down the bumpy gravel road. The road is poorly illuminated by only their headlights and the dim moonlight.

Little is said on the drive home back to Wolf's Creek—a reservation town in southwest Oklahoma that time forgot. The only people who live there are white landowners and their privileged children, as well as Native families who were displaced here a century ago and can never leave.

This used to be a successful small town with a wheat mill that provided jobs for hundreds of folks, Indians included. Since that dried up, there are very few jobs. Mostly at liquor stores, gas stations, the casino, and the local grocery store.

Neither brother wants to bring up what had just happened. Or what is happening now. Five miles west, outside of town on Highway 19, Lee swears he hears whispering from the back seat.

Or, rather, *feels* it..

He is too horrified to look in the rear view mirror. He is too proud to say anything to his brother even as he white knuckles the steering wheel. Lee looks over at Quentin. His eyes are closed, and his head leans on the passenger window. He had fallen asleep on the short drive home.

There is an old Kiowa saying, "Don't look back." He would always hear that in stories growing up. "If you hear something, don't look back. Just keep on minding your own business." It was also used in reference to driving down the haunted highway called "Indian Road." When they were kids and they would drive down it at night, their Mom would always say "Remember keep looking forward. Don't look back or Deer Woman will be in the back seat". They would all say "Yoooooo" and have a good laugh together.

But they aren't driving on Indian Road, and nothing is funny. Lee can feel it isn't Deer Woman in his back seat. It was someone else. Or something else.

Don't look back.

Don't look back.

The boys pull into the driveway of their family home, and Quentin wakes up. He immediately opens the door, and the cab lights turn on. Lee slowly turns his head around to the backseat and sees just the canvas duffel bag, not the Boogeyman or Deer Woman as he thought. He quickly grabs it and follows his brother inside, brushing off the eerie terrified feeling he had on the way home. Lee decides he must have the heebie-jeebies.

They live alone in a torn-up Rez house they inherited when their mother died. Their Uncle Mac lived here for a while, but he moved to Lawton the year prior when they were old enough to take care of themselves.

Their Uncle left the boys his landscaping business, which was basically an old truck, a few lawn mowers, and weed eaters. The truck is a white Ford F-150 with their business logo on the side which features a four-leaf clover. The logo reads, "Mac's Lawncare: You're lucky to have us."

Uncle Mac was 'retired', but what that really meant was he took most of their profit and spent it at the casino in Lawton or whatever he did with it.

Quentin doesn't say anything to Lee and just goes to his room. Lee throws his duffel bag down on the living room floor and decides to investigate his new treasure. He opens the leather bag to find it's got some herbs, feathers, and a few bones in it. No gold, no silver... the rumours were lies.

Not growing up "traditional" as the natives say, Lee has no knowledge of the significance that this leather pouch holds. He grabs a shoe box he has full of wrist watches, silver jewelry, and other contraband he's collected over the years and hides it in the attic. Soon he had a small bottle of whiskey in hand and while getting lost in his thoughts, he falls asleep.

• • • •

Lee stands at the edge of Wolf's Creek, the namesake of the town itself. The creek is said to have magical healing properties. People come from all over and fill water bottles and jugs to hopefully heal their ailments.

In his dream, Lee stands at the edge of the creek and watches as he is taken back in time. Three Indian men are carrying someone over to the creek. They have long black hair and are wearing deerskin leggings and bone chest plates. They move at a panicked pace.

The man they are carrying is an old, thin, dying Indian man. He might be dead already. Even the dying man's face paint can't hide the wrinkles or the bags under his eyes. He watches as they gently lay him in the water, and he sinks out of view.

Lee watches the spot for hours. He doesn't know exactly what he is waiting for, but he knows it is important that he waits. Like a turtle coming up for air, a head and torso pops out of the water. A young Indian man stands in the chest-deep water, staring at him. Water trickles down his face as he looks up and around, taking a deep breath through his nostrils, in and out. This does not look like the old, feeble thing the men dumped into the water.

"Aho for awakening me, you will be rewarded, my servant."

The Indian man speaks in Kiowa and somehow Lee understands him, even though in reality he only has an elementary-level knowledge of his own People's language.

Lee sits on the creek bank in awe of this man and replies "Aho."

• • • •

Lee wakes up to find Quentin is gone. He's probably at his girlfriend's house. Quentin loves himself a good white girl.

Traitor.

Besides being his brother, Quentin is his best friend and probably the only thing he cares about in this world. Actually, he is the only thing he cares about in this world. Lee curses this town for taking away Quentin's bright future. Quentin graduated top of his class, All State in Track and Cross Country, basketball star, but didn't go to college because Indians in this town didn't do that. Quentin's future was stripped from him when he was picked up from the county sheriff for a bogus DUI. His scholarships for multiple universities were rescinded when the local news covered the arrest.

"Star athlete from Wolf's Creek High taken into custody under the influence of alcohol and drugs," read the headlines.

It wasn't until later that the charges were dropped due to lack of evidence. They didn't even breathalyze him, and the public defender called this out before the trial.

But deep-down Lee knows it's his fault Quentin won't leave the reservation. Quentin is the baby brother but Lee feels it's his paternal duty to ensure he himself does not descend into manic depression and become yet another statistic they see on billboards saying, "Native men suicide rate is 2.5 times higher than the overall national average. Call the suicide Hotline 988 to talk to someone."

Pbay-gah Lee thinks, a common expression used by Kiowas to express incredulity and yet an utter lack of surprise at the same time.

Lee goes for a long run that afternoon along the dusty gravel roads that surround the town. A former cross-country star at Wolf's Creek High himself, he seeks to relive the glory days of the only time that the town saw him as a hero.

He runs and runs just to feel the painful nostalgia of winning a race again. Of having his entire future in the palm of his hands. When all the town folk, whites and Indians alike, came together to watch him and his team at State as they fought to become state champions. He didn't lose a race his entire junior year.

Lee runs

The flashback of the State Cross Country meet tortures him like a live entity. A parasite in his brain he can't eradicate. A parasite that has overstayed its welcome.

Lee runs

The day of the State meet Lee knew he was going to win. In fact, he was so confident he didn't even stretch before the race. Quentin was there too. He looked up to his older brother so much he just wanted to be as fast as Lee was someday. Lee knew Quentin was basically just as fast as him at that moment, but he didn't want his baby brother to know just yet so that he could hold on to being the stronger, faster older brother as long as possible.

Lee runs

The starting gun fired and the Wolf's Creek Cross Country team took off. Their tradition was to do a Native War Cry at the beginning of each race, to stab fear into the hundred-plus other competitors. They screamed their high-pitched cries as they went into battle. It was a technique used by his ancestors in a world before people kept track of time. They knew it was possibly a waste of energy, but they felt their ancestors running with them into battle.

Lee runs

He led the pack of runners from all around the state and saw thousands of people lining the course as he passed, screaming for their runners. He had never been more sure about the outcome of a race.

Lee is probably five miles away from his home now, the 21-year-old running harder than he probably should be.

Lee's first mile split was under five minutes. His fastest split ever. The gap between him and the rest of the runners seemed like a mile long.

Lee runs

He tries to repress his memory of the rest of the race. Around the two-mile mark, he felt a 'pop' in his groin area. He finished the race in agonizing pain. His frustration crescendoed as he got passed by each runner and finished in 25th place. He let his team down, the whole town of Wolf's Creek, and worse... he'd let Quentin down.

Lee dropped out of high school in the 11th grade.

Lee crashes to the gravel suddenly and vomits his entire breakfast. He's in agony from having just tried to outrun years of mistakes that changed his life for the worse. He climbs to his knees and catches his breath. Every muscle in his body is aching and his heart works overtime to pump blood through his body. Blood drips down the scrapes of his knees.

He looks to his right and sees Wolf's Creek tucked behind some trees. He's explored every foot of the creek before but doesn't remember this particular bend. He limps over to the creek and sits on the bank.

It's the exact place from his dream. Except, only a turtle swims across the creek in the place of the old Indian man.

• • • •

A week passes. Quentin joins Lee in the living room to watch an old horror movie. "This movie blows, dude." Quentin says just to get a rise out of his older brother knowing *Evil Dead* is one of Lee's favourites.

"You're out of your mind! It goes hard, dude. It's gore galore. Sam Raimi is the shit. Plus, this movie was made on like... a $10 budget so that counts for something," says Lee haughtily.

Looking down at his phone, Quentin follows up with, "It's still got nothing on *Nightmare on Elm Street 3: Dream Warriors* though."

"Agree to disagree," Lee responds, sinking into his uncle's Lazy Boy recliner.

Quentin decides to quit beating around the bush. "Hey Lee.... Do you feel weird about what we did last week? Like.... I feel like we did something really bad this time."

"What do you mean?" Lee inquires.

"I don't know, Man. Maybe it's nothing. I've just had a bad feeling ever since we dug up that grave. You know that feeling that you're being watched?" Quentin asks.

Lee knows that feeling all too well, especially on the drive home from that cemetery. "It's all in your head, little brother."

"I must be going crazy. I've been feeling it a lot," confesses Quentin.

Lee looks over at his brother. "You just need some good rest."

The brothers pause and watch the absurd amount of blood on the TV splatter on the walls.

"Well... I'll see you in the morning, it's time to hit the sack... and after I do that, I'm going to sleep."

"Haha, come up with some new jokes, man." And Quentin walks to his room to get ready for bed as well.

Lee is fast asleep and midway through a dream he won't remember much of tomorrow. He looks down at himself and he is an old Indian on the plains of Oklahoma. But... he recognizes who he is—he's the Indian man from the creek. He feels his strength, but not physical strength.

It's a powerful ancient magical strength, a magical force, forgotten through the generations. He's holding the leather pouch from the coffin.

He is Snapping Turtle, the most-feared dark Medicine Man five-days hard ride on a horse in any direction. The leather pouch in the palm of his hands is the source of his strength and power.

Lee wakes up to the sound of a voice saying, *"Use me."*

Lee jumps up. He looks around and doesn't see anyone in his room. He reaches for the baseball bat under his bed and sees wet footprints. Trying not to panic, he follows the footsteps down the hallway and sees that they stop right under the attic door, which is slightly askew.

Feeling brave, Lee grabs a kitchen knife, pulls the attic cord, and the stepladder descends to his feet. His heart beats madly, and the colour drains from his face. He shines the flashlight up into the attic.

"If anyone is up there you have five seconds to come down and get the hell out of my house," he says with false confidence.

Silence

Lee wonders if he should wake up Quentin. There was something about this attic when they were kids that horrified him. Any time Mom asked him to go up and grab something, an irrational fear of the unknown would shake him to the core.

He is feeling that same feeling now.

Maybe it was because his older cousins would tease him about "The Attic Man." The Attic Man lived in the darkness of the attic; he would crawl like a spider and had an appetite for little kids. If you ever heard creaking in the walls or ceiling at night, it was him. He later found out they made up the Attic Man to scare him.

He's not real

He's not real

He decides against waking up Quentin.

"To hell with it," he thinks, taking a deep breath. Lee climbs up the rickety folding attic stairs. With every creaky step, he is sure something is going to reach down from the darkness and pull him into the inky abyss.

The Attic Man is real, he can feel him in there. He can sense the presence of his lanky legs and his hot breath.

He's not real

He's finally high enough on the ladder to reach the string that lights the attic. He desperately yanks it.

Darkness

The light bulb burns out with a click. He surveys the attic with his dim flashlight and sees nothing.

No Attic Man, no intruder. Just some of Mom's old stuff packed away in boxes and his shoe box of stolen goods. He opens it up and it's the same suede leather bag of herbs and feathers from the dream that he vaguely remembers.

Use me? What does that mean?

He takes the box to his room and puts it under his bed. He wants to keep it close. It is his, after all.

• • • •

Lee is having a good morning. He feels different... strong. He can't explain it. He is on his way to a client's house to do some yard work and Quentin is supposed to meet him there. He brought the shoe box with him and put it under the seat of his truck. He figures he can drive to Lawton after work and pawn a few jewelry pieces that he's collected. As he's passing one of the two gas stations in town, he hears "*stop*" and abruptly obeys and pulls over.

What?

He feels the sudden urge to go inside the Hop and Sack and try his luck at a scratch off lottery ticket. He can't explain it. He just knows that he must get a scratch off. Just one. Lee goes inside and grabs an Ol' Glory energy drink, "America's Energy Drink" it says on the can. He also asks for a $20 Break the Bank scratch off ticket.

He settles back in his truck and grabs a penny. He scratches the first number, a dud. He scratches the second number, $10. "That'll get a 12 pack," Lee thinks.

Lee continues to scratch. He gets to the last number and sure enough, Lee is $3,000 richer.

"Well, I'll be..." He's bursting with excitement and can't wait to tell his brother. He bets he can double this at the Gold River Casino in Anadarko.

Lee pulls out the leather pouch from under his seat. "Did... you help me win this?" He says in short breaths. "You're lucky Medicine, aren't you? I'm gonna keep you close." He has heard legends of 'lucky medicine' before but he's never seen any in person. Medicine of course being the Native American term for Magic.

Lee is leaning on his truck when Quentin shows up at the client's house where they are to do yard work. He's casually fanning himself with his scratch off ticket, a smug look on his face.

"Oh snap, I know that look," says Quentin.

Lee shows him the scratch off card. "I'm feeling lucky, dude. Want to hit up the casino?"

Quentin grabs the card and squints and reads the winnings. "Holy *crap* dude, that's wild. How did you pull this off? And... I can't do the 'Ino today, I'm hanging with Christine. But tomorrow, bet."

Lee walks over to Quentin and pulls the ticket out of his fingers and says, "Deal. I'm feeling lucky."

As the brothers mow the lawn, it gives Lee plenty of time to think. "What is this medicine bundle capable of? What other powers can it give me? It can't just be lucky, there must be more to it."

• • • •

Lee didn't make it to the casino that night. He ended up driving an hour round trip to Lawton to redeem his scratch off. He filled his tank, bought some groceries, and was lost in his thoughts the entire night. He fell asleep with a PBR in his lap and drifted into a dream once again.

Lee dreams he is standing in front of a tipi. He sits and waits for what seems like hours. When the tipi doors finally flap open, there is no one inside. He gets up and walks in. Illuminated by firelight ... his lucky medicine bundle, sitting right there on a stump. The bundle speaks to him in Kiowa, but he understands.

I can give you anything you want. I have all the power you'll ever need.

I can give you riches. I can get you any woman you desire.

I can even resurrect the dead.

Use me.

Lee wakes up from his dream in a sweat. This time he heard the voice inside his bedroom, that wasn't just in his dream. Cautiously, He investigates the house room by room. Quentin is gone. He must be at Christine's house.

Like a thousand needles prickling his neck, he feels that familiar sense of someone watching him. It was the same inkling he felt the night before when approaching the attic. Slowly, he creeps towards the window in his bedroom.

There are a few rules in Indian culture: don't stray far from the powwow grounds when it's dark, don't whistle at night, and don't look out your house windows at night.

Lee parts the blinds no more than a centimeter with his fingers and looks out the window. Under the lone streetlight on the Swift Feet's property, he sees a dark figure, unmoving. Lee's vision isn't the best, but from what he can tell, it's a half-naked man. A crazy neighbour, possibly?

His heart is pounding madly. The man is wearing deer skin leggings, long black hair covering most of his face, staring at Lee from about 75 feet away. Lee stares back. "This can't be real," he thinks. He rubs his eyes and takes a second look. There is no one there.

• • • •

Lee has Netflix playing on the front TV and he's making breakfast for Quentin. He's cooking eggs, bacon, fried spam, and biscuits and gravy. An authentic NDN breakfast.

"How was the 'Ino last night?" Quentin says as he pours his coffee.

Lee looks up at him and says "I didn't make it actually."

"So we can go later tonight?"

"Shoot, you know it. That Mega Moolah slot machine is calling my name." Lee pauses. "Actually, I want to talk to you about something."

"Is it how you're ruining those eggs? Turn down that heat idiot, Gordon Ramsey says cook it on low-medium heat." Quentin says as he reaches over and turns down the heat on the stove.

"I'll throw this entire breakfast into the trash right now..." Lee sighs. "Actually. I think you should leave, Quen."

"Shut up and give me some eggs," Quentin responds. Lee looks down, avoiding eye contact. "I'm serious dude. Get out. Seriously. This town has nothing for you. Take this." Lee sets a bundle of cash on the kitchen table. "And get the hell out of Wolf's Creek. Move to the city, enroll in community college classes like you said you were going to."

Quentin looks over at the cash and then back at Lee.

Still looking down at his feet, Lee says, "You can do so much better than this town. Indians don't leave here. They die here. You're better than that. You're better than me. You always have been..."

The brothers sit awkwardly in silence, as Lee has never been this vulnerable to Quentin. Lee breaks the silence, saying, "I've been holding you back your entire life."

Quentin reluctantly receives the cash and is speechless.

Lee sniffles. "I'll take care of myself, I promise. I'm going to be good. I got this, man. Go be your own person. Don't make the same mistakes I've made.... And just promise me that when you make it, in whatever you do in life that you don't forget about me."

After what seemed like an eternity, Quentin speaks up. "You gonna share some eggs or..."

The brothers break out in laughter.

"I... don't know what to say. I mean, I can call Travis in OKC and ask if I can stay with him for a while." The two finally made eye contact, which for them was basically a hug.

"At least until I can get enrolled in the fall semester if it's not already too late." He looks down at the wad of cash and then looks up at his big brother, his role model since he was born. "Are you sure you're okay with this?"

Lee looks down at his feet and then back up again.

"Yeah Quen, I've been uhh... sure for a long time."

"Thanks, Lee. I don't know what to say."

"Don't say anything, just eat some Spam and eggs with me like the old days. I made them just the way Mom used to."

The two brothers sit on the living room floor like they did when they were kids and instantly, they were both transported back in time. Saturday morning cartoons were playing, their friends were ready to play football outside as soon as they were done eating, and there wasn't a worry in the world.

• • • •

Over the next few days Quentin gets all his paperwork in order and is set to leave for Oklahoma City this evening.

Lee spends his Saturday afternoon working on his F150. This particular year's model was known for oil leaks and keeping it running is a full-time job. He is conflicted about what to do. Something in him tells him to go bury the medicine bundle back in that grave where he found it. But he doesn't want to.

He remembers hearing how medicine could be a double-edged sword if the user wasn't careful. But he isn't using it for anything bad.

His eyes dart back to the leather medicine bundle in the passenger seat.

A new truck would be nice.

I don't want to live here forever either.

I could go to the Casino today and see if this bundle is actually lucky. Maybe life is going my way for once.

I deserve this.

• • • •

"Well, my car is all loaded up brother. Hey, umm. When you see Unc next, tell him I'm going to be in the City for a while.

He probably won't notice anyway." Quentin says as he leans on his '05 Pontiac Grand Am spinning his keys around his pointer finger.

"I'll let him know. Text me when you get there Quen. Drive safe. Watch out for that speed trap in Verden, you know how the sheriff can be towards Indians. They'll catch you with that DWI... Driving While Indian." The Swift brothers chuckle.

"I'll come and see you in a few weeks when you're all settled in. And tell Travis I said I'm sorry for what happened."

The two sit in silence on this September Saturday evening and share a Marlboro. The weather is perfect. Lee stares reminiscently at the old house they grew up in, knowing this chapter of their lives is closing and another is moving in.

Lee repeats, "I'll come and see you in a few weeks when you're all settled in."

Quentin takes a last drag of the cigarette. "Well, brother, I better hit the road before it gets too dark."

Lee isn't the best at goodbyes. He looks up at Quentin and gives him a head nod, and watches his brother back up out of the driveway, and then down the street until he is gone.

• • • •

Lee sits in his truck, chain smoking Marlboros with a bottle of whiskey in hand. "Gold River Casino" flashes over and over, hundreds of tiny lights illuminating his face. The temptation to go in and try to win big is strong. He knows it would be actually, which is why he brought a bottle of bourbon to help convince him it was a good idea.

I deserve this.

Lee slides the leather medicine pouch into his backpack and heads inside. He heads to his 'old faithful' group of machines; the penny machines. He and Quentin often spent hours here betting the same $20 and only walking out with a few bucks here and there. The atmosphere in the casino is sad without his brother, but he's feeling lucky. He knows he's supposed to be here.

The hours pass into the dead of night and Lee has successfully won nothing. He clutches his backpack with the medicine inside and curses at it.

"Where is that luck when I need it? Huh?! You said I could have anything I wanted... I want to be rich."

As if it is God himself, a machine across the aisle comes to life. Jackpot flashed across the pupils of Lee's eyes.

"There's the one."

Lee grabs the last $20 in his wallet and slides it into the machine. It is one of those interactive touch screen machines. It must be new, he's never seen it. The lowest bet is $1. Max bet is $5. The screen is Egyptian Pharoah themed.

Max bet

Lee cranks the slot machine arm, and it is a loss. He tries two more times. Same result.

He stares at the flashing "500 credits" number in the bottom corner. His final $5.

Max bet

Just before he cranks the arm, a message appears on the screen—as if it wants him to know something before spending the last of his money.

Warning: The cost of winning may be more than you're willing to give.

Lee reads the message, assuring himself it is just the Pharoah trying to intimidate him into cashing out before he wins big.

Crank

The numbers scrolled, stopping one by one.

Seven

Seven

Seven

"Jackpot" flashes across the screen as his credit numbers rolls up. They don't stop. His heart is pumping so hard. All the blood seemingly leaves his legs. The red light above the machine flashes and spins around like a siren letting everyone know how lucky he is.

'$67,453' flashes over and over. People around him grab his shoulders and cheer for him. He can't believe it. He clutches his backpack tight until he has the courage to print the ticket.

Lee sits in his truck in denial. A load of cash sits in his passenger seat next to his backpack with the lucky medicine pouch inside.

This can't be real.

By now it is around midnight, and he just realizes Quentin didn't call him to let him know he arrived in OKC. He can't wait to give him the good news.

Ring ring ring

Quentin doesn't answer.

He tries again.

No answer.

Lee checks his location on his "Find My Friends" app. He sees Quentin is still in town.

That can't be.

Lee selects his location and sees exactly where he is. He's parked on Indian Road. *That* Indian Road.

His gut feeling tells him something is incredibly wrong.

Lee dives as fast as he can to Quentin's location. His luck is still with him as he hits every green light in town getting there.

About five miles down Indian Road, just east of Wolf's Creek, in the middle of nowhere, Lee sees the familiar Pontiac's taillights in a ditch. If he wasn't looking for the car, he wouldn't have noticed it.

No, no, no, no.

Lee jumps out of his truck and slides down the hill. Quentin's car is folded in half by a tree. Steam comes out of the engine bay and the scent of gasoline fills his nostrils. The driver's side door is open. Lee frantically scans the area and sees what looked like a lump of clothes in the grass about twenty yards in front of the car.

Quentin's lifeless body lays in the tall grass in front of his car. It looks like he tried to crawl to the road to signal for help but could only crawl so far. He died there alone, in the dark. His body is mangled, and his skin is eaten by mosquitoes and other insects.

Lee reaches for his brother and puts his head in his lap and screams. He screams for help in all directions, but there is no use. Quen's body is cold. He has probably been dead for hours. Broken glass covers his face in cuts so badly that he was almost unrecognizable.

Anger fills Lee's body. His skin is getting hot. He picks up his phone to call 911 and hangs it up. He looks over to the passenger seat of his truck.

I know what I need to do.

I can fix this, little brother, I promise.

Lee brushes off the thousands of dollars in cash and empty beer cans onto the floor of his truck and gently lays his brother's body on the seat and shuts the door. With blood now covering the steering wheel, he looks over at Quentin. His head lays on the window, as if he were sleeping.

They drive to the bend in Wolf's Creek where Lee had that first dream. He puts his backpack on and carries Quentin to the water.

Just lay him in the water.

And like a baby in a baptism, he lays his baby brother in the chest-deep creek. Quentin slowly sinks. Only bubbles came to the top.

Lee crawls to the bank of the creek and sits for hours. He knows all he has to do is wait. He clutches the medicine bundle in one hand and pleads to it all night long.

"Whatever you want me to do, I'll do it. I'll donate the money to charity; whatever it takes. I'll do it."

A turtle swims across the creek and submerges itself where Quentin lay.

His shock is wearing off. He realizes now what he is doing, and he is about to vomit. Dawn is approaching.

Lee stares at the creek.

Slowly, but surely, Quentin Swift Feet rises out of the water. The crown of his dark hair is visible first. Then his face. Then his torso. His body looks good as new. The cuts have vanished. His broken limbs are healed.

Water trickles down his face as he looks up and around, taking a deep breath through his nostrils, in and out.

Lee is breathless, suddenly paralyzed with fear. He has seen his dead brother come back to life. Quentin slowly trudges out of the water and sits on the creek bank. The two are silent, Lee rigid, until the little brother speaks. Not in English, but in Kiowa.

"Aho for awakening me, you will be rewarded, my servant."

PART III
THREE NOVELLAS
BY

ALEX SOOP

PHOTO: DIMA GULPA

～ FIVE ～

BOTCHED LANDING

PART I

THE MOUNTAIN AIR has a tinge of cool to it, even though it is midsummer. We are sitting at an outdoor patio where the smell of the newly installed planks mix with the aromas of barbecue grill and flowers in pots around the deck rail. The spread of nature past the sidewalk and parking lot is magnificent—a vast greenspace stretching wide, then monstrous mountains standing tall.

"You're sure you're ready to do this? It's only been a year since ... well, you know? I don't even wanna say it," says Stan, my best friend for as long as I care to remember.

Sweet, raspberry flavour tickles my taste buds as I inhale a lengthy drag from my e-cigarette.

"You know those things kill you just as much as real cigarettes," Stan says, breaking the silence which is starting to get uncomfortable—for him at least. I keep my eyes trained on the scenery and nod my head like I was hearing a song I liked.

"You're sure you're ready to do this, Chavez? Stan asks again. "You're not even listening to me, dude. You gonna answer my question, or what?" Stan finally sounds off with a hint of anger brewing in his voice.

I stare on without speaking, still nodding my head. Stan and I are enjoying the ambiance of what was her favourite restaurant— a nice, somewhat inexpensive stop in the town of Canmore before we enter into overpriced Banff. A loud squeal emanates from Stan's alfresco chair as he leans forward and smacks me hard on the kneecap.

Newfound feeling of annoyance, I swivel my head sharply and shoot him a cold look. "To answer your question. Yes, I am ready to do this."

"You're absolutely sure? Because I don't want you freezing up at the last minute now."

"I am. And please, have I ever frozen up before a jump?" I say as I suck back another long puff of my e-cigarette.

"She'd be really proud of you, cowboy, I mean the way you've been handling things. Hell, I'm even proud of you." Stan leans forward again, and pats me on the shoulder.

Maria's stunning face comes to mind, with her captivating eyes, and lips adorned in a shade of magenta, all framed by her ever-present smile. Her hair blows across her cheeks, which carry a warm caramel hue.

"Okay here we go," says the short and curvy waitress as she toddles over to our table, one hand balancing a platter full of drinks. "You guys look thirty as caged lions," she says. "...a tall, Long Island iced tea for you, and a mountain-sized Kokanee for you." She places the frosty drinks in front of Stan and me. "Thank you, miss. That was fast," says Stan in his most flirtatious tone.

The fit, blonde waitress flashes both of us a pretty smile, but I just continue to stare right through her at the outdoor scenery. "You are very welcome. And if you need anything more, just go ahead and wave me back over." She gives Stan a saccharine smile before scurrying off and disappearing into the shade past the open patio doors.

"She wants me," Stan says smugly.

"I bet she does," I say nonchalantly and stash my e-cigarette in my unbuttoned shoulder pocket. I grip my tall mug of beer and raise it into the air. "Cheers."

Stan grasps his chalice-like glass and lightly taps the side of my hefty beer mug. "Cheers, bro."

I take a huge inhale of the invigorating air before I take a long swig, smiling as I embrace the cool, crisp taste of the Rocky Mountain beer, still staring past, a thousand yards.

"What's on your mind?" Stan asks curiously.

Everything from this and that is on my mind. Life's fast lane of thinking. I'm finally able to pinpoint my focus on one thing. "That. Right over there." I place my mug of beer down and point past the parking lot.

Stan diverts his attention to where my finger is directed. "What, thinking of getting a new car or something?"

"No, you meathead. Look beyond the parking lot." Stan places his drink softly on the glass table and hovers half out of his seat for a better look. I snicker at his unnecessary action. "You don't even have to get out of your seat to see it, bro."

"Okay then." Stan plops back down in his chair and gazes hard through the clear, tempered-glass barrier. "I see nothing but a long stretch of boring flats and some big ass mountains."

"Exactly. You just said it, bro."

"You're losing me, dude."

I take another swig of my frothy beer, keeping my persistent gaze fixed on the beautiful scenery of snow-capped mountains staring down at us from across the pristine, sun-soaked meadow. "A meadow, surrounded by mountains, just like that one," I blurt out enthusiastically like a kid making the ultimate discovery. "We'll find a meadow like that way out in the heart of the mountain wilderness. That's where we will make the jump."

"Actually?"

"Actually," I echo.

"Okay then." Stan rubs his wiry chin stubble and gazes up at the baby blue, cloudless sky. "That sounds like one helluva plan. I'm game. Let's drink to it." We both raise our drinks, my own beer mug now one-third empty, and we smash glasses. The party that starts at that moment doesn't stop until dawn.

• • • •

"Have a shot, quick, before the pilot sees," Stan says over the hum of the airplane engine. We are loitering around on the runway at the Banff airstrip, checking our gear and waiting for the pilot to give us the go-ahead to board. Drinking or even being hung over is strictly forbidden for skydivers. If the pilot has any idea of our drink-filled exploits from what feels like a mere few hours before, he'll ground the plane and scratch the jump indefinitely. He's a strict one.

Hangover notions get the best of me. I seize the silver flask from Stan's grip and knock back a slug. The whiskey sizzles across my parched tongue and slams into the back of my throat like a breaking dam.

"Blech. That's some pretty nasty stuff, bro," I say with a sour face and hand him the flask like it took a nip at my hand. Pre-celebration. Stan's insistence

Although this isn't my first time being hung over before skydiving, I feel I am making a mistake by going ahead with it today, especially when I'm not feeling hundred percent. More like two percent at best. But everything has been planned out and paid for. To back out now would leave us out nearly a thousand bucks each.

This jump isn't going to be a regular outing like the rest. Stan managed to grub up a pilot in Banff who is willing to fly Stan and me plus our buddy Gris and jumpmaster Frederik two hours into the remote Rocky Mountain wilderness. From there, we are to take a 13,000-foot jump and land into a small, pre-selected meadow clearing. We plan to set up camp for the night, and finally make our way back to civilization by means of inflatable raft. The trip is all in the name of my late fiancée, Maria. Besides being a champion jingle dress powwow dancer, she loved skydiving and took me out on my very first jump.

"Give it here. I need a cure too, badly, fuck." Stan snatches the flask out of my hands and upturns it until there is nothing but a drizzle of gold liquid trickling into his mouth. I nearly gag, imagining the taste of the whiskey blustering across his taste buds. Stan drank twice as much as I did last night, so I know he's gotta be feeling it.

"Alright, gentlemen. The plane is primed for flight, all set to take to the skies. Let's perform a quick equipment check, load up, board the plane, and get the hell outta here," says Frederik, who is our hired jumpmaster and who has also become a friend. He waits for my nod of agreement before returning to the purring plane. Frederik was present during the jump when I proposed to Maria after a 13,000-foot free fall over the sprawling Nevada desert. So, I found it fitting that he should be in attendance for the skydiving venture and camp-out dedicated to honouring her memory.

"How do I look?" asks Gris, a friend of ours since high school on the Rez. Gris, his nickname, stems from his youngster days of rodeo bulldogging as well as to his voluptuous, bear-like size.

"Like a grizzly bear in a jumpsuit, bulldogger. You're lucky you were just under the maximum permitted weight by three pounds," accuses Stan with a sly chuckle.

Gris grins a tobacco chew-stained smile at me.

Nope, not on my watch. "You better spit that shit out before we board the plane," I snap. "I ain't kidding, bro, I'm not riding for hours in a fuselage stinkin' of that nasty shit."

"Yeah, okay cap'n," Gris says with a two-finger salute. "I'm gonna try to finish what's left right now. What about smokes, can I at least bring those along? Fucking guy."

"As long as you don't burn the forest down around us, dumbass," adds Stan.

"You have a lighter?" I ask Gris.

He pulls out a Zippo lighter emblazoned with a pinup girl graphic, and snaps it open with a flick of his wrist.

"Keep that thing safe. We may need it," I say.

"Yes sir." Gris stands stiffly upright and salutes me, British army style.

I nod, snicker, and summon the guys with a beckoning motion of my hands. "Okay dudes. It's going to be hella loud in that plane for the next two hours, and only the pilot and the jumpmaster have headsets. So let's get everything straight right now. First, let's make sure we have everything we need and let's pack in snug on the double. I don't wanna get in the air and realize we didn't pack our maps, or something stupid like that."

"Why can't we just use our phones?" asks Gris.

"Because, dumbass, there's no cell service where we're headed," says Stan, rubbing it in.

Another friendly chuckle. "That's right, bro. We have two detailed land maps. One for each raft, just in case we lose each other—which we won't," I say smugly.

"And the food. Check, a full menu of MRE ration packs," says Gris.

"Man, always about the food with you, eh?" Stan says teasingly, nudging Gris with the tip of his elbow.

"Shaaht up."

"Okay, maps. I just checked. Gris, you for sure double checked the food?" I ask. Gris nods at me with his full attention.

"Excellent," I say. "And how about you, Stan? You've double checked our camping gear and inflatable rafts?"

"I sure did. Three times."

"Good. Well that just leaves us to do a chute check, and then load up the plane. Let's get 'er done, pronto."

We give each other high fives, double check our parachute rigs and then commence loading up the airplane with our gear. The plane is free of the paved runway and in the air within ten minutes.

An hour into the flight. I take a moment from studying the map to gaze out the window and appreciate the splendid view of the mist-enveloped mountain peaks below us. At 17,000 feet, the rugged, slow-moving terrain gives me the impression of a tidal waving sea in a hundred shades of green, grey, and brown, the low clouds hovering below the peaks acting as the calmer waters. Knife-edged peaks of a thousand monsters seem to be trying to claw at our airplane's undercarriage.

A quick glance across the aisle and I establish the fact that the deafening roar of the airplane's twin engines, mixed with the cruising elevation, are making Stan's hungover head swim in wooziness. It was his idea to go so hard the night before. No pity for him. His skin is pale and he looks crazy, blinking his eyes tightly and shaking his head. He abruptly catches me staring and feigns a smile.

"Damn, I think I'm gonna be sick." The words come out in silent mouthing as I stare at him from across the aisle.

I snicker at the sight of Stan, looking like he is about

to lose his stomach's contents at any given moment. I sure hope he skipped on a huge morning breakfast. "Dumbass," I mutter to myself, although I could barely hear my own voice over the drone of the airplane motors. Getting back to the task at hand, I return my concentration to the paper map through a small plastic magnifying glass until my eyes begin to strain and my head feels faint. My own hangover symptoms, probably.

Letting my eyes return to normal focus, I reach into my breast pocket. Hands shaking, I extract a pocket-sized picture of Maria encased in thin plastic. Her university graduation picture. My heart skips a beat every time. She looks stunning. Her flawless smile drew me in from the very first moment I set eyes on her. That same beautiful smile greeted me as I revealed to her my grandmother's gleaming diamond ring, from my one-knee posture.

Those happy days are now long gone.

I take in the scene of Maria's memory in my mind. Her lean silhouette against the backdrop of a swiftly moving river captivates me like a black hole's infinite gravity. I feel as though I am hovering as I take small, gallant steps toward her. For each step I take, she shifts further away from me and seems to be blending into the darkness of the evergreen trees looming all around us. I know it is her by the familiar scent of her vanilla fragrance, and by her distinctive posture. She slowly turns around, but her beautiful face is shrouded in midnight shadows.

I stutter her name.

With a violent bump, I am jolted by the plane's midair turbulence. Maria's name is still on my lips.

Feeling totally taken by surprise with a rising mingle of anxiousness, I survey the airplane's compartment. Gris is fully alert in his seat, staring with intrigue out of his circular porthole, earbuds jammed into his ears. Frederik, the jumpmaster, and Jordan, the pilot, are sitting in the cockpit, deep in discussion as they chat with animated hand gestures. A look across the aisle. Stan is politely getting sick into a paper bag. No surprises there. A witty grin crosses my lips at his situation, and it brings some calmness to my battered nerves, still feeling the lingering effects of my own hangover.

Why, oh why, did I fall for Stan's insistence on going so hard the night before? I glance at my wristwatch just as the plane cabin grows substantially darker, like an evening under a rain-cloud, and the time only reads 2:32 p.m. It's approximately 30 minutes until the drop zone. Driving the anxious feeling away, I try to rest my eyes, but my darkened vision starts to spin like I am on a roller-coaster. The ultimate hangover dizziness. I peer out the fuselage porthole and see shifting, demon-faced storm clouds encircle the plane. The ground from 13,000 feet is virtually undetectable through the malevolent billows.

A hard tap lands on my shoulder, and I whirl around to meet Frederik's concerned gaze staring into mine. "We have trouble." I can't hear him at all over the roaring twin engines, but I manage to read his lips loud and clear.

"What is it?" I scream back over the deafening hum.

He hands me a headset with shaking hands, and I position them on my head as though my life depended on it. "What's the problem?" I ask.

"This storm." Frederik's voice crackles through the headset.

"Okay. It's bad, I get that. But what else is there?" I ask.

"It's a big one. We've lowered our flight altitude, but storm clouds are spread all the way down to a few hundred feet above the ground. We go any lower and we could fly right into a mountain face—and not to mention the fact that you want to do a thirteen-thousand-foot jump."

A blend of despair and anger brews in my head. I take a moment to dwell on the situation. Our safety is more of a priority over which altitude we exit the plane at.

"What's the highest altitude we can safely jump from without getting too tangled up in the storm clouds?" I ask.

"Three thousand feet," Frederik crackles on the headset.

"Damn it, that's so low though," I groan. The disheartening news of having to do a jump at such of a low-slung altitude stabs me like a serrated blade. The boys and I did not wrangle up big money just to do a low altitude jump over such beautiful scenery, now sadly compromised by heavy rain and midday darkness.

"Well," Jordan says, "for an extra four-hundred big ones, he'll circle around for a bit until the heavy clouds dissipate over our jump zone."

I didn't think it over for but a second. "Let's do it," I blurt out. The boys and I will sort out the costs later.

A satisfied smirk creases Frederik's lips. "You got it cap'n." He nods at me, politely retrieves the headset, and stumbles back toward the cockpit.

I reach into my pocket and once again pull out the plastic encased picture of Maria. I stare hard into her tantalizing gaze. "Look out for us, baby," I whisper and close my eyes. Her enchanting smile seeps through my mind's eye once again. Without forewarning, I feel gravity rip hard on my chest and stomach as the plane gains altitude. My unsettled hangover nerves begin to quiver in sync with the vibrating airplane cabin.

Anxiety begins to make itself known.

Air sickness as well.

I breathe. Deeply. In and then out, keeping my mind focused on the calming aspects of an midair free fall from the plane, hopefully soon. My mind stays occupied by those thoughts working like a natural high until the pilot does a split-second nosedive indicating we are back to our intended altitude. Nausea hits me as my head goes weightless and my stomach soars to my chest. I gaze out my condensa-tion-smeared porthole to see that the skies are still dark. Flashes of dazzling white and blue scrape across the black-ened skies, leaving trails of split-second light in their wake. No longer am I afraid. I am now enthralled by the brilliance of Mother Nature's fabrication that one would otherwise never get to witness from the ground.

Absolute beauty.

I stare through the window in astonishment like a kid at a fireworks display, when suddenly, the high-speed glimpse of a human form comes sailing past my peripherals. I twist my head around and see Frederik lying in a slumped posi-tion over his chute rig at the rear of the plane. My happy face drops. He is out cold. Panic makes me scream out for him and I grasp for my seatbelt. An enraged state of alarm trig-gers me to heave a barrage of unnecessary swears as I wres-tle the buckle to free myself.

I am just free of the seatbelt when the plane jerks left, then right, and I am tossed around like a ragdoll. Regretting unbuckling myself, I clasp onto the sturdy armrests for dear life. As the plane levels out momentarily, I get a split-sec-ond to gather myself. I glance around the plane to check on everyone's well-being. Jordan is in the cockpit struggling to control the plane by himself. Stan is struggling to get out of his seat. I am unsure as to why he would want to do that. Gris is still seated with his head against his headrest; his earbuds no longer crammed into his ears. He is crossing himself and speaking lightly. A prayer, I presume, since Gris is Catholic.

I wait for a moment until I presume it's safe to go and check on Frederik, then let go of my death grip on the arm-rests and leap out of my seat. I bolt for the rear of the plane, working my body overtime to battle against the tilt of gravity slamming me on all sides. Frederik is out like an exhausted battery, but still, I try my best shake him conscious.

"Come on, someone give me a hand," I scream to no one in particular, my voice barely making it through the noise of the cabin. Gris has heard me, or at least has seen my discernible hand gestures. He is out of his seat and wobbling toward me down the small aisle while Stan is staring at us with terror-filled eyes.

"Here, hold onto his head. I'm gonna go tell Jordan that we need to turn around and return to Banff," I scream over the hum and wait for a reply from Gris. He only stares at me like a clueless dog. I make deliberate hand signals until he finally nods in comprehension.

I have to force myself up against gravity pinning from all sides as it yanks down on my 200-pound frame. I shakily make my way down the aisle toward the cockpit. First, I stop to tell Stan that we are heading home. He reads my lips and nods with worry swimming in his large brown eyes. I place a comforting pat on his shoulder and carry on down the aisle. The final few feet to the entrance of the cockpit are harrowing as I feel the forces of gravity pulling me back hard like an invisible cowboy tether. The weight of the parachute rig strapped to my back doesn't make matters any easier.

Finally I reach the cockpit after what feels like wading through thick, viscous water.

I begin yelling for Jordan when I am suddenly sent soaring back from whence I had just so tediously trekked. I land hard in the middle of the cabin aisle, winded from the sudden plunge and the slam of my robust frame onto the floor. The force of gravity changes just as I push myself to a kneeling position, and I am sent tumbling toward the front of the plane like a rolling boulder. With quick reflexes, I catch myself hard on the aluminum frame of the cockpit entrance.

Jordan swiftly whirls his helmeted head around. "We might have to abandon ship," he screeches, his distorted words easy to perceive.

As I look on helplessly through the porthole, I see nothing but brewing clouds and aggressive lightning, the thousand shades of the malicious clouds made more intimidating by these flashes of fleeting light. With Jordan hard at the helm, the plane finally levels out and I am able to stand tall. He hands me a headset and I hear him clear as day. "Get everything we need and prepare to get everyone out. Now!" he screams. He begins activating a makeshift autopilot using a stick and rubber band, then brushes thrusts past me.

I am hard at his heels. "What the hell are you talking about?" I demand as I trail him down the centre aisle.

"The GPS—hell everything electronic is fried. I won't be able to safely fly us through this electrical storm. It's best that we jump now while the plane is still at a safe enough altitude." Jordan keeps on moving until he reaches the main fuselage access. He tugs on the safety latch and slides open the hatch. A squall of freezing wet wind infiltrates the calmness and overpowers the already loud cabin. I have to grab on to the roof suspended safety railing just to stable myself.

"Frederik's hurt," I say through the crackling headset.

"What?" Jordan stops what he is doing and faces me with shock-riddled eyes. "How bad?"

"I have no idea. He's at the rear with Gris."

"Okay—shit! We have to get him off the plane first. He's priority. Someone will have to jump with him, maybe even two of us so we can guide him safely to the ground."

"I'm on it," I say. I begin striding toward the rear of the plane to begin assisting Frederik when another violent jolt of turbulence rocks the aircraft. I lose my relaxed grip on the safety railing, stumble a few feet forward like a drunk, and once more go tumbling down the uncluttered aisle.

There I go. Clean out the open hatch.

••••

PART II, Maria

Maria, you are always on my mind. These survival log notes are letters meant for your eyes. You have always encouraged me to be a writer, so here I go. I dream of you only. I know you are looking out for me.

August 16th, Day 1:
Dear Maria,
   Yesterday I regained consciousness in a tree in a state of toxic panic, but your soft whisper breathed my name. Lucky me. Somehow, someway, I was in a seated position on a large, bristly branch stabbing out from a thick tree trunk, staring through a tangle of ruffled leaves. The red ball of burning, daytime fire was situated far beyond a tall mountain peak, its rays of warmth barely enough to penetrate my freezing body and soul. I probed the grey skies hanging over top of me. An obvious path of man-made destruction draped above me in the forms of twisted and broken tree limbs. The white strings of my chute rig were tangled like Twizzler licorice and the canopy of my bright red, nylon chute was in tattered strands with jagged green leaves and branches stabbing through it.
   I glanced at my sky-reflecting wristwatch, a great pawn-shop buy of a once-rich-man's extravagant time piece—until he ultimately decided that it was time to buy another, more expensive piece, I suppose. It was either that or a good steal by a meth-head. One way or another, still a steal of a deal, but utterly worthless in my current predicament. The silver timepiece read 4:22. I'd been out cold and in the cradle of a half dead tree for almost two hours.
   My throbbing head was still hungover, with an added touch of fatigue like I had suffered some kind of a beating in a forced boxing match. I ached, but pulled myself to a more comfortable position using one of the strings still attached

to my harness. Then that I realized that my whole lower body had gone numb from the hugging tension of my harness rig. I disengaged the clicking fasteners and my body dropped like a rock to the solid ground. I landed hard, grunting as I hit the ground, feeling lucky to have only fallen a few feet. Well isn't that something lucky, if I knew any such luck. My face was lying in a heap of dead and damp leaves. I pushed myself to my feet, looked around and tried to process my whereabouts. Nothing but the scraggly twists of sun-borne evergreen shadows surrounded me. I patted myself down and realized I had nothing on me but my uninsulated jumpsuit, with my $6,000 parachute rig and harness still in the tree. Money wasn't an issue at the moment. I fished around my pockets some more, taking the time to feel around, until I found your picture, holding it for dear life in my numb, shaking fingers. A large bending crease was streaked across your beautiful face in the shape of a jagged lightning bolt. I ransacked some more and found my cellphone and my e-cigarette. Both were cracked. I tried the power button on the phone but it was as dead as the branches scattered all around me.

I felt defeated.

Fuzzy flashbacks of the preceding events streaked across my mind's eye. I scarcely recalled my choppy free fall, mere seconds after I had tumbled out of the open airplane hatch. My mind replayed the sounds of the deafening blasts of air as it ripped past my face and enshrouded my eardrums like a broken record player. The recollection of the plane's silvery fuselage, rapidly diminishing from my tumbling view and becoming just another speck amongst the dark clouds, suffused my thoughts like a bleary hallucination. I don't remember for the life of me how I recovered from my spinout and safely reached the ground by way of my open parachute.

Safely. Barely.

Then I remembered Frederik. A sudden sense of alarming shock overtook my senses. "Oh shit. The guys. Frederik," I shouted to no-one in particular, well, or, maybe just to you, Maria. I have a wholesome feeling that the guys are faring just fine. Hopefully. Unlike myself. No, they have to be. They had Jordan at the controls; an ex-CF-18 fighter pilot (with experience in field dressing). The best in Canada by all means.

Feeling drained and sad, I gathered what was left of my primary shoot. I pulled the tattered strings from their tight grip winding around the unbroken tree branches. No way I was going to get out of this mess alive, only to leave behind a $6,000 rig. It took me almost an hour just to piece together the nylon strings and canopy. Once I was finished stuffing my chute remains together, I shouldered it like a backpack and looked up at the empty skies of slow, shifting clouds.

Hearing nothing but the eternal whispering hush of the mountain breeze, the dreaded feeling of being fully alone ate at me. Only the faint chirps of far-off birds and the calls of the wild engaged my weary senses. I cupped around my eyes with my hands and carefully scanned the skies for a few minutes. There was absolutely no sign of any neon-coloured parachutes, or the drone of an airplane in search of me. Only ridge-lined mountain peaks and tree-covered mounds as far as my eyes could see.

I sighed again as my heart dropped into despair. But I have to stay strong and resilient for myself. Hope will get me through this. Hope ... and you.

I had to make a choice of taking a particular direction. And yet, I had no idea which route would eventually lead me to safety. If that. A literal life or death situation at its finest. It might be weeks of walking before I finally come across a logging or service road; my clothes nothing but rags, my body gaunt like the walking dead. If I even make it that far.

And still, even if I manage to survive that long with no food or water, it still could be an eternity of hiking absolutely nowhere into the expansive Rocky Mountain wilderness. Treading into an untouched world of oblivion with only my teenage air cadet training to rely on.

I loosened up my harness, closed my eyes and did a few spins. And then like a gambler, I played a game of absolute chance and chose to follow an animal path criss-crossing through a clearing. The lowest of the mountains surrounding me was my intended destination. Hope. Perhaps.

Falling asleep was almost impossible beneath the open, starry skies. I tossed and turned, trying to find the least bit of comfort. The gathering of pillowed leaves and solid ground for my bedding kept me in a lucid state of dreaming. My dream was that I was encircled by the swishing sounds of a swift river. Cool dampness from the soft grass tickled at my bare feet. I followed the waterway until it broke into a large Y intersection, where the river branch connected to smaller body of rapid, roiling water. Despair seeped in at the feeling of nothingness. But I decided, not-so willingly, to follow the more powerful of the streams with the setting sun parallel to the river's shifting horizon, its tint of rose gold rays leaping off the unsteady surface like a jagged mirror.

Twenty paces inward and I saw a form standing at the riverbank's edge. A woman. I knew it was you by your long flowing hair waving, like a flag in the wind, and the scent of vanilla. Like a kid seeing Santa, I cheerfully trotted over to you. "Hey Hey!"

You had your back turned to me and you were completely motionless except for the wind fluttering your hair. You was dressed in an all-white satin gown which was bizarrely unmoving in the breeze.

I told you I was lost. You twirled around and your long hair was like a flowing river. The sun beams shone upon your face like divine spotlights. I was torn from my trance of fear. Your familiar face struck warmth in my cold-running blood. I said your name like I've said it so many times over. "Maria."

You smiled, making your delicate, rosy cheekbones reflect the sun's warmth. Then you said, in my dream, "You have to trust him." Your voice came out like an angelic rustle on the breeze.

But who? Who am I supposed to trust?

You didn't answer me. You turned to face the river.

I called your name again, Maria. I took another step toward you with outstretched arms. My hand caressed your soft arm.

Thinking back, I know this survival log is keeping me sane. I will write more tomorrow for you, or for someone to find if I don't make it out of here

August 17th, Day 2:

This day got very strange, dear Maria.

Although I still felt useless and drowsy today, I fought against the cold attacking my nerves. I am so tired. The bed of gathered leaves is not enough comfort for my two hundred pounds. I wondered where the hell to go. My stomach grumbled, I was and I am so hungry.

The sun was high when I set out, almost directly above, so it must have been about noon. It was almost impossible to tell which direction was which. My legs were wobbly. Surrounding were three clearly visible mountain peaks towering over green valleys. I took a gamble and headed in the direction of the lowest valley, thinking there might be a river at its base. I hoped studying the map had given me some memorable knowledge of rivers or lakes in the vicinity.

First, I stopped to examine a grouping of tightly arranged

trees. No dice. The full ring of bark was void of any moss, indicating the direction of north.

I kept moving.

Summer is still in full swing. Thirst and hunger has invaded me. I walked for hours on end, dreaming of flowing waterfalls and immaculately detailed water fountains. The abundance of wild grass surrounding me was knee high and damp, marinating my polyester pant legs in an immersion of wetness I wished I could slurp up.

In a shadowed area, I paused to catch my breath. From my side of the hill, a splendid view of a steep, evergreen-lined decline presented itself. The thorny canopy tops rippled downward until they crashed into an opposite incline and again sloped up in a surge of hazy green, straight out of an enchanted dream.

Shit. I would love this had I'd not been so damned lost, and you would love this nature too, Maria. But all I felt was a long streak of loneliness and desolation. On my journey today, I listened closely for the sounds of a river. The pungent air was graveyard silent though, except for the constant whisper of Mother Nature's essence breathing through the foliage. Not even the sounds of chirping birds were around to break the serene quietness.

I found an animal trail and opted to follow it in hopes of coming across any signs of life.

Anything.

I walked carefully, keeping my eyes on the path and behind me, hoping a predator animal wasn't following my scent. Above my head, the greying pillows of clouds shifted slowly around the misty horizon, blocking the direct view of the mountain's summit. When the blistering sun made momentarily peeks through the clouds, I tried my best to keep my polyester-covered body hidden in the tree shadows. It was much cooler in the shade of the towering trees.

As much as a ten-degree difference. A difference my dehydrated body couldn't afford to ignore.

As I walked on through the never-ending Canadian outback, a dull cramp of pain began to bite at my calves. I forced myself to keep going until the trail levelled out, then I stopped to take another breather. Tiredness eating my body, I took a longer break than I should have, nearly passing out from exhaustion.

It felt like I closed me eyes for only a few minutes. Nope. A few hours later and the sun was setting over the horizon. West. Good. I knew if I kept on following my route, I would eventually come across a mountain town like Radium—or maybe one of the hot-springs streams that pours into it. Eventually.

Hopefully.

I carried on but my hope was waning. I trekked for another hour or so—up and down, and up and down—before the animal trail abruptly ended and the assembly of trees cleared into a large meadow. Meadows sometimes meant water, so I kept pushing forward, straining myself, even through the severity of swampy terrain. But at least there was water. The large meadow was a flat of muddy wetland, but I was sure I should not drink the smelly water. I trudged on, keeping my thirsty gaze fixed to the potholes of muddy water, just wishing I could hop face first and lap up until my dried-out stomachs content.

But of course, I didn't. Couldn't.

I had no other choice but to reach the other side of the meadow, hoping I would still have enough energy to set up camp. Hoping I wasn't being eyed by a ferocious and hungry bear or a pack of wolves.

Near the closing of the wide-open expanse, there was a an even worse smell. Probably decomposing animals in the bog. Then I heard a crashing in the woods and my heart began to race. I saw the unmistakable silhouette of a tall man striding casually near the rocky base of the mountain. I bellowed out to him, "Hey!"

He stopped. He heard me.

"Hey. Over here!" I screamed as loud as I could. My voice sailed through the open air and bounced off the sheer rocky precipice perched beneath his place of stride. I knew for a fact that he had heard me. And he did, indeed. The mystery man stood still, just staring. I felt like I should turn and run the other way. But then the man started waving at me with two huge, flailing arms.

My welcoming gesture. I was saved.

Ignoring my aching legs and lungs, I broke out in an all-out dash for the hills. I moved like a gazelle and kept my eyes shifting from the man to the rough, rock-strewn ground, and back to the looming man. The smell remained in the air. I kept up a steady stride, leaping over ankle-breaking rocks and foot-luring marmot holes.

"I'm coming to you," I yelled. My spirit was as high as the pitch of my ecstatic voice. I took another few wide-footed strides before I finally stopped at the base where the wet, jerky ground met the inclined rock face, decorated in patches of green moss and dirt mounds. I glanced up; eyes full of teary optimism.

He was gone.

My heart and soul dropped. As did my face.

All I could do then is cry out, "No, no, no. Come back. I'm just lost, I'm not going to hurt you." Like a crazed and desperate animal, I was. I scrabbled up the hill, dodging treacherous stones and skeletal tree branches that seemed to claw at me, preventing me from reaching the stranger.

"Hey wait. Don't go, don't go," I screamed at the stranger over and over again, until the mixture of climbing and yelling made me stop dead and plop face down into a heap of pillowy moss. That's when I passed out from exhaustion.

When I woke up, the sun was setting. Then I remembered the man. I knew he wasn't a dream or a hallucination. He couldn't have been. Perhaps I had just spooked him off. Isolated locals surely wouldn't like strangers in their territory of pure freedom. And I understood that I might have looked crazy in the way I was dashing toward him like a rabid dog eyeing a would-be meal.

I got to my feet and for a second time I began my climb up the incline of the mountain. I was hard at the heels of the setting sun. As I hiked up into the uphill nothingness, I began to contemplate my sanity. I thought to myself, "Could I have hallucinated the man?" It's been known to happen. Besides, I was certainly dehydrated, to say the least.

My mind kept busy wondering about my sanity until the incline finally levelled out into a small, oval plain, dotted with shrubs, and evergreens. Tired and worn out, I decided to sleep under a large tree with a low-hung canopy for me to crawl under. Maria, tonight I was too drained of life to even build a comfortable camp.

August 18th, Day 3:

Dear Maria, Success, I'm alive to tell you about another day. I awoke today still feeling groggy. My body felt cold and achy but at least there was no fever, only aches and pains from the constant tossing, turning, and shivering. And hunger and thirst. Oh, the hunger and thirst. I hadn't felt that kind of hunger since my days as a kid growing up with a single mother of four.

I got up and carried on moving, still dragging my defunct chute rig. I chose to keep mounting the hill because a feeling kept nagging at me that there was hope resting somewhere beyond the scraggly horizon. Maybe a 360-degree view of the surroundings. Of a town or village—or even a lake full of fresh, thirst-quenching water. Or the unusual stranger I saw yesterday.

At last, after hopeful hours of wearisome climbing, I reached a gentle incline and busied my conscience with deep thoughts of what to do next. Then my eyes caught a glimmer in the low-lying distance. It was like the fluctuating reflection given off when light hits water.

I raced for the glimmering speck, once again ignoring my stomach pains, wheezing lungs, and burning leg muscles. Within a few feet of the reflection, my weary mind was in a state of frenzy. The glimmer was a one-litre bottle of spring water. I snatched up the bottle, tore open the cap and slammed back until there was nothing left but a two-drop sprinkle.

I brought the empty water bottle to my shocked face and examined the clear container. Dasani spring water. Gris's favourite—if he had a choice for a favourite water.

I blurted out, "Gris, you sly son of a bitch of a bulldogger," I looked around the surrounding area in search of more water bottles, keeping my twitching eyes bonded to the grassy ground and outlying treetops. After minutes of hopelessly searching, I was ready to give up in anguish. I looked up toward the skies, ready to scream at the heavens in distress.

And there it was. The bright, neon-yellow bag was wedged tightly between the thorny branch arms and tree trunk, a large tear slashed through its side. One of our emergency packs. The guys had managed to toss the bag of supplies out of the open hatch not long after they noticed me gone.

I calmed myself, eyed the sky once more, and gave them thanks, "Thanks, you guys," I said right out loud to the cloudless azure.

I wasted no time and scaled the tree. Maria, remember me telling you how I'd spent many a summer climbing trees when I was young. Whenever I saw trees, I was immediately putting my climbing skills to the test. After what seemed like an hour of careful climbing, the bag was safely in my grasp. I attached it to my harness rings and descended the tree, grabbing onto the thickest of the branches. The climb down was rougher than the climb up.

Finally on the ground, I zipped open the pack and inspected the contents. To my complete satisfaction, the pack was crammed full of the good stuff: four bottles of Dasani water, space blanket, plastic tarp, waterproof matches, candles, tin bowl and cup, water purification tablets, durable LED flashlight, extra batteries, sunscreen, sun goggles, gloves, folding knife, first aid kit, and best of all, four MREs. Yes. One of our emergency kits.

But there was no compass and no map. Damn. Oh well. In that dire situation a beggar couldn't also be a chooser.

Then I came across the final items, which made me smile: Gris's pinup-decorated Zippo lighter and a tin of tobacco chew.

With a new state of cheerfulness brewing in my mind, I immediately got busy, setting up a camp for the evening on the oval hill crest overlooking an immaculate spectacle of oceanic shades of green. The small plastic tarp worked magic in its use as a temporary tent. I gathered up armfuls of wood and kindling did just fine for a small campfire. Sitting happy with my small inferno of mortal warmth, I tucked into one of the MRE's; slowly, so as not to make myself sick. Even after my small meal, I was still hungry, but I still chose to ration the remaining three, knowing I may be stranded for the long run.

I fell asleep for a good long while by the small red glow of the crackling fire coals, my stomach no longer growling. I dreamed I was back at the Y intersection of the swift moving river, but, Maria, you were not there this time.

"Maria?" I called out for you but you did not answer my call. There was only the melodious hissing of the river rapids at my feet. I turned and started moving away from the river, when I heard a strange noise. I whirled around to face the river's edge again. Still nothing. Cautiously I moved away from the swishing water and joined a trail that extended far through the shadows, snaking its way through a curved clearing beneath the impenetrable awning of trees.

The sound came again. It sounded like an owl's screech, only larger and deeper, sending chills running down my spine. It was as though the bird was the size of my own physique—perhaps bigger. I turned again and saw it clearly. The large silhouette of the man was standing on the opposite shoreline, waving its arms as if to be saying: come over here.

Ignoring any sense of caution, I stepped to the rocky shoreline and carefully placed one foot in the water, followed by the other. The smooth rocks were cold and slippery. I paused to have a look at the man. He was still there, waving at me. Waving me over!

I called to him, "Hold on, please wait up for me this time." I nearly lost my balance on the slick rocks. I resumed my upstream battle, taking another step against the raging current when I felt the oily-like substance scrape against my numbing foot. I immediately lost my balance on the slippery rock resting beneath the water.

Face first, I went crashing down to the icy water, hands out. My vision was obscured by the rush of the cool, biting froth, falling and rising, and plunging and climbing through my distorted field of vision. The sheer coldness compressed my chest like the pressurized deep of a bottomless ocean. My ears were filled with the rumbling ambiance of the rushing water as it sliced past my face. I began to feel myself drowning in the murky iciness, my slashing limbs giving up their fight to get me to the surface.

A crash, loud and deafening, forced me to a sitting position before I was even fully awake. I pushed my lungs to try and breathe through a fit of coughs. My hands flailed wildly about, causing my makeshift tent to crumble on top of me, soaking me wet from the downpour of the freezing midnight rain.

Waking sleep is what I once read in an old high school textbook. It's a state in which the sleeper can hear and even respond to questions. In this case, the question was the roar of thunder which tore me from my sleep. I answered it. I rolled over onto my stomach in an effort to shield my face from the freezing torrent.

In a state of lingering misery, squirming my body to hide from the icy moisture attacking my body, I waited for the storm to pass. Rolling onto my back, I scanned the blackness of twinkling of stars, their glow broken in segments by the sprouting evergreen pine needles above my head. I wasn't beaten. Not yet.

In a desperate move full of aggravation, I folded the crackly space blanket tightly around my sopping body and shivered myself back to sleep. I wish you were really here with me, but your memory keeps me going.

August 19th, Day 4:
Dear Maria, I was parted from my diary for a few days, but I will remember as best as I can.

On Day 4, I was welcomed back into the world of magnificent sunbeams warming my face. My body was damp but not soaked; the benefits of polyester clothing.

Envisioning myself in the comforts of my bed, I lay back and stared up at the cloudless ether, thinking about what I was going to do next. At least I had some provisions. And hopefully they were enough to keep me alive and going. But for how long?

Before I could get too comfy in my newly acquired bedding, I was up and nourished from my second helping of a spaghetti-flavoured MRE.

I walked to the middle of the oval clearing and took in the sights before me. Spread out on the opposite mountain's edge, lustrous shades of green spread downward and ended off in a steep precipice. Further beyond that, a heavy cluster of clouds hovered over a smaller mountain peak, with gloomy shades of green twisting around the hilly horizon.

For some reason, joy filled me entirely. The looks of the hills extending down the distance seemed promising. The kinds of promises that spelled out civilization.

I was packed and ready to move out within minutes.

Within a few hundred metres into my trek, the excursion was daunting—even though I was travelling downhill. Dead pine needles and loose dirt riddled the sharp pitch of the downhill climb, which made me stumble. I managed to scrape my exposed arms on the thorn-like tree branches reaching for me like emaciated fingers.

In the shadows, my spirit began to dwindle. I kept up my feeling of chirpiness by fantasizing about hot showers, a fat, steak and egg meal, and a warm bed. With you.

The entire day was spent trudging downhill, as I tried not to lose my footing and tumble the whole way down, killing myself in the process. You don't realize how hard it is travelling downhill through dense bush until you've spent an entire day balancing yourself with your aching calf muscles.

At least I knew I was still heading west, when the sun began to conceal itself beyond the western horizon of a black, thorny ridge line. Without a compass I was only able to depend on the sun.

I kept my mind busy by pondering over my thoughts and ambitions. Ambitions like me taking the time to study the stars, much like my ancient forefathers. At last, I reached another gentle incline, and trekked upwards. But the endless hike got the best of me. So, I forced myself to set up camp even though it had grown dark. I whistled a tune as I made my encampment on a small flat of open ground and cracked open the third MRE. Steak and rice flavoured.

Feeling somewhat full, I dozed off into sleep. This time my sleep was dreamless and peaceful, until it turned for the worst, as I was torn awake by a bad smell and the sounds of my makeshift tent being violently shaken, sounding like a large sail flapping in a squall. Adrenaline at full tilt, my heart felt like it was beating in the centre of my throat. In a desperate hurry I wriggled out from under the tent, grabbed the trusty flashlight and flicked it on. Curiosity getting the best of me, I skirted around the tent perimeter and scanned the darkness enshrouding me. The LED light beam lit up anywhere it touched with the brilliance of a white sun.

Could I have been imagining it again? Much like the man I thought I had seen? I was dehydrated and delirious before. Now I was not. I skulked back to the tent to investigate the outer shell. There was no wind, so therefore, it would have been impossible for it to flutter like a rogue flag. I sprayed the bright beam over the slanted sides and came across what looked to be a large mud-smeared, humanoid handprint. My blood ran icy. My heart jumped back up my throat.

And then I heard it. A deep, guttural growl from behind me. I pivoted around as fast as my throbbing calves would turn my body and flashed the beam like I was carving through the air with a sharp sword.

I counted six sets of closely spaced eyes. They reflected the bright LED beam, giving them the appearance of twelve lone stars in the dead, blackness of space. My fear sent me sprinting in the opposite direction of the perilous sets of eyes. Over my heavy breathing, I could clearly hear the wolves' ground-thrashing footsteps and growls gaining on me. I kept moving, keeping the flashlight beam shining ahead on the path.

I had no choice but to slow my pace as the grassy ground before me curled downward like a closing fist. A cliff's edge. And before I even had a chance to fully stop and think.

I was airborne.

The splash clouting my ears was all I heard before my face was shrouded in freezing murkiness. I saw the flashlight beam tumble like an out-of-control car as it careened from my grasping fingers and got lost in the depths.

This time it was not a dream.

I kicked wildly until my legs gave up and stabbing pains jolted through my lower body. I was left pitching and tossing like a weightless puppet through the airless murk of black. I held my breath and closed my eyes.

Through sheer luck, my partially numbed bare foot touched the grainy bottom. I pushed up with what strength I had left, taking a crucial gasp of air before my head was sucked back beneath the raging current, which tossed me in all directions. I repeated the action three or four times until my knees eventually scraped a rocky undersurface with my head still above the water's bustling shallow.

I crawled out of the freezing water and, like a broken man, collapsed onto the gritty shore. I rested, shivering and coughing until my breathing normalized. My inner voice told me, "Get the hell up."

The full moon glided from its cover of black clouds, drowning the surrounding area in a cold white light, similar to my bright LED flashlight—now lost forever in the raging black river. A treeless, sandy beach spread out, the moonlit sand extending to the water. The sloshing, white-light-glistening river was bent like an elbow. Just beyond the raging water, a steep rocky cliff soared upward, looking like the devil's mural of a thousand deformed faces, with its jagged features, snapping at me. Trying to take me in.

"Holy mother—"

My words of surprise were abruptly cut off by the siren-like whines of the wolves chanting and wailing their songs of failure. Failure at having lost their chance at a late-night snack. I tried my best to ignore the wails which pierced my waterlogged ears.

"At least I found water," I said to myself.

Hope was restored once again.

August 20th, Day 5:

Dear Maria, Between day 4 and 5 I stayed awake all night like a sentry on duty, contemplating my imminent death. Death, which was just a hidden monster, ready to jump at me when the right moment arrived.

At last, the rising sun made itself visible on the eastern horizon, the warming rays battling to cut across the mountain and evergreen tops. But I waited, fighting my shivers, until there was sufficient sunlight and I was dry enough to be comfortable. My mission was to get back to my gear. I backpedalled the sand and rock-riddled shoreline until I was able to find a shallow spot in the river where it met the lowest elevation of the cliff. Lucky for me, I had taken those rock-climbing classes, remember that, Maria? I was ready to use those barely recollected skills. As cold and miserable as I was, it was also the morale-upping thought of another MRE which was enough to make my body spurt some energy out of nowhere.

The placebo effect. I was in full energetic mode.

I scaled the cliff in no time and was back at the top, edging along the overhang until I reached the spot where I had stepped off, right into the raging river below. I skulked, hunched over and slowly craned my head to take a peek over the grassy verge. There were no signs of the peckish wolves in wait, ready to devour me. I took a look behind my shoulder. Distant ridgelines crisscrossed each other, giving the outline the appearance of a sideways view of a glass-encased ant farm. I looked down. From the top of the grassy cliff edge, I wondered how I managed to not get seriously hurt after taking such a fall.

I recalled my cadet survival instructor saying that falling into raging water is safer than falling into calm waters. Who knows if that is really true, but it was what I heard in my mind as I scurried up the incline and back to my campsite.

Canine footprints were evident in the soft, damp ground surrounding the camp. But something else also caught my eye. It looked as though the wolves had been involved in some sort of melee with another animal. A much larger animal. The abnormal set of strange footprints sent another jolt of shivers through me. It looked like a bulky bear's paw with lengthier fingers—and no visible claws.

I shuddered at my mind's depiction of such a larger, more prehistoric creature, and myself just barely missing meeting it head on. My body might have been the tug-of-war rope between the skirmishing beasts.

I had to leave, and fast.

First, I examined my belongings. Miraculously, my remaining MRE was untouched by the hungry visitors in the night. This notebook was right where I'd left it. I realize, Maria, that if I am going to make it out of here I need to keep my mind on my escape, and I must be vigilant of the strange man and the wolves. Please know you have helped my body and soul survive, and I love you.

• • • •

PART III
Survival in the Present

I waste no time gathering my gear and wrapping up my tent. Like a fully equipped soldier, I hike back to the cliff's edge and scale back down. By the time I reach the bottom, my heart is on fire and my body is drowned in sweat.

Once at the bottom, I fill my empty bottles with the clear river water and drop in the purification tablets, just in case. I work on another steak and rice MRE, gathering my thoughts of how to go about the next leg of my journey. I choose to follow the raging current of the river, keeping my senses acutely attuned to my surroundings. Wolves are cunning, and they will stop at almost nothing to get their anticipated meals. This I knew.

The large foaming river twists and snakes through the bush. At some intervals, I am forced to distance myself from the river's edge, because the ground becomes too soft and deep with mud.

The setting sun is falling directly ahead of my path when I see two specks of glimmers spread out on the flat horizon. I keep my pace going until the river splits into the shape of a Y.

I already know this Y intersection. It is where Maria was standing in my dreams, looking beautiful and unmoving in her motionless white gown, saying, "You need to trust him." Thinking back at that, I wonder who she means I need to trust. My radar will be up. I choose to take the branch of the river with a more powerful current. Just like in my dream of Maria.

I seem to be walking more and more into the world of nowhere. Deja vu strikes me hard while I peer up at the crimson sun aligned with the river sequence, its transcendent shafts of light piercing the water surface in a crisscross of golden rays.

An eerie and overwhelming feeling seizes me, and I am forced to stop. I shoot a sideways glance over my right shoulder.

There he is again.

He is closer than ever. The stranger stands tall, on the opposite shore, waving at me with both arms like a madman jumping out in front of a moving vehicle. And there is that rotten smell again.

I turn my head away, biting my tongue, and gaze down at the thick undergrowth of rippling knee-high grasses gliding past my unseen feet. I mutter, "You're losing it, man. You're absolutely fucking losing it." First the man at the meadow, then the shaking of the tent . . . now this? I am going nuts.

I keep my head trained to the ground and walk a few paces until curiosity gets the better of me. Taking my sweet time I look back at the gleaming river surface.

The man is still there, seeming to have walked in step with me along his side of the riverbank. He is no longer waving, but is now unmoving with broad shoulders and tree trunk arms resting at his sides. I feel his shadow-concealed eyes staring hard at me. The realness of him feels genuine. I know that I am not dreaming or seeing a mirage.

"What the hell do you want?" I ask him. My loud voice sails across the rushing river surface.

Still, he doesn't move, only stares at me.

"Fine," I scream. I tightened up my shoulder straps and storm into the raging river. It is not as cold as I thought it would be. I just take another step when I feel and hear the rumble of footfalls coming from behind me. I turn, almost losing my balance, my keen eyes catching the swaying movement of the bush tops lining the river's edge. And just like that, like a parade—a deadly parade—the pack of wolves jumps out of the bushes in unison, the biggest of the pack lunging and stopping just before the water. The large snapping teeth and snout just miss my outstretched hand, both my arms spread out for balance, as I stop and stand motionless. Fear has gotten the best of me.

Then I face the man on the opposite shore, looking for an answer to yet another disastrous situation. Maybe it was how abruptly I turn my head but I lose my balance, my feet slip on the slick, rocky riverbed, and my low back slams into a concealed rock. My vision turns black, then a hundred tones of white and grey as my head submerges below the water's surface.

All I can think of at that moment is the unidentified man. To hell with the wolves. To hell with the sudden onslaught of another dip in a raging river. I use my hands and elbows to push my face to the surface, twist my body so that I am belly down in the water. There he is. Still there in my wobbly, water-withered vision. Standing tall, the man remains unmoving. I feel my short-lived sense of reassurance sweep away as I am carried down the river, the man once again just another speck disappearing into boundless wilderness.

Have I finally given up? Accepted the fact that I am meant to die alone out here in the Canadian wilderness? I turn to lie on my back, sipping small breaths as my body and head dip below the surface. Bad turns to worse as I feel the rubbing rocks withdraw from the balls of my feet, the water turning deeper and colder. Even the banks seemed to be retreating from my teary field of view.

But no, I am not going to give up. I duck under the water again, to try and push off a bedrock with my flailing legs. But the water is too deep. I panic, the river now trying in vain to make me whole with it, dragging me under with its magnificent undertow.

I scream, accidentally taking in a mouthful which stings my lungs. Too late. I am surely dead. My body goes limp, my thrashing arms go still.

But what is this?

My head strikes something floating on the river's wild surface. My elbow bends and stays put on what feels like rough wood bark, giving me enough of a boost in morale to regain some strength and pull my head out from the water. First my head, then my other arm, plunging from the cold and wrapping around the log. Yes, it is a log. A thick log with the circumference of a garbage can that had saved me.

I try to pull myself up so that I can sit safely aboard the thick cut of tree trunk. It is futile. But at least I am safe from the icy depths of this unknown river, half my body out of the water. I watch, holding tight, as the river carries me down its treacherous rapids. I would surely have drowned by that point had the log not appeared from out of nowhere.

Or did it? In either case.

Sleep comes fast, like the breakers I was riding down. In no time I fall into a tumbling world of slumber.

• • • •

My eyes open. Rushing water is at my back. I am holding onto my pack for dear life with the remnants of my shoot, my soaking wet notebook, and probably still that pesky tin of chewing tobacco. Then I remembered the log that had appeared from nowhere to save my life. It was now long gone. But it isn't the thought of a log that snaps my eyes fully open. No, it is a different sound. A sound that makes my senses jump in pure and utter joy.

Traffic. The not-too-distant hum of passing motorists.

I am instilled with energy that comes from the heavens. I push myself to my feet and run. I don't care how dark it is, but I run. Run until my feet touch the road pavement. I follow the road until I come across a sliver of light in the distance. Streetlamp glow. But I have no more energy to run. I slog my way up the slight incline until I finally meet with the first piece of man-made construction I have seen in five long days.

The sign is lit up by an overhead lamp. My mouth drops at what it is painted in black on the yellow sign. Its arms are as thick as legs, the same brawny outline I have seen three times in the past five days. It is the stranger.

The sign reads, just below the black silhouette of a large, ape like man. The man I had encountered. Barely.

"Sasquatch X-ing."

⌒ SIX ⌒

BLACK 'N BLUE

PART I

SOME DAYS I feel as though Creator has blessed me with a gift from his own divine powers. Most of the time, I love having it, especially for my own safety in the mean streets of New York City. Other times I feel it is my own curse; being able to hear what people are thinking.

I am a 26-year-old Native American woman. I reside off-Rez in uptown New York where I have been employed in the dynamic life of Manhattan as an assistant to Mr. Oscar Jones, going on three years. What a name, Oscar Jones. To be honest though, I love the man, he's great. If it wasn't for him, then I may have had to move back upstate to the reservation I once called home. Now don't get me wrong, I love my home on the reservation, but it's just that a woman like me with a degree in human resources doesn't get much work up there.

So here I am, working as a cross-examiner for potential

employees coming in to work at Mr. Jones' prosperous company: Desired Straits Insurance Underwriters.

At least I am not alone here in the big city of New York. The Big Apple. Two of my brothers decided they'd better move down here to keep an eye on me. But their move wasn't just on my behalf. Steady employment on the Rez was hard for them to find too. Currently they are employed in the solid profession of iron working. Guys working in this line of work are called "Rod Busters." A hell of a tough line of work to be in, but hey, they love their careers, just as I do mine.

• • • •

The man perched in the leather interview chair before is me tall and handsome. His raven, slicked, Elvis Presley style haircut gleams in the fluorescent lighting of the boxy interview room like shiny strands of black gold. His three-piece suit makes him look stylish and intelligent at the same time.

I don't know if this man is rude or trying to flatter me by occasionally gazing at my bare legs. It's been a long winter so they're god awful pale in colour. Despite being Native American, light skin runs in my genes. I knew I should have put on some pantyhose on today.

He says, "So, there you have it, that's my work life's story. Is there any more you would like to discuss about my career highlights?" His name is Michael ... or Michel. His last name I have already forgotten, but I can always look back on his résumé once I have completed this thorough interview.

"Hmm, no I don't think so," I say. "I believe you have informed me well. Very impressive, to say the least."

His thinking voice trickles through my ears, *'You're the one who is impressing me. Oh, how I would love to have those long sexy legs wrapped around me, as I steadily lick... your neck'* ...and it doesn't end there. His lusty thoughts merge from one to the other like an annoying unseen mosquito. An annoying mosquito that must be swatted dead.

I should be used to it by now. But I am not. Men are pigs. And just when I thought we maybe had a decent man on our hands, he goes and thinks that. But then again, no one can get in trouble for thinking, only doing. Right?

I quell an instinctive glower as his smile meets my gaze. "Well, Mister . . . uhh,"—I take a skimming glance at his professionally typed résumé—"Zamen."

"Samen," he cuts in. "The Z is pronounced like a S. You see, I'm European," he smugly asserts to me, adjusting his sleeves as if he felt a spider run up his forearm.

"Oh. My apologies, Mr. Zamen." I pronounce it right this time, stand up and extend my right hand in a gesture of professional etiquette. "If you are selected for the position we will be in touch with you."

'Oh, I'll show you a position.' He thinks as he reaches out and gently pulls at my hand, shaking hard enough to make my legs wobble. "Yes. Thank you, Misses Miller—"

"Ms. Miller," I correct him and politely retract my hand while he ogles me, smiling that sucky smile I have seen from so many others coming through the HR office.

"My apologies, Mizz Miller. Well, I guess I will be on my way now. I do have a busy schedule for the day planned. It was very nice meeting you, and I eagerly anticipate your response."

I'm sure you do, bud, I think coldly. "And you as well, Mr. Zamen. I will show you to the exit." Head held high I lead him out of the interview office passing by the receptionist's desk where Mary the chocolate-loving receptionist smiles and gives him the once over. Clearly, she's taken a liking to his Elvisstyle hair or finds some other aspect of him appealing. I escort him over to the main elevators.

"Thank you for coming by, Mr. Zaman," I say, pushing him far back into the elevator with my impactful stare.

"Please, call me...," he tries to blurt out his first name but the metallic doors briskly shut between us. His thinking voice trickles out, *"I have a passionate kiss in mind for you if I get hired."*

I smile, nod without speaking, watching with bitter anticipation as the elevator doors seal completely, and whirl around and rest my head on the sturdy steel. "Great. Another horny asshole," I mumble to myself.

"Who's an asshole, now?" Mr. Jones asks with the bluntness that is characteristic of him. The tall, robust man, always dressed to impress, strides into the corridor through his private office door, holding a mug of steaming coffee. The mug in hand reads: OSKAR, in bold lettering on a big red maple leaf. I bought him that mug as a souvenir while on a trip to visit my cousins in Ontario.

"Oh, just a text I received from an obnoxious guy friend," I say with an awkward giggle. I absentmindedly pat the sides of my skirt, a futile search for pockets that aren't there.

"I see. Well? How was the latest interview?" asks Mr. Jones in his most serious yet lively tone.

"He was. . ." I gravely want to reveal that he was just another horn dog. But then again, he was remarkably qualified, and his skills exceeded any other applicant for the job. "He is strong contender for the job with his skill sets, Mr. Jones. Probably the best applicant we've had so far," I respond honestly.

"Excellent." His exclamation startles me, unintentional as it was in its volume. "Call him back. Tell him he's got the job. And when he gets here, send him to my office, ASAP, would ya?"

"Yes sir, Mr. Jones. I'll get on it right away, Mr.—"

"For Pete's sake," he courteously steps closer and pats me gently on the shoulder, "I've told you over and over, Alycia. Just call me Oscar. You're more than my assistant. Shoot, I'd even go as far as calling you family. Now call that man and tell him he's hired." Mr. Jones, Oscar, strides off toward his office before I can say another word.

For reasons I am unaware of, I cannot read Mr. Jones—Oscar's—thoughts, unless if make an unusually intense attempt, which would make me look crazy. The wild stare I must enact as I try to penetrate the minds of men make me look like a Star Wars Jedi Master. It is obviously for the best that he doesn't think of me as a sex object. Maybe he really does see me as family. Whatever the reason that I can't breach his thoughts, I'm sure it is noble. And I am truly fortunate to have Oscar Jones in my life.

The women's bathroom is painted an extravagant blue, with delicate specks of white paint, most likely meant to convey heaven-sent clouds. Whatever imagery they intend to portray, these patterns offer a soothing visual treat. Positioned at the centre of the washbasin counter, a basket of potpourri sends off a subtle yet pleasing aroma, a detail that elevates any washroom experience. I thoroughly wash my hands. The suds lather up and emit a sweet aroma like springtime in the tropics. Not that I have ever been there. I haven't. I just assume that's what spring would smell like down there in the tropics.

Taking a closer look at my reflection in the mirror, I observe my dark brown hair cascading just above my shoulders. This new haircut was an experiment I decided on, resulting in a resemblance to Kate Micucci, the actress from my all-time favourite TV show, "The Big Bang Theory." Kate Micucci portrayed Raj's awkward girlfriend. I even almost have her nose, and my skin is ridiculously pale for an Native American woman. Maybe that's the reason why so many people in New York routinely assume I am Italian. And they are awestruck when I tell them I am not, but I don't go into detail. I'm pretty sure I have a great, great forefather who was of European descent, but that's too far back to fully comprehend for my own family's personal history pages.

I stare into my hazel eyes. They have changed. When in a relaxed mood, they are a caramel hazel. When in a bad mood, they turn different shades of green. Right now, I know my mood is irritated—perhaps from the encounter with Mr. Zamen—for they are emerald lake green. Another gift from God, my friends would say.

Just below my left eye is a night-sky purple bruise I've tried my best to conceal. And I did a damn good job at it. It's a snub of a bruise, could be called, I suppose, a 'shiner.'

As I leave the washroom, I hear Oskar Jones' loud voice, "Well? Is he hired yet?" I can't tell if he's angry or tranquil. He's got one of those voices that are always loud and overbearing, even when he doesn't want it to be. I head back to my office to reluctantly phone an incoming workmate.

••••

My trusty sidekick earbuds and the embrace of my favourite music help me keep my head screwed on right. Keeping voices out of my head is the main reason I bring them along with me everywhere I go, but music also drowns out the random craziness of the New York City subway system.

After years of feeling ensnared by my powers, I've finally managed to control the voices in my head to a remarkable degree. Let's say if I look at a man and truly try to gaze into his mind, that's when the voices will come. They usually dance around themes of desire and lust, though not exclusively directed at me, thankfully. It seems the male mind often fixates on sex. These voices are not eerie whispers or full-on ranting; they sound as if the man is standing right next to me, speaking in a cool yet authoritative manner.

Then there's the regulars. When I'm not concentrating

on a specific individual then I will usually hear the minimal murmur. Picture a continuous hushed whisper reverberating down a long circular tunnel. This is when the earbuds come into good use. I have no idea what the inaudible whispers are saying, they're just always there. Creepy yes. Again, that's what the music is for.

Not all the voices and thoughts I peruse are bad, though. I gaze hard at a handsome man from the corner of my Ray Ban covered peepers. He is nervous because he is going to ask his long-time girlfriend to marry him. His thinking is of love. I wish more men's minds were thinking the warm and tender thoughts like this gentleman.

'Lisa, look. You and I, we've been together for five amazing years now, and . . .' His thoughts trail off in indecipherable musing I can't read. Perhaps he is still trying to memorize how he is going to go about in proposing to his love. He adjusts his red silk tie and shuffles into a comfortable sitting position atop the blue, imitation leather train bench. The vibrant bouquet of rainbow-coloured flowers he holds emits a sweet scent which drifts through the stale aroma of the commuter train.

I smile and continue to observe the man through the corner of my sunglasses as the monotonous, computer lady comes on the intercom and announces the next stop. The train slowly whines to a halt, and the man gets up and casually strolls off like a man full of good intentions. And what better intention than to ask his sweetheart to marry him.

Two thuggish-looking young men rudely board the train before anyone has a chance to disembark, tenaciously bumping shoulders with a stout woman and the man with good intentions. One of the thugs then twirls around and flashes him an intimidating smile of golden teeth. A grill is what I've heard the rap superstars call it. The thugs then plop down on the empty train bench right across from me.

Oh, how much I hate the seating arrangement of these inner-city subway trains. There is no outdoor scenery to enjoy since it's mostly underground tunnels. You're practically compelled to awkwardly stare at the person or people sitting directly across the aisle from you

Thankfully I have my sunglasses on to hide my shiner but also because these two thugs look dangerous. They won't stop staring my way.

I start to feel the hot sensation of uneasiness begin to surge from within me. I angle my nose toward the narrow glass openings of the train's exit doors, purposefully avoiding direct eye contact. Yet, this subtle maneuver proves futile. That doesn't help. Their lecherous intentions are strong.

'Damn girl. I'd eat that thang right up,' ponders the one with the grill. In addition to his golden teeth, he has a tattoo of a rolling teardrop just below his left tear duct.

I mind-scan the other thug while trying to keep my attentive gaze away from their eyes. *'Mm mm mmm. What I wouldn't mind doin' to you if this train was just the two of us,'* he thinks. He could be handsome if he wasn't dressed like such a delinquent of society.

Both thugs have their eyes locked dead my way and my face twists in disgust. I am starting to feel the beads of sweat ooze their way out from my pores. That feeling like needles stabbing at my face from the inside starts to arise.

I hastily hop off my bench and move toward the sliding exit doors. I don't care if my stop is still four stations down the line. I need to get away from these two unsavoury characters and their foul-minded intentions. I yank out my earbuds and wait impatiently at the door for the train to come to a complete stop.

"Next stop, Fifth Avenue, 53rd Street Station," belts out the monotonous tone of the robotic intercom lady.

I feel a more at ease when five other passengers rise

from their seats, joining me to get off at 53rd. My comfort is short-lived as the two thugs also join our group, all the while continuing to stare me down intently. I step out of the train onto the concrete platform, overwhelmed by the musty and unnatural odors that pervade the air. Which way has more people? As I step out of the stale-smelling train and onto the concrete platform reeking of mustiness and unnatural aromas, I look left and right towards the exits.

The disembarking group of five splits up and go their separate ways. Two women head together up the lonely cement stairs leading to the dim winter evening streets. Another passenger seems to have made an error in his stop, as he walks towards the tunnel exit on the other side of the platform, presumably awaiting an incoming train. Two other passengers stand and chat each other up, their puffy jackets protecting them from the chilly elements. I choose not to hover around them—for they may think I am just another eccentric traveler.

Faint but lively music drifts from one of the exits through the cool, stagnant air of the underground station. Music usually means people, so I follow the sound. To my dismay the two thugs trail me, maintaining a short distance. I hurry my step, round a corner underneath the escalator where assembly of teens are standing in a circle in the dead-end corner with one fluorescent bulb situated overhead. One of the teens is in the middle, spinning on his head on a flattened sheet of cardboard. The rest are cheering him on.

These assholes won't try anything here, I whisper to myself as I take up position outside the group's circle. One of the young people in the circle may have overheard my mumbled whisper. He grins at me, and I reciprocate with a smile of my own. *'Well, hello there, pretty lady,'* he thinks. He turns back to face the circle. *'Now's my chance to show off my skills in front of this hottie. Hurry up and finish, Julio, cause I'm next.'* I smile and giggle at the teenager's thoughts. At least he wasn't thinking obscene intentions like so many male minds do.

Assuming a sense of permission, I position myself to watch the ongoing performance, for the time being anyways. Or at least until the two thugs decide to leave—whenever that will be. They maintain their position a short distance away, shrouded within the obscurity of a pillar's shadow. Their vigilance appears fixed on our group, or potentially solely on me.

Nervously, I stand and watch the dancers and they gradually draw me in to the mesmerizing rhythm of their breakdancing routines. Among them, the one who had been spinning on his head steps out from the circle and places his bucket hat bottom side up on the cement floor. I know what this means so I rummage through my purse and pull out a wrinkled 5-dollar bill and toss it into the overturned hat.

"*Gracias,*" he says. Puerto Rican accent perhaps?

"*De nada,*" I reply. I had learned some Spanish phrases from some co-workers. "Some really good moves you got there."

He nods with a grin and returns to his circle of friends, with high fives and knuckle bumps.

I throw a quick glance over my shoulder to see that the two thugs are still standing there, gawking my way. They seem to be deep in discussion with their eyes darting around the subway, before settling back on me. I could focus in on them, but I choose not to. Giving them any sort of attention could escalate matters for the worse.

Feeling somewhat safer, I stay put, hanging about nervously whilst watching the amazing moves of the teen who smiled at me upon my approach. He's really got some skill. I am especially impressed when he starts doing a tricky dance move I know of; the Windmill.

I wait until he is done before pitching another glance over my shoulder. The two thugs have temporarily stepped away from their cover. One is on a cellphone, while the other is inhaling a long drag from a cigarette and peering out at the open blackness of the dark spherical subway tunnel.

Suddenly, the rumble of an incoming train delivers a puff of dank tunnel air. A train heading back toward lower Manhattan.

People, I figure.

Lots of people. Regular people.

Recognizing the impending influx of people, I toss additional loose change into the upturned hat before dashing toward the inbound side of the platform

I hear shouts of thank you's and *gracias* behind me from the circle of teens. I don't bother looking over my shoulder again as I run. I swiftly board the halted train without hesitation. As I take the first available seat, I steal a cautious glance out the large square window. Through it, I see the thug with a teardrop tattoo discarding his cigarette and grasping the sleeve of his companion on the phone. They make a frantic dash toward the train, only to be thwarted by the swiftly sealing doors. Danger gone; I have time to focus on myself now. My heart races. I exhale a long breath like I had just surfaced from the deep of a dark, abyssal ocean.

My gaze sweeps around the train. The passenger car is virtually empty, minus a few commuters sitting in their seats. A young woman dressed for a night on the town has her face glued to her smartphone, she is grinning as she cheerfully thumbs texts on her latest model iPhone. A grandmother, accompanied by her grandson, maintains a tranquil demeanor as the boy engages in a muted video game on his iPad. A middle-aged man dressed like a lawyer has his eyes closed as his head nods to some music blaring from a pair of Beats by Dre headphones. Stylish, I think to myself.

For a moment, my thoughts stray from the specter of my pursuers and what they may have had in store for me. I check my smartphone. No service. No abnormality there. We are underground, under God knows how much tons of impenetrable concrete. I fish my earbuds from my overcoat pocket, place them in my ears and sit back and relax.

Sugar crash. Adrenaline crash. Whatever it's called, I had fallen asleep. Inadvertently, I've missed my intended stop in inner Manhattan by several stations. My eyes flutter open, and I jolt upright, consumed by a sheer wave of panic.

They could be back, I think. My gaze darts around the train, now populated by an assortment of different people. Some stare at me strangely—perhaps by the look of distress plastered on my own face. Again, I feel uncomfortable heat begin to emerge from the core of my body. And my thick overcoat intensifies the heated situation.

I disembark at the next stop for a much-needed breather and cool off. The Lower East Side. Cool winter winds bite at my overheated face akin to magma encountering the frigid ocean's surface. I sense the essence of steam rising off me as I speedily stride toward the nearest set of exit stairs. The moment I'm at the top of the dirty cement stairs, the wind gathers up in an immoral amplitude. A mixture of sweat and sub-zero cold can be a deadly combination.

The city streetlights cast a full glow on the scene. Archaic apartment buildings share the landscape with skyscrapers that glitter vibrantly, illuminating the flurries of snow falling sideways from the ebony expanse above.

A coffee. What I need right now is a nice cup of steaming java to warm my blood and wake me up. I had been to this area before for lunch with co-workers. There is a nice little café owned by a Italian family, just out of the way, not a block from where I stand.

PART II

A tinkling bell announces my entry as I step into Frankie's Italian Café. At once I am revived by the tantalizing aromas of freshly brewed coffee and oven-fresh pastries.

"*Buonasera, Signorina.*" A short and rounded, middle-aged man walks out from behind a handmade curtain and greets me. "A please, do have a seat." He waves towards an open table that overlooks an aquarium adorned with fluctuating hues. I smile gracefully and take a seat.

The coffee hits the spot. Sharp and spicy notes arouse my jaded, winter-pummeled senses. I struggle to recall the last time I savoured a brew so delicious. I was used to the same old fast-food chain and convenience store coffee brands. I guess I never really took the time to come out and enjoy a real cup of coffee from an authentic little New York café as this. Frankie's Italian Café.

I look around and notice that I am the only patron. I admire the rustic Italian design of the tablecloths and translucent window curtains. The spotless floors are covered by white and ashen granite tile, looking like an ancient Roman palace floor. The tables and chairs are all immaculately handcrafted wood, most likely by an Italian American company. Walls, sand-coloured, are adorned with paintings depicting the homeland—mountains, white beaches, the old Romanesque rooftops in the backdrop.

In broken English, the owner introduces himself to me as Frankie and gives me a complimentary *pastiera napoletana*, baked by his wife. As he waddles from his station, he starts cleaning up, wiping down the empty tables. He glances up at me and smiles again. There is a charm to the short plump man. He reminds me of Super Mario with his warm smile, thick shaggy mustache, and grey paperboy cap. I smile back at him. Right away I sense that I cannot read his thinking mind—much as is the case with Mr. Jones. Perhaps Frankie is a man with only good intentions. I can truly feel it from the perception of warmth emanating from within him.

On the final sips of my coffee, a man storms in. The door's bell jingles like a distraught canary, ushering in the chill with him. He is covered in snow and breathing heavily as though he had been running for a period. I try not to stare, but there is something in the manner of his abrupt movements. I divert my gaze as he sits at a distant table, eyes locked on me.

'What the fuck are you looking at?' His thoughts assail my consciousness, as if he's perched right there in the vacant chair across from mine. I am astonished since I didn't even try to read him. His crude words had automatically invaded my mind.

I'm consumed by a fervent urge to return his gaze, to delve deeper into his thoughts, but the coldness from his glowering gnaws at me like the gust that blew in with him.

"More coffee, Signorina?" I snap out of it and meet Frankie's warm, grin.

"Umm, yes, please," I reply with enthusiasm. I would much rather be off and away from the threatening eyes of the other patron, but at the same time I feel it would be rude of me to say no to a second helping of this man's delectable coffee. Frankie fills my cup to the brim and walks over to the man's table with the same question. They begin casually conversing.

Now is my chance.

I fixate my gaze on the man and focus hard on his thinking mind. His stream of consciousness comes to me in broken phrases, perhaps because he is busy chatting away with the café owner.

'I better . . . she's dead . . . cops . . . what if . . . but first. . .'

I withdraw my probing eyes from the customer just as they finish talking, and Frankie returns to his post behind the counter. Once more, the man's stare locks onto me. I drink as fast as I can but the scalding coffee sears the roof of my mouth and back of my throat. Collecting myself, I sip slowly until the cup is drained. I stand up. "Thank you," I say to Frankie, retrieving a 10-dollar bill from my pocket and tossing it on the table. "That was some really good coffee."

"Please, you do come again, Signorina," says Frankie in his warm-hearted elegance. Something definitely not learned in New York City.

I nod and offer a smile. "Of course, I will, Frankie. See you later." A polite wave goodbye and I promptly exit the warmth of the café.

As I take to the streets on foot, a single thought reverberates—I just want to be home, in the comfort of my bed, safely shielded from the prying eyes of malicious inner-city men. Especially the latest one who has inserted himself into my thoughts. I have no idea of what it was that man was thinking. Amidst my haste, questions churn in my mind. Who was it that he implied was dead? Me, or could he possibly have already killed someone? These questions battle through my mind as I hurry through the flustering, streetlamp-lit snow, my boot stomps sounding like fresh carrots being snapped in half.

Either my bewildered mind or the winter's wailing wind provided the perfect cloak for the man's stealthy steps through the snow. His actual voice matches precisely the way it had echoed in my thoughts only moments before. "Hey, wanna see something real funny? Watch this," he proclaims, seemingly emerging from thin air. Literally from out of nowhere.

Before I have a chance to react or turn, a blast of grey and white froth engulfs my face. Natural reactions kick in, urging me to twist my face away, but I am too slow to oppose the sudden surge of deadly mist. I scream, and some of the bitter compound floods into my mouth and burn away at my gums and tongue. My eyes are immediately balls of reddened flames. My throat scorching with a swelling heat and seizing up like melting plastic.

Abruptly, a force yanks my hair, wrenching my head back. A pair óf icy fingers clamp around my chemically overwhelmed throat. I try to scream again, but all that comes out is a gurgling wheeze like someone stepping on an already deflated balloon. Eyes still open, all I see is dual silhouettes within my bubbling vision of kaleidoscopic greens and browns.

As he socks me in the stomach, the only sounds coming from his mouth are loud grunts and indiscernible slurs. Another futile attempt at a whimper escapes my mouth as every ounce of strength leaves my body, my legs going limp and doubling over like a finished book snapping shut.

Feet dragging on the snow-caked cement, my eyelids are begging to be shut from the corrosive effects of the unknown gas attack put upon me. I try my best to take one last look around me. For life or death. Where am I headed? Where is he taking me?

At last, my eyelids surrender to the assault. My last hazy spectacle is the bright streetlamp glow drowning away from me like I was a boat drifting away from the sparkling island of civilization.

PART III

I surface into awareness as if awakening from a bad dream. My brain thrashes me with a sense of all-around pain shooting up my neck and delivering severe blows within the boundaries of my inner skull. My vision remains blurred, akin to peering through a windshield glazed with frost.

Cold—nothing but cold. The frigid air stings at my eyes

and body as though I am standing in a chamber of chlorinated, sub-zero gas. I realize that I am in the dark, except for an oscillating red glimmer dancing away beyond the halfway drawn blinds of the lone window at the far end of the room. Stretched out upon something unyielding and flat, my chilled form discerns the contours of a table, perhaps. In vain I try to wiggle my arms free from the sides of my body, but they are tightly constricted by a rope with coarse prickles that stab into my skin. I stroke at the side of my body with the tips of my frozen stiff fingers. Naked. Or at least, very near to it. Aside from the rope that binds my wrists, the outlines of my frosty bra straps and underwear waistband register. I attempt a feeble wriggle, grateful for the comparative freedom in my legs. I wriggle, shift, until my feet touch the floor, enabling me to utilize my toes to explore. Yet, the texture beneath me remains stiff, like bristles of a toothbrush.

Taking a shot in the dark, I barrel-roll like a baby to my left until I roll right off the table's edge and plunge to the floor with a dull thud. A flash bursts behind my eyes as my head slams into the floor, the brief flash like a star before closing in on itself and going dark, forever.

Half winded, I thrash my legs around attempting to gauge my surroundings with ice-clad feet. The ground is carpeted. Cold and rough like a floor mat left too long outside. I make another attempt, my hands straining, only to be met by the unyielding resistance of the tight rope.

Lying alone on the cold and rigid floor, nearly fully exposed and forsaken, a involuntary whimper slips from my throat, even though I know only he will be able to hear me. His merciless scowl then flutters into my mind, his hate-filled eyes searing with so much animosity it burns. With the realization of bringing myself further, potential suffering, I immediately stop my whimpering. It will do nothing for me in my dire situation.

Vanquished and consumed by fear, I lie still and listen, hoping my icy-hot ears will catch familiar sounds that will orient me to my whereabouts. A dreadful silence has enshrouded the dark chamber. I realize that my ceaseless whispers have hushed. I have no idea what this means.

But why?

I have to get a grip. I listen again. The lateness of the night becomes evident, borne by the tranquility of near-silence seeping through the thin windowpane. No sounds of the constant city traffic drone or chatting pedestrians. Only distant wail of emergency vehicle sirens punctuates the eerie silence, mingling with the mournful wind howling outside the building like a broken set of flutes.

And then the sickly familiar odor hits me. A tang of copper fills the air, clinging to my senses like a haunting melody. You see, my supposed 'boyfriend' fancies himself a connoisseur of currency, a collector of pennies. Our bedroom walls are lined with one cent pieces that bear this same smell. Smelling it here reminds me of how wrong it is to smell there too. My fingers brush against the shiner bruise on my cheek, small potatoes compared to what's likely in store for me now.

Lying uncomfortably, I writhe on the bristles of shag carpet as I try to regain my composure. I haven't given up yet. I muster the strength to roll over onto my side to try and wriggle free of the rope's body-hugging restraint. I roll into something thick and stiff, my efforts leading me into contact with something solid, its form hardly discernible against the shadows, but roughly my own size.

Another sound choruses in my ears, besides the spine-chilling howl of the wind.

Flies.

In the middle of winter?

Nevertheless, my wandering eyes are quickly adjusting to the dimness enshrouding me. With patience, I await the gradual retreat of the utter darkness, examining my surroundings. Inspecting the room. I am in some kind of small bedroom, or storage room, with translucent black curtains hanging over the solitary window in the far corner.

I twist and fold my body and kick at the floor using my unbound feet, slithering like a caterpillar around the stiff mound beside me. My destination: the window. The smell of tainted copper is now stronger, sweeter like the odor of corroded metal dipped in more corroded metal. I almost gag at the sickly, overpowering odor. I hope it is not what I think it is. I keep my body squirming in an effort to try and move away from the lump for a better examination.

Then I see it.

By way of the dim, fluctuating light seeping in, I see her face. It is fully exposed unlike the rest of her lean body wrapped in some kind of old blanket. The lower half of her mouth is cocked sideways and agape as though it was snapped clean from the upper jaw beneath the unbroken skin. Her hair is streaked messily over her face and open, unblinking eyes.

I scream.

"Welcome back, my love." A serene, masculine voice drifts through the dark, blood-tinged air, along with the scraping sound like chair legs rubbing against a wooden floor. At the proclamation of the unnatural calm, yet eerie tone of his voice, my already-chilled skin breaks out in gooseflesh.

With a distinct click, a solitary lamp flickers to life, casting its feeble glow upon the corner junction of the brick-walled chamber. I see clearly that I am in a small bedroom void of beds. The setting is old-fashioned, with the walls constructed of uninsulated, red brick which is chipping at the worn edges. Spirals of cobwebs hover in the corners, the shadows cast by the lamp giving them the eerie spectacle like mini, pitch-black vortexes of doom. Dominating the space is a sizable table, the very one I fell off, flanked by towering stacks of brown packing boxes, rising like ominous mountains, encircling the room's perimeter. An ancient carpet, the one that cushioned my fall, lies neatly beneath the rectangular table.

I turn to face her again. Something I immediately regret. In the lamplight's glow, she emerges into stark clarity. Her face is battered like she had been beaten severely, blue-black skin abrasions decorating the tender skin beneath her blackened eye sockets. The lower half of her mouth is no longer in line with the upper half. Wide open eyes emit no twinkle, rather, they shine like oily marbles of death.

I scream again and briskly turn away.

"Oh, her. No worries, now. She's dead—as you may already know. So she will be of no harm to you or to me." The man, the embodiment of madness, giggles with an unsettling glee, a child who's cracked a knock-knock joke.

"W-where am I?" My own words come out like a small frightened child.

"That I cannot reveal—for our own safety. But as you can probably already hear, yes, we are still in the City That Never Sleeps, he calmly declares as though I am an invited guest.

A lump forms in my throat. The kind that arises just before you let out a burst of uncontrollable sobbing. Conversing with a man harbouring unspeakable intentions toward me is the last thing I want. Yet, somehow, my mouth opens, and words tumble forth. "Please... I have some money, take it all," I sputter, striving to suppress a wave of whimpering.

Again he laughs and giggles like a deranged scientist after finally realizing the missing element he needed to finally conclude his experiment. His thinking mind asks: *"You want to know why I've taken you and what I am going to do to you, don't you?"* His eerie silence is more terrifying than if he was to be screaming at me. Tears begin to stream down my face.

"Oh, come now." The sicko approaches, his gritty hand stroking the tender skin of my cheek. "At the café. You knew what I'd done, didn't you? To her." He gestures to the lifeless girl with a grimy finger.

I remain silent, locking eyes with him, a blank stare that refuses to gaze again upon the face of death mere feet away.

He stares emotionlessly back at me, his waxy face glowing like a Halloween mask with a candle lit on the inside. "No use trying to hide it. I saw you reading me—my thoughts. Your curious and startled expression said it all." I feel a fire of hatred burning from within his dark, puffy eyes.

I want to scream, but I don't. "What are you talking about?" I casually solicit in a dry, hoarse voice. My mouth is like sand.

He steps ahead of the glowing corner lamp, his glossy head eclipsing the light like the moon blocking the sun. The lamplight generates dark shadows around his eye sockets, giving the impression there is nothing behind them. A smile creeps across his face, a deathly grimace that exudes the triumph of a predator cornering its prey, his thinking mind saying, *"I've got you now, and you're utterly defenceless."*

"You just sit tight for a little while longer," he finally says aloud. "But if you'll excuse me, I have to get my late night eats before I commence with the crucial business at hand. Oh, and I'll grab a lil' something for you, too, of course." He grins again, this time like a madman with demented intentions, and snickers boldly as a dark cloud seeps into his voice. "We're gonna need the energy for this aren't we? But hey, don't worry it'll all be over very soon." His smile fades again and he rubs at his wiry chin stubble. "Hmm, maybe too soon." He abruptly leaves in anger, slamming the antiquated wooden door behind him with a resounding boom.

My heart thrashes against my ribcage. His boots shuffle noisily in the hall, fading out briefly before rushing back. He bursts through the door, a blanket draped over his forearm, and his face is lit up like a kid on Christmas morning. "Oh, where are my manners. Here you go, honey bunny," he says calmly, tottering toward me and placing a woolen blanket over my shivering form. The wool blanket reeks like old sweat and a stale wretchedness.

Beaming with pleasure, his teeth, yellowed like ancient bones, gleam in the dim light. He kills the lamp and leaves the room. I am once again left alone with my thoughts and the decaying presence of the dead girl beside me.

But at least I am warm.

I whimper until I have no energy to whimper any more.

• • • •

I awake suddenly to the gloominess of the room, not realizing that I had dozed off into a deep slumber. Outside the building, the wind sings its daunting song. The corner lamp is still out, but for a second time there is a trace of rose-gold illumination spreading into the room from somewhere beyond the room's lone window.

Footsteps. On the pavement below. And the chatter of people. I may be, after all, on a floor that is closer to ground level than I had originally thought.

With sheer desperation I squirm and twist like a jagged log beneath the windowsill and unleash a piercing scream, "Hello, somebody? Please help me!" I pause and wait for a reply. The shrill coldness of the floor beneath the window pierces me like an invisible knife.

"You need to get out of here, before you end up like me... murdered and missing." Her words reverberate from her mind through the room, pronounced with an eerie clarity as

if the speaker is here with me, her voice ragged and strained, as if she's attempting to speak through a sutured mouth. I pitch a swift, fear-stricken glance over my shaking shoulder. There she is, seated in a twisted, knees-up position at the opposite end of the small room. Red, then yellow neon afterglow from outside shimmer through the window blinds, landing on her disintegrating, olive-coloured face like prison bar shadows. She is gazing directly my way. Her soulless eyes are like depths of black tar. Her vacant gaze is fixed directly upon me, eyes like pools of inky tar, devoid of any humanity. Her once-beautiful face now a canvas of disfiguration, a cruel masterpiece of agony.

"*Didn't you hear me?*" she screams. "*You need to leave. Now!*" Her ear-splitting thinking voice explodes off the bare brick walls. The glass window above me trembles and then shatters under the intensity of her voice. Instinctively, I shield myself, closing my eyes as the glass rains down.

When I dare to open my eyes again, the scene before me is nightmarish. Her lower jawbone has detached clean from her skull, thick blood dripping from her mouth and trickling into a viscous puddle over the bottom half of her teeth resting on the floor.

"No! You're dead!" My words tremble with disbelief and terror. She stays silent, upper teeth jangling, and only staring at me with her murky, lifeless eyes. Determined to communicate with me, she scrambles to her feet, pushing at the floor with contorted limbs like a string-less puppet doll. Standing on her hind legs like a mutilated animal, I see that her feet are smashed, and positioned in abnormal postures. She limps toward me in a broken gait, slowly like an undead creature. The buzzing of flies and the putrid stench of death and decay grow stronger with each of her stumbling steps toward me, her leftover teeth exposed like razors of death, while her eyes shed tears of blood.

A scream tears from my throat, a primal sound of pure terror that strips away the last remnants of my composure. My vocal cords ache and tighten, as if trying to close off the terror that has taken root in my very being. The cold, barren room has once again gathered in near total darkness. All I can conjure up are her walking dead steps towards me, my mind set off in a state of total alarm. Fully awake. At the thought of her still lying dead in the same room as me, I abruptly sit up in a curled ball and raise my knees to my chest.

The smell of blood is heavier.

Decay is percolating.

In an effort to get as far away as possible from her, I kick at the floor with my bare feet until my back slams into the brick wall. I peer up at the swirling black ceiling, my head swimming in agony from the lack of having anything to drink for so long. My skull feels a few sizes too small for my throbbing brain. Peering through the darkness, I can only wait for the door to be opened and slammed. To be once again in the dark with him. Besides the haunting flashes of my night terror, I am almost dead of thought, every detail of my concentration wrapped around my battering heart and the spine-chilling howl of the wind chanting beyond the darkened window.

An eternity of waiting passes, when at last I hear the menacing sound of footsteps reverberating down the hall. My captor bursts through the door and stares down at me lying helplessly on the floor. He slams the door shut behind him. He heads for the lamp and pulls the power cord on, his careless eyes darting for the unknown woman's lifeless physique. A sick and twisted smile adorns his face and he places his fingers over his crinkled nose, shooting me an unamused look, saturated in sick humour. "Well I guess it's time I get rid of this other woman's body now, wouldn't ya say? She's starting to stink." His words come out like the dead woman is nothing more than an accidental road kill left too long uncooked.

Unblinking, I stare back with a blank expression. Saying nothing. Not wanting to initiate any behaviors in him that would make me end up like the poor woman beside me.

Nevertheless I can now clearly see my captor's profile in the lamplight. He is balding and built like an out of shape gorilla. Only he is wearing glasses now. The thin wiry frame sits snuggly on top of his red spotty nose. Thick and greying, his sullied mustache wiggles and hides his upper lip, stained a sickening brown and yellow. A loud, yellow and green Hawaiian shirt is wrapped loosely around his body, making him look like one of those out-of-place tourists in any destination. In the draft of the room, I wonder how he isn't feeling the cold.

With his small, beady grey eyes, he gazes down at me with a sly grin on his face, holding it for a brief moment before snatching up a loose end of the blanket the woman is wrapped in, and dragging it out into the hall. I catch a clear glimpse of her. She has black wavy hair like my own. Her face is too distorted to precisely know her nationality, but I presume she is either Hispanic or Indigenous ... like me.

Perhaps it is the shock or other symptoms brought on by my unforeseen kidnapping, but as her head drags on the dusty, wooden floor on her way out of the room, she winks at me. I withhold a gasp and turn away in horror.

He ceases his movement in the hall, releases his firm grip on the rolled up blanket. Hunched over and panting, he twists his neck to face me, lines of wrinkles undulating across his forehead. He thinks, *"You will soon love me too, my new love."* Then aloud he says, "I will be right back. I got you some food," he says with a wink. Groaning as he catches his breath, he wrestles to drag the dead woman's body further down the hall before finally returning to close the door on my face. But not before I catch a glimpse of the long, wooden constructed corridor leading down to what I presume is his living room.

I am left alone in the dark once more. This time I will not give up and fall asleep. Something larger than fear has overwhelmed me, making it possible conceive a new notion. Hope. It's all I have left. The outside world begins to glow. A striking parallelogram of red and yellow illuminates and radiates across the darkness.

The window. A light.

Hope has reignited my drive to move forward. It propels me to combat the hollowness that attempts to seize my heart and soul. If the window is truly as ancient and fragile as it seems, then I should be capable of shattering it with a swift kick. My desperate pleas might pierce the air to the streets. A surge of anticipation courses through me as I realize that my irritated eyes have almost completely healed. I drag my body toward the window, the dark circles swirling around it like a celestial halo. The atmosphere grows more hostile with every inch I traverse. At last I reach the window and have a listen first before attempting anything.

Screams. From the outside. Screams I recognize. Playful, like a small group of women who have been out on the town. My heart pounds against my ribs, feeling too grand for my chest. Now might be my one and only chance to bring about my liberty. Relaxing my body as best as I can, I pivot and line up my body so that the balls of my feet face the window. I elevate both legs, steadying them with the remaining sources of leftover energy, and then I kick hard. To my satisfaction a section of the window breaks free from the aged sill and goes crashing to the pavement below with a loud, but somewhat distant smash.

The playful screams turn for the worst. Frightened.

Electrifying pain shoots up through my legs. First cold, then warm as blood oozes out from gashes caused by the razor-like windows. I clench my teeth and slowly bring my blood oozing legs in from the piercing draft. Even before my legs touch the floor, they have gone numb. Too numb for me to elevate myself up to the window so that I may yell for help.

I have lost my chance as the women's screaming voices fade away. Death is imminent. I curl up in a ball beneath my smelly blanket and whimper. I have given up and now I can only accept my fate.

My fate to die.

Minutes pass as I lie on the floor sobbing and contemplating my inevitable end.

The door opens with a loud creak.

His thinking voice says, *"Well hello there, my new love."* Then aloud he says, "I have brought us something special." My captor's voice drifts through the dark before he flicks the lamp back on, and closes the door once again. His eyes dart around the room—from me to the broken window, and back to me again. In due course his smile fades, and his voice goes dark and malicious like a beast. "What have you done?" he growls. He drops a paper bag from one hand and heaves a bottle from his other hand at the red bricked wall adjacent to the window frame, now mostly empty of glass. The bottle shatters into a thousand pieces and I am showered in sticky wetness and glass shards.

I open my eyes in time see him gliding across the floor with sheer anger smeared across his face. *His thinking mind screams "You bitch!"* as he strikes a blow to my face. I am once again knocked out cold.

• • • •

PART IV

When I come to, I hear, "I'm so sorry. I did not mean to lose my temper like that," my captor's hollow voice is whimpering like a little boy, sounding fuzzy as though I was hearing him through distorted headphones. I hear his thinking voice, fading now into near silence, *"You're missing already but not murdered yet—"* His thinking voice sputters out. I see him sitting on a foot stool beneath the newly boarded-up window. The side of my face is throbbing and I can hear ringing in my ears. I try to move my legs and arms, but my legs are zip tied and my wrists are bound in chrome police handcuffs. My leg wound is draped up in a bandage that is stained a bright pink.

He says, "I have patched your wound up—even cleaned it. We don't want any infections getting in the way of our fun, now, do we?" Without uttering a word, I fixate my gaze on him, my eyes expressionless.

"Come now. I suppose you are dying for a drink of water, yes?" he says, and flaunts a glass filled with a clear liquid, turning to face me at a snail's pace. I nod enthusiastically. He waddles to my side and takes a knee. "Here you go, love. Now don't try anything funny okay?" Not waiting for me to answer, he reaches around and unlocks the handcuffs around my wrists. "Take a sip now." He holds the glass in front of my face, maintaining the position until I feel comfortable enough to slowly extend my hand towards it.

I tighten my grip around the cool glass, upturn it to my lips and let the liquid splosh to the back of my throat. I swallow a mouthful, then gag and cough as the firewater sweeps across my parched taste buds and courses down my throat like a stream of liquid fire. The back of my tongue goes instantly numb from the potent liquor. My warm stomach feels like it has been poisoned.

Once again he laughs hysterically, nearly falling from his stool. "It turns out I had an extra bottle, just hiding away in the rear of my freezer. Firewater. It's much better than normal water, isn't that what your people think?"

My people? I realize at that moment he is targeting me for being Native American. I wait for this sick feeling to subside. My mouth lets out an uncontrollable, enraged grunt and I toss the half-emptied glass across the room like he had done with the bottle. The glass smashes and falls into a bristly heap below the red, cinder bricked wall.

My abrupt action has surely enraged him furthermore. I close my eyes and turn my face away from him in anticipation of another harsh blow.

Nothing.

I gradually open my eyes and face him again. He is staring at me like a mother taking her first glimpse of her newborn child. A sick, demented mother. "Don't worry about the glass. Perhaps I deserved that one." He giggles uncomfortably. "Now before we start, I must dispose of Jenny's body properly before she starts to stink up my entire apartment. I will be fast, and then—oh boy—we can start our fun."

I begin to feel those lumps of sobbing building up again. But I control my outburst and say the first thing that comes to mind, "Water. Please, just water is all I want."

"When I return. And I'll be back in a jiffy." He looks down at me and his eyes transform from dark to light. The happiness in his eyes is far more disturbing than his spells of anger. I haven't heard anything from his thinking mind. Has he learned to block me? What is he going to do? He exits the room and closes the door. I recognize the click of the door being locked from the outside.

I wait until his shuffling footsteps leave the apartment, and then I realize that he had forgotten to re-engage the handcuffs. But my ankles are still tightly secured in the unbreakable zip tie. I look around the room. Nothing useful. I analyze the pile of glass, the shards are much too small to use as a cutting tool.

I am left in a state of hopelessness and have no choice but to wait again for him to return. Involuntarily I fall asleep once more, brought on by weakness.

SLAM!

His voice and the slamming of the door shock me into an awareness of my desperate situation.

"Shhhh. Don't talk," he says, ambling over to me while pressing a dirty finger over his puckered lips. I squint in the dim light and see it clearly.

His eyes are filled with fear.

"What are you talking about?" I keep my voice low so that I don't anger him.

"I made a booboo. Oh Jesus, I think they seen me," he exhales in a whisper like he is out of breath.

BOOM-BOOM-BOOM

The pounding on his door echoes down the bare apartment corridor. My captor looks up at the ceiling in utter shock and crouches to his knees.

I am very pleased to finally see terror—like my own—in him.

"What? No, it can't be. I lost him. I know I did," he quietly says and rises to his feet. "You just wait here and shhhh." Taking baby steps, he creeps out of the room and closes the door gently behind him. But not before remembering to lock the handcuffs and gag me so that I cannot scream for help.

I lie motionless with the only sound I hear and feel being my racing heart. I have a sliver of optimism about this visitor. I listen, nearly choking on my gag, until muffled yells, and clamouring like a scuffle breaks out; sounds I hear through the small crevice between the door and the hardwood floor. I pick up on shouts and grunts, and shatters of glass with the ruffling of furniture. This goes on for a few short minutes until finally a gunshot rings out.

The commotion I cannot see falls silent.

As silent as a cemetery on a windless hill.

My captor enters back into the room dragging the limp body of a lifeless man by his leather jacket collar, a streak of blood oozing from the man's mouth and dripping onto his chest. As he struggles to drag the lifeless corpse, I notice the silver handle of a pistol tucked snuggly into my captor's belt.

"Oh don't you worry hun," he says, almost fully out of breath. "He tried to pull a gun on me, but my years of childhood karate got the upper hand." He coughs out a forced laugh and finishes dragging the man's body to the far end of the room. He plops the body down where the woman, Jenny, had been sitting. The dead man's bullet-ridden mouth is open and cocked to the side exactly as Jenny's had been.

Hunched over and fighting to catch his breath, my captor stands straight and clasps onto his lower back with both hands, stretching outward until his back cracks. He then reaches for the pistol on the dead man's body and inspects it closely. "Wow, a Beretta A1. I could really use one of these," he says as he coils his head toward me and flashes a twisted smile. I look away from him in horror and face the dead man again. A loud gasp escapes my mouth when I realize I have seen the man before. His face is too bloodied to fully recognize but I recognize a tattoo of a rolling teardrop just below his left eye. His golden grill gleams from the within his bloody mouth.

The captor seeing my awe-struck expression, says in sweet, yet terrifying manner, "Oh, is this awful man scaring you?" He slips the pistol back into his belt and snatches up another old blanket from the top of one of the boxes.

A mean, crinkle-nosed expression crosses his face as he tosses the blanket over the dead man. "There. That's better. Now before we begin, any last requests?" he asks, walking toward me, removing my gag.

"You promised me water," I cry out. I am still staring in disbelief at the now-covered-up dead thug who had been following me. He had followed me all the way here! It's almost an impossible irony that he was a hair's breath away from becoming my salvation.

The captor pulls the Beretta out of his belt and the gun catches my weary gaze, gleaming like a lone star in the midnight sky. I had seen these Berettas many times before, back on my home on the reservation. The men in my family had always had a love for them. Even when my two brothers moved down to New York with me, they each purchased one for themselves—and even tried to get me to carry one.

My captor was so entranced with the Berreta that he missed seeing the switchblade tucked halfway into the thug's black leather belt. This thug may just still be in my fate's path to salvation.

"Water!" I burst out, trying to buy myself some valuable time. I look away from the dead man, hoping the captor doesn't also take an inspecting glance to see the knife.

"Yes. Very well, then. I will be back in another jiffy," he says in a sickly sweet manner and leaves the room.

I wait and watch until the captor disappears around a corner down his long apartment corridor whistling a happy tune. Then I curl my body up and do a series of barrel rolls until I collide into the reclining dead thug. With my back to him, I wriggle my hands and feel around until my fingertips touch the man's leather belt. I keep shuffling my fingers upward, until the solid cold steel of the switchblade body grazes my fingertips. I grasp in like the bucket of a backhoe and take the knife into my palm. Then I roll back to my starting point. I kick the knife, with both feet, under a loose end of the thick shag rug and wait patiently.

He finally re-enters the room, smiling like an accomplished man. "I got your water, my love." He takes a knee beside me and hand feeds me cool water from a large steel chalice. I purposely lap sloppily at the water, making splashes until it streams down my lower face and onto the floor.

"Aww jeez, you're making a mess of yourself," he says sympathetically, placing the chalice on the floor. He stares at me carefully.

"I'm so thirsty," I utter like a lost child.

"Okay then. I trust you won't do anything stupid now. You know what happened the last time? Let's not have that again, shall we?" He hunches over and unlocks the handcuffs. "There, now you don't have to make no more mess of yourself." He gets to his feet, turns his back to me and slides out a red tool box from beneath the table. Humming a happy tune, he begins unwrapping items, arranging them neatly on the lone wooden table.

I immediately notice the long, dangerous-looking curved blade and other tools for torture.

It is now or never.

I use my feet to slide the knife from under the rug and towards my waiting hands. I nudge the trigger switch with my thumb. The blade pops out with a flick sound and I immediately saw at the plastic zip tie. Soon my legs are free.

"No, no, no. You can't!" screams the captor. He drops what he is doing and sails across the room toward me. My last thought is of how grotesque his face is, and the sensation of cold steel rubbing against my thrashing fingertips.

• • • •

PART IV

My head is still swimming like I am suffering from a bout of sunstroke. My neck is tender and sore like a bruised piece of fruit. I clasp on to my temples with a soft touch and begin gyrating my fingers. My blurry eyes have yet to normalize.

The stout detective sits on the other side of the ancient, desk, flicking and rotating a ballpoint pen in his fingers while he eyeballs his computer monitor. He clicks the pen one last time before tossing it onto a stack of messily strewn papers. "You are one helluva lucky woman, Misses Miller—"

"Ms. Miller," I cut in with a rasping voice.

"Oh, sorry about that. My apologies, Mizz Miller. I am just finishing skimming over my final report here. I have the full incident leading up to the victim's death as self-defence. The knifing and whatnot." He leans across the table toward me and continuing to say, "And the sick bastard deserved it, if you ask me."

"So, I'm not in any kind of trouble?" I choke out.

The detective looks and states, "Lord Jesus no. Like I said. It was obviously self-defence."

I wince and croak out forced words through my aching neck, "And what of the other girl?"

He leans back in his chair and interlocks his fingers. "Her name is Halona Williams. She is from upstate," he says in an expression like he has recited it many times before. "She was reported missing five days ago by her family. Turns out she was the fifth victim of that sick asshole."

His words echo in my mind, each syllable a chilling whisper. Halona's grim confession comes back to me in a haunting refrain, as if she had whispered it to me in the dead of night herself. She had been one of the vanished, her existence snuffed out in the most sinister of ways, a victim among the ranks of murdered and missing women.

He leans back further in his squeaky chair and regards me with a sombre look. "It also turns out that the son of a bitch had a sick knack for..." and he pauses, possibly wondering how to phrase, without stereotyping, his propensity for victimizing Native American women. He came up with, "It also turns out that the son of a bitch had a sick knack for women with naturally dark hair. Like yours."

Detective Jones takes another look at me and nods just as someone opens the door behind me and enters his small office. "Well, you heal up good now, ya hear, Mizz Miller. I'm going to have the sergeant here drive you home. Are ya sure you'd rather not go spend some time at the hospital? Those marks on your face look pretty unkindly."

I shake my head. "I'd just rather be in my own bed right now." I force the words out of my blocked up throat. Immediately I regret speaking. I agonizingly swivel my stiff neck to have a gander at the freshly arrived officer.

A hushed gasp escapes my mouth.

"Where are my manners, this is Sergeant Stakos. He's from a precinct closer to your home," Detective Jones begins. "Sergeant Stakos, this is—"

"Alycia Miller," interrupts the sergeant. "Yes, I've crossed paths with this one before," he says arrogantly like he had cracked his own unfunny joke.

"Excellent. You will take her home then?" asks Detective Jones.

"I'm on it, Detective. Come on miss, I already have the car warmed up outside." The sergeant slides out of the way of the door and motions with a gesture for me to exit the office.

I hesitantly obey the sergeant, pacing past him with my head down.

• • • •

The first few minutes of the ride are eerily silent. Sergeant Darius Stakos waits until we are well away from the police station before voicing his concern.

"So. How the hell did you end up at that son of a bitch's house?" Darius asks sharply.

"So just like that, huh? No 'How are you, babe? I hope you're okay.' Just right to the blame game," I angrily retort.

"Better watch your damn tone with me," he snarls. "Now answer the fucking question."

"I was on my way home—didn't you read the report? You obviously knew I was at that police station."

"That sounds like a crock of bullshit to me. I hope you know, I will get to the bottom of this . . . oh, you'll see. I will."

"Wow. Really?" I roll my eyes. "And I see you're still keeping our relationship on the down low. I wonder why?"

"Oh please. Take my advice and don't start with that race card bullshit. I keep you and our relationship on the down low out of strict professionalism. Take my advice, do the same."

His thinking mind continues, loud and clear, *"... or you'll be in a world of sorry, just wait and see."*

"Professionalism?" I scoff. "Whatever. Just take me home."

"Oh," taunts Darius, "you'll see what surprise I have waiting for you when we get home." He eyes me acidly. I grimace and keep my absent-minded gaze fixed on the rows of old timey, interconnected dwellings blurring past his cop car. As I peer out at the coldness, a chorus of whispers chants out to me: *"Know your limits ... get rid of him ... survive."* The chorus, sounding like a small stadium of Halonas and her sisters, bring me courage.

I won't let him win this time.

Enough is enough.

No more hiding black eyes and blue, puffed up lips.

There will be no more of Darius Stakos hiding behind the safety of his police badge and uniform. No longer will he get away with the never-ending mental and physical abuse. No more listening to his phony advice that forever tests my limits, bringing nothing but grief and mistrust.

Darius's surprise from me when we get home is that I'm throwing him out for good. After what I have just been through I have the courage to get rid of his sorry ass—expel him, along with his realm of sorrow, his ridiculous penny collection and police badge, immediately and without a moment's hesitation. My work and my trust of good guys like my boss Mr. Jones inspires me to believe that a good many men in this world are pigs, but not all of them.

⌁ SEVEN ⌁

WHEN THEY RETURN

PART I

WHY HAD SHE TAKEN THIS SHORTCUT? It was the dead of night and the massive, four-story building she found herself cutting through had masses of unsettling shadows hiding in every red bricked corner. No wonder; it had been built in 1892 as an Indian Residential School. Every person who had to do with the construction and the first generation's staff and students were long since dead. The very fact that it continued to function as a high school in 1991 was utterly bewildering. As fate would have it, it was *her* school: Iverson High. On this night, it wasn't the creaks and thumps that had 16-year-old Lucinda Baxter hurrying her step. It was the voices—clear and evident as the wind forcing itself through the building's dust-filled eaves. Whispers that she knew were after her. Following her. People behind the voices hushing and craftily hiding themselves each time she would turn around to have a look.

She might have been better off finding a route outside the building itself, cutting through the school's courtyard of clustered trees. But even more shadows loomed over that area. They would have been safer, outdoor shadows at least; where she would have been able to alert anyone within earshot with high-pitched shrieks of terror. Sound journeyed further in the chilly outdoor air.

She surveyed her surroundings—a wide hall stretching ahead for what looks like an hour's worth of speed walking. And the empty, cavernous cafeteria to her left, where she has eaten countless piles of french fries with gravy, is masked in oily blackness, adding to the fear factor. Too many places for an army of stalkers to conceal themselves. She scolded herself silently for being such a nerd, where studying late into the night was routine.

Her father's stern voice rebounded through her panicked wits, "Just breathe and keep on walking. Always have a can of pepper spray close at hand." His voice was loud and obnoxious as if he was walking right next to her—or behind her pressing her with the pointed end of an assault rifle bayonet. But still, she wished he was walking with her. His extensive military training would be more than enough to scare the grey socks off any stalker or potential predator.

There was that word again. *Predator.*

For all she knew her surreptitious pursuers were just a group of hoodlums who had broken into the school. Hoodlums looking for a place to sleep and perhaps a bite to eat. Hoodlums who got off on scaring smart schoolgirls out of their wits.

Predators.

The word rattling through her mind was like a dire warning from her overly strict father. A father who wished he had a son or two instead of an only daughter. The early years, starting right after she took her first steps, were nothing but drills and sports. Drills and sports. It wasn't until her primary teen years that her father finally gave up on the hopeless drills and sports undertakings and made her focus on what she was actually good at: academics. "West Point Academy fully acknowledges academic overachievers—even if you're not the best at sports. And even then, the PT instructors will make a man out of ya." Her father's stiff words streamed through her conscience again. But this time it was a faint echo, like he was standing tall inside the smallest fissure in her brain. The fissure where she stored all her most unpleasant memories.

Predators.

She had to stop and let her breath catch up to her racing memories. Catch herself before she fainted in the middle of the old school's lowermost corridor. Past the time of night when most people were already snuggled comfortably in their beds. If she dallied or, worse still, fainted, it would be a free-for-all buffet for the creeps in pursuit of her.

Across from the massive cafeteria was the school's reading room and bookstore. The all-steel security barricade, with shatterproof windows sandwiched between the unbreakable slits, stretched across the whole of the store's frontage. A lone light shone from the bookstore's main lobby, above the checkout counter, enough so that she could perceive the basement level corridor at last ending. The green glow of the running man exit sign posted above the double door exit was her peace of mind. She breathed a final exhale and made ready to break out into a jog.

So she did.

Not more than a few widened strides and there it appeared. A shadow. The lone silhouette stepping across her point of exit, the obvious lanky height of the person standing below the exit glow. And something long and ugly clasped in their hand.

She backed up a few paces and readied herself again, only this time it was to turn and run back the way she came. Back to the safety of exit stairs that were inconveniently located a football field away. An old-fashioned design indeed. And an eternity of running. But at least it was better than what the shadowed delinquent had in mind for her. Just as she turned there was another shadow. Only closer. Dead on closer. She ran face-first into the shadow and then face-first into the person. She chirped out a muffled grunt as her face buried into the person's bulky jacket chest.

The far-end shadow caught up fast, the heavy thuds of running stomps drawing death nearer—

And that was it for Lucinda Baxter. All she could do was exhale her last breath and let her essence of life escape her body borrowed from Mother Nature, while her lungs and heart fought overtime to keep her alive.

They failed.

• • • •

"Two new students? Both in the same week?" asked the English Lit teacher, Mr. Randall Munro. "And here I am still trying to process the loss of my dear best student; Lucinda Baxter." He bowed his head in heartache, slamming his hand to his paper-scattered desk. It had only been a week since the gruesome murder of sixteen-year-old Lucinda Baxter, right there in the school. And the killer or killers were still on the loose.

"I know, I know," harmonized the high school's principal, Mr. Charlie Dent, who had come to Mr. Munro's classroom to give him the news about the new students. Mr. Dent was a tall, skinny, bald man who reminded everyone, students and faculty, of Montgomery Burns from the Simpsons; a new cartoon sweeping the nation's TV airwaves. "She was one of our best indeed." He exhaled a deep and wheezy breath. "Well, I just hope they find the goddamn sons of bitches who killed that poor girl."

Munro clenched his teeth, his focus drawn to the closest vacant student desk—the one belonging to Lucinda Baxter. Lucinda Baxter's desk. Always at the front, ever since her first day of high school inauguration. Her exam scores consisted of straight A's. A true whiz kid. Now she was just another statistic who would never get to wear the customary blue cap and gown on her big day, which would have been less than six months away. Her exceptional grade-point average had been paving the way for a promising future, making her deathly absence an incredibly disheartening loss. Such an awful shame.

"Have you talked to anyone?" asked Dent, fiddling with a ballpoint pen.

"Anyone?" asked Munro, his tone leaning on a mesh of anger and frustration.

"Yeah. You know, one of the counsellors here at the school, perhaps? I'm confident they would help." He leaned in close, almost hunching over his best teacher's drooping shoulders. "And look. I know how close you were with her. Hell, I saw nothing but greatness in her future, myself. Maybe she could have one day even been a teacher here."

"Professor," Munro spoke softly, his gaze still lowered. Gradually, he lifted his head, his eyes moist. "I'm certain she possessed more intelligence than either you or me. She could have risen to the ranks of a distinguished professor at one of America's top universities. Not a soldier, like her ineffectual father wanted her to be."

Dent maintained silence, a solemn nod affirming his agreement. Making lighthearted or unexpected comments might only deepen the sorrow of his most esteemed teacher. He, too, was aware of the military-oriented upbringing that the unfortunate girl, now resting peacefully in the nearby cemetery, had endured. Glancing at his watch, he fabricated a quick excuse to be on his way. Thoughts of a sandwich and a can of Coke from the vending machine occupied his mind now—scholarly demeanor notwithstanding.

"Well look at the time," Dent said, rocking on his loafer heels. "It's getting to be about that time I go and make sure there's no more dropout delinquents combing through the teacher's lounge. You know they tend to think that we, the prestigious teachers of Iverson High, bring valuable and leave them lying around. You believe that? As if..."

Munro straightened out his back, took a sip from his cold coffee and rubbed at his temples. "Yeah, I get you."

"And most of these punks aren't even students here. They just—well they just piss me off," Dent said, slyly shuffling toward the classroom's only exit. "So, you'll be okay then?" he asked, his head looking like it was popping off his shoulders as his body was already out the doorway.

"Yes, Charlie. I'll be just dandy. I'm going to just finish grading these papers and then be on my way home."

"That's my boy," said Dent in his cheeriest voice, adding, "two more students..." Neither he nor Munro were considered boys. Mr. Dent was in his early fifties while Mr. Munro was in his seventies; well past the age of retirement. But if Mr. Munro wanted to teach until his heart desired to give up, then that's what he would do. "Have yourself a good night, Randall. Don't work too hard, now. Remember, it's Friday, Thank God it's Friday. Oh and that new boy—Wilton Heller is his name—will be in sometime next week I believe. Monday, perhaps. That's what his father said, anyway. And as for the other kid, I'll have to look up his name. Hispanic as I remember. Goodnight?"

"Right," said Munro. But there was no one to hear him, as Principal Dent was already walking briskly away.

••••

The car ride home was dreary, as it had been for the past thirty odd years with no one to keep him company but his roving thoughts. Randall Munro wasn't a married man. He had a short stint of a marriage when he was in his early forties, prior to graduating to full-time teacher. But that had only lasted a mere eight months. Failure to communicate. Or maybe, in the hippie era, he and his false love were too messed up on acid and other mind intoxicating substances to realize that they weren't anything right for each other when they came down and went straight. A new, full-time career in teaching can do that. Munro was a Johnny-come-lately to the teaching world, compared to the rest of the profession who usually got the kickoff in their twenties. He had gone back for an education degree after living a tedious life of being an orderly for most of his young adult years. But booze caught back up to him after the marriage ended, even though he had said a big no to drugs.

Munro pulled up to his driveway and shut off the engine, his ears catching on to the light ticks and taps stemming from the inactive motor. He could already hear the loud yelping barks of his only companion, Mr. Wiggles, from the inside of his locked house. He looked up and over the vehicle's dusty dashboard. He cracked a modest smile as he observed the little head of white, brown, and black fur popping up and down over the living room windowsill. The Jack Russell was always full of energy.

Munro did a double check of his messy car interior, seeing if he needed anything more to be brought inside with him, besides that fresh bottle of Stolichnaya vodka. In his late stage of age and life, he hated to have to scamper outside in the middle of a cold January winter just because he forgot something, such as a graded paper or a flask of spirits. As he searched with his combing eyes and fiddling fingers, his breath already became visible in fluctuating puffs. It didn't take long for the winter air to seep inside his ratty old car when the engine was off.

Of course there was nothing but the regulars to bring inside the house. He had graded all the required papers at the school. He had just wasted two minutes of sitting in the bone chilling cold only to figure out he needed nothing else.

He gathered his cheap vinyl briefcase and leftover McDonalds' bag and got out of the car. Along with a high count in age came along the low count in body warming blood cells. The January weather, well below the low point on the thermometer, felt like another 20 degrees colder.

But at least his walkway was shovelled. The paid kid down the block was always on point when it came to keeping up with the weather. Ronnie was his name. The fifth-generation Italian American sprog with a jagged accent like the hoodlums from the Bronx movies. Yet this part of town was smack dab in the middle of the Pacific Northwest. Maybe the boy's accent was fake, maybe it wasn't. But who gives a shit? All that mattered was the kid did his job. He earned his $10 a week well.

Munro's glove-less fingers had already iced over, just from the 15-foot hobble from his beat-up Ford to the front door. He unwittingly dropped the McDonalds' bag in his juggling effort to unlock the door. Ah who gives a fuck? Damn burger tasted like it was left under the heat lamp for a few days, anyway. At last, the door creaked open and out sprung Mr. Wiggles, jumping at Munro's thighs before catching a whiff of the floored food bag.

"Yeah, you go ahead, boy. Papa brought that home for you," Munro said, watching with satisfaction as the dog stuffed its twitching wet nose in the bag and took out the partially eaten burger. The dog was smart, unpacking the loose wax paper wrapping around the meat and bun mixture with his nose and teeth, and right away scarfing the leftover burger down in one chomp.

"Thata good boy," Munro said as he scootched the dog inside the house and closed the thick wooden door behind them. He leaned his weary head against the closed entryway, checked his watch and leaned back again, eyes staring into the silent nothingness of his inner household. It was customary to let his bones warm up a touch before he went on with the Friday night evening routine of flicking on the TV; heading to the kitchen for a cold one; slamming back the cold one and then sitting in front of the TV to get drunk off his ass on Stoli for the remainder of the night. *Hell,* he thinks, *it's Friday, why not.* Maybe he would pass out on the couch. He was done marking that week's papers, and his old legs were too sore to lob him up to his depressing bedroom.

On that evening, while he reclined across the couch, the TV murmuring softly in the background, he found himself revisiting a haunting nightmare. He always knew how it was going to end, but his boastful, dormant mind made him sit and live through it anyway. Front row seating. Like being dragged to the same movie for years on end while also being strapped down tightly to the uncomfortable theater seat.

• • • •

The kid in his dream is always the same 15-year-old boy. He had enough of life in a boarding school which operates more like a reform school. There are daily beatings by the older kids, food full of decay and the occasional bed of maggots, and worst of all; sexual molesting by the older boys—and by the occasional faculty member too. Sleeping with your face against the wall so that the sexual deviants wouldn't hover around with bad intentions was becoming too much. The kid wants to sleep a soundless night and be able to awaken peacefully so that he may witness a God-given sunrise.

It's the middle of the night. The 6 a.m. wake-up call lies at least a few hours away. He knows this by the taint of grey overtaking the dusky black wall in front of his face. He needs the faint source of light to make his final getaway through the forested land. He rolls over slowly and sees no one stirring. Everyone is soundly asleep. Good.

Arms moving as quietly as possible, he slips the stiff and itchy blankets off his body, drops his hand to the cold floor and begins feeling around under the cot. With little to no personal effects allowed on one's person, the staff never checks under the beds unless it is the weekly sleeping quarters shakedown. There it is, right where he left it. A split-in-half broom handle with an old handkerchief tied to the end. The contents full of extra socks; extra bread; extra undies; unwashed bed sheet; one apple; one rusted tin cup. And last but not least: a notepad so that he can keep his mind busy. It could be weeks of running before he finds a safe haven.

He grabs onto the curved headrest rail and pulls his scrawny frame through the roomy opening. Rolling sideways off the bed would only add pressure to the rusted springs and thus get him busted by the loud squeals and knocks the beds emit. On his feet, he drops to a knee and reaches for the makeshift travelling sack. And just like that he's out. No more locked door due to the past days of kids pissing and shitting in the room's corners because they were locked inside the room while the lavatory is situated down the hall.

He peeks out into the eerie greyness of the empty corridor, his breath coming out in frosty wafts as he stares down the darkness. It's cold but it won't last. And it's early summer so freezing to death isn't the worst of his concerns. Food on the other hand is. But he remembers the farmsteads and ranch houses only a few miles away. Farm people are usually nice, and who wouldn't want to help out a high and dry 15-year-old kid put off course in the mountainous backwoods.

Clouded darkness greets him as he makes his exodus without delay, skulking on the tips of his chilled bare feet. For some mysterious reason, this is the part he hates the most. It's almost as if the whole inside of the darkened school transforms. While he runs silently down the hall, everything suddenly seems so different. So strange and alien to his young mind and eyes. Even his body seems different. But he keeps on running. The end of the elongated hall is always nearer than it seems.

At last, he makes it to the double door exit. He unlocks the deadbolt and ... too late. The doors make a lurid, un-oiled squeal. *Scrrrrrr*. Still, he makes his dash for freedom down the cement staircase.

The fresh country air has a nose nibbling pinch to it. He doesn't remember the last time he has smelled such natural freshness. Much better than the reek of twenty unwashed little boys' and adolescents' bodies.

But he took too long taking in the silvery view of endless trees and smelling the scented crispness.

"Hey you! What the hell are you doing out here you little shit!?"

He whips his head around so fast that his neck cracks and shiny little specks appear above his vision. The worst of the worst of the school's malicious personnel is standing tall between the open doors, all robed up in his usual attire of a black smock. The Prince of Darkness is what the other boys call the wicked orderly. A large stick is in both of his hands. The club. Many students have felt the wraith of that polished black wood bruising the tender skin of their backside, including himself.

He runs.

At the end of the long stone walkway the kid turns around. There are three orderlies now standing at the top in between the open doors. But the Prince of Darkness is storming down the last sets of concrete steps, grey sky reflecting the club in his hand. His eyes are jittering as he bounces down the steps, his mouth is agape, his teeth bared like a ravenous beast about to attack.

Go! he says to himself in silence. So he runs, his heart is wound up like a gold-plated timepiece and his lungs expand like black balloons. As fast as his 15-year-old leg muscles can take him, he dashes for the nearest cluster of overhanging trees. As he rushes through the woods, he shields his face from the onslaught of stinging branches and clawing twigs. His face and bare hands hurt from the sapling lashes which have drawn blood. And so do his lungs. His breath is coming out in wheezy puffs.

There seems to be no end in sight. For all he knows, the woods go on forever and ever, around the world, and ending right back where he started. But no. He keeps on running, driving his body against the weakness now enveloping all the body parts beneath his wheezing throat.

BOOM!

Was it a stick—a thick trunk of a tree? Whatever it was, it is enough to floor him.

And then they catch up.

All he hears is himself, gasping perilously for the breath of life. But you see their upturned faces drawing nearer. Their smiling faces. Devil's faces. Their lips are moving but their words are indecipherable through the ringing in his ears.

His last sight is the raising of Dark Prince's arms, and

then more blackness following the first strike. Followed by too many to count.

• • • •

Fighting his way out of his dream, Munro rolled over fast and abruptly on the couch, his arms and legs flailing so wildly, that he smacked shoulder first into the carpeted floor. Mr. Wiggles' loud yelp accompanied his own grunts. Instead of getting up off the floor, he opted for staring up at the his ceiling of discolored stucco. Brownish stains, from years of a pinhole leak within the copper pipe plumbing system, decorate the ceiling like grotesque polka dots.

His recollections of a Billy-club initiated walloping came first. Then came the hangover headache and dizzying spins followed by a cascade of licks as Mr. Wiggles lapped at his dried-out lips and oily cheeks.

"Hey there, my boy," Munro said casually as though he hadn't just woken up screaming and flailing from a recurring nightmare. "Good weekend morning to you too."

PART II

It was still the opening stretch of the new semester and there was already that ragtag group of slow learners—the special group—who were already lagging in grades. Snoozing in the back rows of the classroom, not handing in assignments, disrupting the class, tardiness, and no-shows were only a few of their usual up-to-no-goodness. But Munro wasn't paid to be a glorified babysitter. That was the school security's job. He was paid to teach and that's exactly what he would do. Monday morning's lecture was on the proper way of keeping an essay's thesis on target. A rather laidback topic for Munro and for a few of his good learners at least.

"Can anyone tell me how you should always establish the last paragraph on an essay? No matter the topic at hand," he asked the classroom of 28 students. All he received was a small crowd of bland faces, and needle-drop quietness. It was at this moment in time when he truly realized he missed Lucinda Baxter. She would always be the one to raise her hand and have the correct answer. But nope, she was dead. As dead as the expressionless faces directed at him while he stood at the front of the classroom with his thumb up his ass.

"Anyone . . . No one?" he asked glumly.

Still no hands in the air. But at last, a self-important pair of snickers broke through the dead-air silence. The regulars sitting at the back. The regular lesson disruptors. Two boys that seemed to have no real problem being kicked off the basketball team due to a low grade-point average. These two were on that road. And that road was ending soon.

Munro had enough bullshit. "How about... Josh Roddick," he said, and pointed to a kid at the back. "How about you? Since you're so keen on interrupting my class, I figure you must know the answer." Roddick adjusted his posture and arrogantly flicked up the collar of his leather jacket, his smug eyes shifting between the front of the classroom and his closest companion, Terrence Stanton, positioned across the aisle. "Uhh," he started, his voice loose and wiry, "to be honest, Munny, I didn't read the book. Look, I'm real sorry, but I had a wicked crazy weekend of—"

"That's Mr. Munro, to you!" snapped the teacher. He exhaled, inhaled, and exhaled again, his breath coming out like a cornered dog ready to strike. "Your answer by the way has absolutely nothing to do with today's lesson. Please, stay after class, would you? I would very much like to have a word with you." A wave of oooh's and jeers sizzled through the classroom, causing Roddick's face to turn beet red.

Feeling content that he received no rude retorts from

the affronted student, Munro decided to take a minute to clear notes off the board. However, there was a light, two bump knock at the door. The door opened up and in stepped Principal Dent, his bald crown glowing conspicuously under the classroom's bright fluorescent lighting. "Morning, Mr. Munro. Your new student has arrived," he said with a forced smile, his right hand guiding in the new kid on the block. "This is Wilton Heller. A transfer from Seattle."

Munro placed the bulky chalk eraser back in its track. "Good morning, Mr. Heller," he said, extending a welcoming hand. The new kid, head lowered, just looked at the teacher's outstretched hand like it was smeared in a repugnant substance. "Hey," he said, not bothering to look Munro in the eyes or offer a handshake. He snapped his head up and scanned through the still and indifferent faces of the 28 students—him now putting the number to an uneven 29.

"Okay," said Munro, clearing his throat and withdrawing his greeting gesture. He turned and scanned the small audience of disinclined learners for a place to seat Wilton Heller. The only empty spots were Lucinda's chair at the front and an empty seat right next to Terrence Stanton at the back. But he didn't dare to have a new guy fill Lucinda's spot. It was all he had left of her bright classroom embodiment. "Over there at the back. There's a spot for you to sit," he said, hiding his disappointment while pointing to where Roddick and Stanton were eyeing the empty seat like they were ready to recruit the newbie to their degenerate clique.

At last Heller trained a glimpse toward Munro, taking only a split-second to flash a grazing set of cold-filtered eyes at him. Familiar eyes. Munro had watched Heller stroll down the aisle and take his seat, his memory speed-reading through thoughts of where he might have seen that face. He was ready to distinguish where, when a student's hand raised in the air.

"Yes. Miss Sandford," Munro said, pointing at the pretty blonde with his wrinkled, stubbly chin. "I imagine you have an answer to my question from a few minutes ago?"

• • • •

After class, Josh Roddick sat with his head heavy, sweaty black locks almost covering his eyes, and his distraught face reeling in tongue-tied thoughts of dismay. It wasn't the news of his failing grades so much, but rather it was the bad news that he was about to be kicked off the school's championship basketball team that had him so disheartened.

"Did you let that all sink in?" Munro asked as though he was a teacher who gave a damn. On the inside he was the Fourth of July in the big city. Fireworks of pure exultation were bursting through his head. Only his stern, pokerfaced eyes were able to mask the kidlike giddiness. "Mr. Roddick?"

"So, if I flunk out, then I'm off the team. For good?" Roddick asked, a clear dribble of hopelessness falling from his lips and landing on his lap.

"Not for good, no," Munro said. And that was the truth he hated to disclose. He'd rather the kid be gone from his teaching life altogether. Forever. "Tell you what. If you manage to up your marks—let's say to a C minus, then I don't see why we shouldn't allow you to continue playing ball here at Iverson High."

"But I just can't grasp onto this stuff, Mr. Munro." At last, he looked up, a variation of hate and sadness fighting to win over his countenance. "I'm pretty damn stupid, in case you haven't noticed."

Pity now replaced the pleasure. It was his good-teacher morality coming into play. "If you need tutoring, I often stay late after class." He opened his mouth again to speak but nothing came out. Just emptiness as his mind fought him to backtrack what he was about to say: "I can tutor you, if you would like."

The flare of hate in his face seemed to subside as Roddick eagerly said, "And what about Terrence? Ain't he doing really bad too? Can he also be in our tutoring session?" There it was. He hated Roddick enough. Stanton even more. And he couldn't even imagine the two of them. The three of them sitting alone in an after-hours session of advanced learning. "You know, I think I would much prefer to do it one-on-one. That way seems to produce better results, I once found."

"So just us two?" Roddick asked, his face now an immoral twist of revulsion.

"Yes," Munro calmly replied. "If that works for you."

"Well it doesn't," Roddick snapped, his voice bold and unfriendly. "You fuckin' sicko. You just wanna have me alone inside your classroom, don't you?"

Again, Munro opened his mouth to speak up, but nothing came out. His skittering eyes moved down to the bulky student's fancy leather jacket. The radio's current hit song, "Smells like Teen Spirit" came to mind as he acknowledged the glossy, all leather jacket with a popped collar and huge gold buttons instead of a zipper. He wasn't fond of the grunge song genre and what that era's young people called music or their taste in fashion either.

"That's not what I was getting at. Not at all, Mr. Roddick," he said peacefully, keeping his screaming inner voice on wraps. "So, we don't have a deal, then? You would rather flunk out in my class and risk being discharged from the basketball team."

"Fuckin' rights we have no deal!" Roddick leaped out of his chair, brusquely knocking it to its plastic backrest. He towered over the naturally hunched, 75-year-old teacher. His right hand was balled into a fist.

Munro remained stoic and calm. This wasn't his first outburst from a disgruntled student. "So what, then. You going to just up and hit an old man? A man who wants very much to help you with your failing grades?" He placed his steady hands atop the table, palms down, and closed his eyes as if in anticipation for a striking blow.

Nothing of the sort ensued.

Munro opened his eyes, Roddick was standing with his shoulder leaning against the steel frame of the doorway, his sideways glare burning into the teacher. "If you dare flunk me, Mr. Munny, we are going to have some major problems, ya hear? Me and my boys, were gonna just have to retaliate if you fail me. That's right. You're fuckin' dead if that happens. Ya hear?" In a flurry of anger, he spun around and exited the classroom, but not before clouting his fist against the door.

As Munro quietly listened to Roddick's footsteps fade down the hall, his brain scanned over not-so-old memories. He visualized the folder reading, Roddick, Josh Trevor. There it was, pinned by paper clip; that year's most recent school snapshot, which looked like a police mug shot. He skimmed past everything superfluous, heading straight for the only footnote worth noting: "Mental health issue: suspected to be a sociopath."

● ● ● ●

Driving home from school, Munro realized he was more shook up than he had originally thought. Maybe it was his old heart working overtime for no good reason at all. Maybe it wasn't. Maybe it was the fact that he had just been threatened by a hulking student who looked like he could hit like a sock full of bricks. It had been almost ten years since his last threat. And even then, it was just some recently failed students driving by while tossing out a barrage of insulting intimidations and adding in a strawberry milkshake. The milkshake missed his face but it did ruin a brand-new pair of loafers. He'd rather the viscous drink had struck him square in the face. That would not have been as expensive.

In his daze of daydreaming about the past, he almost ran a red light, his foot slamming onto the brake and causing the car to skid to a sideways stop on the icy blacktop, mere inches from the pedestrian crosswalk. Good thing there was no traffic in his lane. But there was a group of teens pushing their bikes, all of them tossing him cruel glares of disapproval.

He watched with a phony smile as the four kids strolled by walking their bikes alongside them. Once they were gone and free of the crosswalk he fumbled for his nearest, unemptied bottle of Stoli and popped the cap off, downing a slugging drink until his throat muscles burned like a match against sandpaper. He cared little if the driver sitting at the opposite side red light witnessed his in-the-act exploit of driving under the influence.

Lowering the bottle, he coughed as the blazing firewater scorched his throat, his heart vigorously protesting against his chest as if trying to batter-ram its way through his lungs. Chasers weren't necessary in his veteran days of alcoholism, but he suddenly wished he had a root beer—a beverage that had been contraband during his government-sanctioned residency inside an all-boys school. He had also used the tasty drink as a way to torment the 'bad' students for the duration of his days working as an orderly.

"I need a fucking root beer," he said to himself, licking his lips uncontrollably. He locked onto the red traffic light with an intense gaze, almost as if he could manipulate it with his mind. Eventually, the light yielded, turning to green. His foot slammed the accelerator down to the carpeted metal, slewing the sideways sitting car to a straightway as he headed for the nearest 7-Eleven.

Once home, he was ready to start his routine, which had worked for him for the past unknown number of years. Get drunk—for he once again stayed late to mark the mostly failing essays, followed by Burger King—and pass out. And wake up. And it was only the beginning of the work week.

Tuesday would come. But as of recently, he wished the next day just would stay away.

Forever.

• • • •

Principal Charles Dent liked to keep tabs on his teaching staff. Especially his most prized teachers. It wasn't even a day after seeing the early term exam marks of Josh Roddick and Terrence Stanton, that he strolled down to the basketball coach's office to demand that they both be thrown off the team as of immediately. All this was done without Mr. Munro being aware.

Period two, and Munro was already to call it a day. He mixed his preceding evening of vodka with a little too much of the six-pack of root beer he had bought at the 7-Eleven. It was two nights in a row of root beer and vodka. Too much of a sugar and alcohol infusion tended to lead to a crueller hangover. He learned this in his early years of being a drunk—all before he was enrolled at university on his way to becoming a teacher. But still, he did it anyways.

He dawdled his way up the second story staircase constructed of pure brick with a glossy finish. He often envisioned himself slipping and falling to his death after heading to work on the days when the alcohol, still lingering from the prior night, wasn't quite cleared of his system.

As his classroom always remained locked when he wasn't present, the regular early birds stood loitering around Classroom 27, laughing merrily while throwing rubber erasers and paper planes at one another. Once seeing their teacher on approach most of them seemed to straighten up and quiet down, minus the few Pepsi-aroused boys that remained smirking and eyeing the three girls. These early bird specials were also the brightest of the class. After Lucinda Baxter of course.

"Good morning class," Munro said, lifting his head competently while he strolled past the students and reached into his pockets for his keys. He received a few undertones of haughty giggles and friendly replies. He stopped fiddling with the keyhole when he saw what he feared the most. But knew he had it coming. He almost dropped his keys.

A short distance away in the corridor, Josh Roddick and Terrence Stanton sat with their backs against some yellow and purple lockers. The sports team colours. They were in deep and worrisome conversation, their shrewd laughter erupting and bouncing off the steel lockers as the new kid, Wilton Heller, ended his dialogue with a gesture with his hands of an explosion. It was as if they all felt the staring eyes of their despised teacher pressed upon them. At the same time they turned their heads slowly, their gazes converged in a fiery lake of pure hatred.

It had taken less than two days for the Delinquent Duo to become the Terrible Trio.

"Good morning, Mr. Munro," said Wilton Heller, straightening out his knees as he towered to his feet and tucked his fingers inside his leather belt. He stood a good 6'1" tall. "You look like you're feeling awful good today, if I might just say."

Munro felt the teen's off-putting stare sucking in his consciousness. He snapped out of his daze, finished opening the door, and stepped aside for the good students to go in. His eyes darted to the troublemaker boys still sitting with their backs against the lockers. "And will you two gentlemen be joining us for class today?"

Roddick remained staring blankly at the glazed flooring between his bent knees, while Stanton pushed at the ground and used the slippery locker as his backslide. On his feet, he snapped his head to Munro, his blonde undercut tresses catching up to his face. "Sure, I'd—we'd like to join ya. But you see, me and my good friend, Josh here, well you see we were just kicked off the basketball team. This morning. Because of our grades in your class, sir!"

Munro sensed a cocktail of anger and frustration brewing in his blood. He knew that these two delinquents were not only failing his class, but others as well. "No one is forcing you two to be here. If you would like to skip today—skip forever. Be my guest." He then turned to Heller, a sham of a smile fighting past his angered, baring teeth. "Mr. Heller. You are new. So therefore, you are welcome in my class. Will you be joining us today?"

Heller kept cool under fire, flashing a nodding smile at his new friends before turning to face the teacher with a jovial face. "Sure, Mr. Munro. I would be delighted to join your prestigious class." At least he had a good hold on admirable vocabulary. He exhibited another showy smile to his new friends, remaining quiet and composed as he then nodded at Munro and scooted politely past him, with Roddick and Stanton in his wake.

There was that reminder again. Munro knew for a fact, standing at close range, that he had seen Heller's face before. But he didn't want to waste any more time delaying his 'prestigious class'. Class for the entire day's schedule went as planned; with no interruptions from the disturbing duo causing a ruckus in the back row of the 6 by 5 desk arrangement. Munro instructed the entire second period class without looking at the new kid, Heller, who sat mutely at the back of the room, hands resting innocently on his desk. But it was harder than it should have been for Munro.

Heller was constantly locking his own baby blue eyes onto the teacher like he was some kind of unsympathetic android from the future.

The remainder of the day went by relatively quickly. Again with no interruptions from the disturbing duo: Roddick and Stanton. There were always others, in every class, but none of them even came close to the double delinquents. Munro was just ready to pack it up and not quite call it a day. A detour to the basement sector's information and personal files room was his last stop. He had to know who this new kid, Heller, was, and where it really was that he came from. Knowing he transferred from the big city of Seattle alone wasn't enough information to fully satisfy him.

He used his teacher's key to unlock the padlock leading into the boxy storeroom, and the same set of keys for the hulking filing cabinet. With impatient hands, his numb and trembling fingertips flipped through the H grouping of student family names. Helena. Helton. Heller. There he was, his surname not yet cataloged in the proper order. Maybe the principal's secretary said she would get to it later. And why not? There seemed to have been a hell of a lot of students who had come and gone throughout Munro's twenty-five years of teaching at Iverson High. And the staff were still waiting on another one for this week.

He carefully pulled out Heller's file like it was made of antiquated paper, the kind that turned to dust under the natural oils encasing human fingertips. It was new, of course, not a single water stain streaking across the beige Manila paper. He went right to Heller's student personality profile. IQ 125: Superior percentile. Outstanding aptitude skills test scores. Even his personality test was rated excellent.

Munro placed the file on the lonely desk and took a seat in the ratty chair. He breathed out and gazed around him at the dull white walls and the chain-link strongbox holding surplus sports equipment. "Heller is an all-around smart kid," he said to the dank air. "Why the hell would he be wanting to hang out with those two future felons?" He flicked on the aged lamp and began reading more.

The disciplinary history summary was what finally caught his eye. The kid wasn't such an angel after all. Fights, fights, and more fights. He had been expelled from four different schools. All of them for fighting with team-mates and once; a football coach.

His parents? Maybe their names would say something to Munro's tip-of-the-tongue ruminating.

And there it was. Just what he was looking for.

William Fielding. The new kid's father was William "Dasher" Fielding; a slow learner from twenty-two years prior, whom Munro had removed from the school foot-ball team due to failing grades. But unlike Stanton and Roddick, William Fielding possessed a clear-cut future in football. NFL perhaps? Definitely the NCAA. But as Principal Dent would always declare: school guidelines were school guidelines. Fielding was dismissed from the team, missed the remainder of the varsity season and the all too victorious championship game, and thus never received his all-inclusive university scholarship. No one knew what ever came of old William "Dasher" Fielding.

Munro flipped back to the front page and stared hard. The resemblance was like looking into a police station's two-way mirror of the past, Wilton Heller standing in place of his father. The same mischievous grin on both father and son's faces. He remembered that part well. Like something was always up his sleeves. And there was always some disobedience hanging low inside William Fielding's rolled up cardigan sleeves.

The kid, Wilton Heller, was obviously smart—beyond smart. Up to par with the late Lucinda Baxter. But sometimes the apple didn't fall far from the tree when it came to settling scores. And he had found the right clique he needed to exact his revenge. If he had any in mind. Which he surely did. It was inevitable.

Munro slammed the folder shut and breathed out a rattled exhale. A sudden burst of all-out dread broke into his stomach and remained, curling and twisting like a malicious snake made up of pure, all-consuming acid.

He needed a drink.

• • • •

The nightmare came flooding back that night. Only there was a slight difference. Typically, the kid never make it further than a few hundred feet past the dense tree line.

But this time he did.

He ran into a fantastic meadow of tall trees and swishing rivers. Very unusual. And again, he stopped to take in the surroundings, almost forgetting his devilish pursuers. He turned just in time to catch a blow to the face. After coming to on the ground, after a few seconds of black, he watched as the Prince of Darkness caught up and raised his arms, ready to bring down·the death club.

Munro stared aloofly at the Prince of Darkness, his face compressing by absolute horror as he began screaming hysterically. That was him! Thirty or so years younger. The face of the horrific man whom 15-year-old Munro was staring into was also his own. A wicked frown of a smile creasing his ugly lips as he brought down the club for the death producing blow ... upon himself.

He awoke with a shriek on his lips, kicking and flailing alone in the darkness.

• • • •

PART III

Thursday morning. Three cups of black coffee and sugar before class started only worsened the screaming hangover. Munro felt the sugar crash closing in on to him as he stood at the front of the class, lecturing about that week's topic of the novel, *White Fang*, by Jack London.

He needed a respite. Vodka respite. "Okay, students. I would like you to read chapter five for the remainder of today's class." He took a scanning once over of the students, his stare landing on the three young men sitting precociously at the back of the room. He was slammed by an unsettling suspicion that crawled up his spine like a litter of freshly hatched spider newborns.

They were sitting quietly, not a peep from them. All three of them. But still, their faces held looks of masked wickedness. Roddick and Stanton slowly eyed Heller as one, grinning vindictively, and then watching without a peep as the seemingly new leader winked appallingly at the teacher before opening up his book and reading on.

It was some kind of a ploy. It had to be. Munro wanted to scream until his lungs hurt, and lob his hardcover edition of *White Fang* across the room at Heller. And he would have had he not been interrupted by another unexpected knock at his classroom door.

"Morning, Mr. Munro," said Principal Dent in his cheery voice, opening the door and stepping in. "We finally have that other new student we chatted about. Better late than never," he said with a chuckle. He stepped inside the classroom and motioned with his head for the new student to move into the room. "Hello, Mr. Munro's English class. I hope you will all treat this young man fairly like he is already one of you. His name is Francisco Flores. I believe he hails from—"

"It's just Frankie," the new student shyly said. He

marched two nervous paces inside the classroom, head held high, hands shoved in his camouflage jacket pockets. But his eyes were not trained on the throng of gawkers. He stared at Munro like the teacher was going to attack him. He stopped within a few arm lengths of Munro. Principal Dent cleared his throat. "I beg your pardon?" he asked the new guy.

"I just prefer Frankie, if you wouldn't mind," he said, his dark brown eyes again flickering to Munro.

"Oh. Well, okay. That works for me. Frankie," Dent repeated, puckering his lips and nodding in approval. He then looked at Munro, his raised eyebrow, helpless expression asking for him to be saved.

Munro sneered at the principal's unnecessary pretence. "Thank you, Principal Dent." He eyed Frankie Flores. "Welcome," he said, motioning for the teenage boy to take the only empty desk. Lucinda Baxter's desk.

Flores took a seat without question, letting his backpack slip from his shoulders and drop to the floor. He looked to his left: a kid judged him icily. He looked to the right: a sweet and pretty girl eyed him like a piece of candy.

"Let's learn now," hollered Stanton, prompting the rest of the class to break out into an amused titter.

Dent, still loitering in the room with his hands in his pockets even laughed. "Well, you heard the man," he said, holding his turtle shell paunch and giggling some more. "I guess I'll leave you right to it. Good luck," he said as he exited the room with a hobble.

Munro watched the principal leave, then turned to face the new kid, stepping up to his desk. Lucinda's desk. "Well, I'll have to wrangle you up a new book from the storeroom. But here,"—he handed off his own limited edition hardcover book—"you can read this one for today."

"Uhh, thanks, sir," Flores uttered timidly, taking the book in hand while his eyes continued evaluating the teacher.

"Please. 'Mr. Munro' fits better. Now you go ahead and begin reading, Frankie," Munro said with a wink. "We're only on chapter five, so it shouldn't take too long for you to catch up." He patted the book's cloth binding and stepped back, pivoting around to at last take his informal 'coffee' break. But first he stopped at his bureau to pick up a book, to make it look as though he was going to attend to some photocopying, and his coffee mug. "I'll be just a few minutes, class. Just carry on with your quiet reading, if you will," he said as he sauntered out of the classroom.

An anxiety attack was in the works. Another dreaded characteristic to go with his daily hangovers. But the bottle of 7-Up was always where he left it; at the back of the faculty's fridge past the different assortments of other capped bottles and canned drinks. It was a wonder that no other teacher had sniffed out the masked vodka. But that was a good thing. The teachers of Iverson High were of the noble kind. Not like the first school he taught at, where sandwiches and soft drinks would often go missing from the teacher's fridge.

Munro tossed back a shot, followed by two more. His heart rate decelerated once the warming sensation in his stomach began to coil. The teacher's lounge was as empty as a ghost town, the rest of the faculty were most likely teaching their daily lessons. Munro wouldn't have it any other way while he was stealing shots at 9:45 in the morning.

He poured himself a cup of the lounge's cheap and fusty coffee—no one wanted to fork out the money for the premium stuff—and threw back a few sips. A supplementary caffeine rush wasn't something he desired for his already hung-over and compressing skull, but he needed something aromatic to mask the firewater breath.

Now feeling recovered to some degree—for an hour or so at the very least—he sat back in his squeaky chair and reminisced. What would you do if you were in the shoes of a kid whose father was flunked by yours truly? He pondered this to himself, taking his own personal experiences into account. And yes, he had once been that no-good delinquent. Following years of a rough upbringing in foster care, no biological parents ever in the picture, he went down a short and dirty path of life until he was at last hired to help out with the kids of a boarding school. Much like the one he had been forced to endure as an adolescent. But that was so long ago. It hadn't been a part of him for well over thirty years. That's two lifetimes worth for most of the kids he was teaching.

No extravagant ideas flowing to his 75-year-old mind, he decided just to head back to class. Twenty minutes of being away was long enough. Young students tended to get restless when there were no adults present to keep them grounded.

"Hello class," Munro said, a usual greeting whenever he returned from somewhere—the shitter or the photocopy room was what he presumed they thought. He received no direct replies, only a few heads popping up from their books to curiously look his way. Some smiled back courteously.

Trembling coffee mug in hand, he took his seat behind his large bureau of a teacher's desk. His roving eyes went right to the Terrible Trio. Of course, they were pretending to be sitting graciously, all three with their interlaced fingers resting on their desks. The trio of boys displayed gratuitous smiles, their gazes going nowhere near the timeless novels resting under their praying hands.

Munro held back on an instinct of verbal lashing and opted for busying himself instead. Maybe a short, personal read would settle his drifting mind. He reached for the nearest big book in front of him, titled *The Key*, and turned to the last page he had bookmarked. He inhaled a short wind of alarm, almost soundlessly so as not to alert his students, his hand nearly ripping out a blank sheet that read: Dead Men Tell NO Tails in blotchy red ink made to look like it was written in blood.

That was the firecracker setting off in his brain. And to anger him even more as an English Lit graduate was the fact that they were in his 11th grade English class, and they had spelled 'tales' incorrectly. He grit his teeth and snapped his head upward so fast that it hurt his neck and made his dizziness strike out. They were all staring at him again, their smiles gone and replaced with straight-lipped looks of boastful composure.

Alas, the next best-of-the-worst thing was yet to come. Frankie Flores, looking bored out of his mind, caught a glimpse of the glaring teacher's evil-eyed scrutiny cruising over his head. Then he looked over his shoulder, stared on for a few seconds, then turned back to face Munro.

He smiled. In that instance, sitting right there in Lucinda Baxter's desk, his petty, beaten-dog look was gone.

And then, again, it was as if Munro hazily recognized the familiarity of a new face, turned old. It was a real-life horror scenario. A teacher's living nightmare. In less than a week, his predicament doubled from two demons to four. Quadruple trouble. Munro felt like thrashing out as he rummaged through the new kid's file.

There was almost nothing for the teacher to use against the new kid. And he wanted to use something. That smile. He knew that the kid's dangerous smile alone was more than enough evidence to confirm his possible upcoming recruitment into the Terrible Trio's clique—after only five minutes of being in the school. Frankie Flores' beaming face coordinated with the rest of the three devils, dead-on.

• • • •

What the hell was a timeworn 75-year-old man supposed to do against four kids whose combination in ages still didn't reach his number in life? At least keeping Frankie at the front of the class in Lucinda's desk wouldn't make it Quadruple trouble. He knew the Terrible Trio were up to something. The kids in the books he read and the movies he had watched about teaching gone wrong always were. And it usually ended on the bad end of the spectrum for the poor teacher. And the threat. Tales spelled wrong in blood-red lettering. Where was Munro supposed to go? To the cops? In reality, it was hardly a threat much less a sign that the kids needed an English tutor in their lives.

The mixture of pessimistic thinking, waning drunkenness, food hungry stomach, and caffeine-initiated over-excitement was beginning to feel like too much. He pulled over into the nearest gas bar and parked in the back lot beneath a swell of illumination, where the tarmac abruptly ended and a steep cliff dropped over the edge. No decent-sized protective barrier or even a chain-link fence was there to stop anyone from going over. Only a row of parking stops.

As Munro stared across the vast void with the foggy, moonlit outlines of the mountains as a backdrop, breathing hard, a grisly image came suddenly. He envisioned himself starting up the car, slamming the accelerator and plummeting headfirst overboard, like an Olympic diver. He shook his head free of the botched notion and decided he needed more drink. But he needed to be in a somewhat sober state of mind. He needed to think on his toes and vodka would only impede his ingenious rationality. Beers. A case of beer was the answer. Slow and steady wins the race.

And beers are what he purchased. Twelve of them. Something strong and smooth. Molson Canadian would do.

Canadian beers were like smooth malt liquor. He popped open a cold one as he carefully drove home, keeping the paper-bagged can down when passing another driver or pedestrian. A DUI was the last thing he needed when he needed to be at home thinking up a counterattack against the Quarrelled Quartet. That last tag was something he made up on his short drive between the school and the gas bar.

He pulled hard into his iced-over driveway, the car's steel bumper thumping into the already damaged garage door. He looked around to make sure no one had seen the mini collision. Even in his own driveway, a drinking and driving charge could still be handed down to him. Seeing he was in the clear, he gulped back the rest of his beer and tossed the can into the passenger seat foot compartment, along with all the other empties.

Looking up and at his doorway, he smiled. But the smile was for nothing. There was no excited head of fur popping up and down on the inner side of the living room picture window. Maybe he's just sleeping. He is getting old—like me. Munro grunted as he pushed his creaky door open and studied his passenger seat. Beers. All he needed to carry in on this Thursday night was his case full of brews. Minus the three he had already downed.

He placed the rattling case of beer on the stoop and dug in his pockets for his house keys. The door swivelled open on its aged hinges. The loud squeal should have been more than enough to arouse the dog. But it wasn't. The front, shoeless porch stayed as empty as the high school on a Friday night.

Munro stepped in the rest of the way, kicked the door closed and enacted his usual stance of resting his head against the closed door. He was about to think of what to do next when his nose crinkled and twitched. He detected the off-putting scent that he usually only tasted each and every morning following a bottle of Stolichnaya.

Blood.

Eyes stretched open he rushed his old legs into the kitchen where the smell seemed to be growing stronger. It was as plain as day, for all to see, as he rounded the corner and met the same handwritten message that had been doodled in his teacher's answer book.

Dead Men Tell NO Tails.

The message was scrawled on the wall beside the small dining table. By the iron smell being excreted from the red lettering, it was real blood. Munro, terror-swamped face, took a step closer. His suspicions were confirmed as he looked upon what was once Mr. Wiggles thin and bristly tail, the brown and white twist of fur ending off in a fray of dangling blood, bone, and sinew. It lay on the table as a message to him. A message of mortality.

He knew now that they deliberately replaced the word tales with tails.

Too bad it had to be poor little Mr. Wiggles' tail.

Sure, Munro had enough evidence with the scrap of paper in the textbook and the dining room graffiti, along with a dead dog, to get the Quarrelled Quartet taken in by the police. But for how long? They had killed his beloved dog. Killing a dog didn't get you a capital punishment sentence. A few measly months in the slammer would only aggravate them furthermore. And then they would surely be out for blood. His blood.

He buried the tailless dog carcass in the backyard, and after a good cry and another case of beers, he was ready to bypass the mourning stage and head right into acceptance. Payback was an addition to Mr. Wiggles' untimely commemoration.

It was time to settle the score with the little punks. His age-old thinking—terrible thinking—had come back into a play. He decided to call in a sick day on the Friday following the death and one funeral-goer burial of his only real friend in life: Mr. Wiggles. And yet another old friend came to mind. One he hadn't seen since the 1970s. An old, and real friend who had survived the Korean War and had a lifelong fixation with collecting firearms.

PART IV

"You look like you might need a little crash course training on that thing," said Ethan Demonte, a 31-year veteran of the United States Marine Corps. He snatched the steel cold M1911 from Munro's fragile grip and thumbed a small and round button which made the unloaded magazine slide out into his waiting palm. He was only four years younger than Munro, but he carried himself like a man still in the prime of his early fifties.

"Got anything smaller, perhaps lighter?" Munro asked.

Ethan gave his estranged friend a lopsided, pencil-eye regard. "Where the hell you plannin' to be usin' my guns, there ol' buddy, ol' pal?"

Munro articulated his own crash course update to his onetime best friend, the two 'graduating' from the same boarding school as teenagers. He added more to the story than necessary, and left out nothing, especially the gruesome details of how the Quarrelled Quartet had butchered poor little Mr. Wiggles.

After the disheartening narrative, Ethan spit angrily at the ground, and took a seat, in shock. He called one of his three German shepherds over and rubbed at her pointed ears, pulling her head close and embedding a kiss to her snout. "The damned dog?" he asked in utter disgust, shaking his head. "The damned dog."

It pained Munro to relive the details of Mr. Wiggles' ruthless killing. But what had to be said had to be said to win over his old friend. "Yeah. So, I imagine they won't stop until something bad happens to me. And I'm too damn old to be worrying about such troubling business. So, I would much rather just defend myself if I must. You know, some good old Texas style justice."

"We ain't in Texas, dontchu remember now," Ethan reminded his old friend, itching his bushy backwoods beard with his chubby, dirt-caked fingernails. "For you to be able to use this here gun,"—he pulled a small snub-nosed. 38 from a toolbox at his feet— "on those sons-a-bitches, they'd have to have you by the throat. You would have them dead to rights once they put you in any morsel of life-threatening danger."

"And that they will, my friend. And that they will."

Ethan furrowed his lips and bobbed his head in consent. "Now listen here. I know our pasts—remember them dark days all too well. Way too well." He rose to a standing position, eyeing the revolver in his hands. "This here. I don't think I much trust myself—you—with something as this. You get me?"

Munro breathed through his teeth, lost in a reflection of thoughts. "Hey," he said, all too coolly. "Got any of that new stuff? What was it? Heroin?"

Ethan flashed a grin and nodded.

• • • •

That entire weekend Munro did something that surprised even himself. He stayed sober.

The weekend drifted by like a car being dragged by a huge turtle. He yearned for a drink each time he woke from a power nap and let his hand fall to the floor. Mr. Wiggles' sleeping spot. Nothing but cold carpet greeted his slumped hand each time.

Monday morning. Period two. No hangover. Munro sat

at the front of the class reading his own composition he had written back in university. His 49-page thesis on the Walks of Life was his go-to paradigm whenever it was composition time for the class. The grade of 98 percent was the best he had ever received. His endorsement to finally becoming an English Literature teacher.

Curiosity killed the cat as he glanced up. To his sheer dismay the Quartet was seated together as one. Lucinda Baxter's seat was now filled by the all-star football player, Tommy Johannes; a once-stupid ape who actually seemed to be refurbishing his grades this year. Probably bribed by one of the delinquents to switch desks. The four troublemakers had their heads down, throwing each other some kind of sign language from behind cover of the student's physique sitting in front of them.

Munro cleared his throat and spoke up. "Flores, Heller, Stanton, and Roddick. I sure hope that's open book composing I see happening back there." Half the class relinquished their paper jotting and looked up and over their shoulders. Some looked up at Munro like spooked animals.

"Uhh, yeah, sure Munny Man," said Heller. "We're super busy over here just chatting about that Jack London guy and how much he musta loved dogs. Don't you love dogs, Mr. Munny? I know I do."

"Yeah Mr. Teach," added Flores, his peculiar accent sloped like he hailed from a whole different part of the country. "I wickedly like dogs too. Wish there was a—oh I dunno—a Jack Russell running around the classroom right now. That would very much bring some life to this boring class, don't you think?" The four boys broke out into a raucous titter, Stanton, and Roddick slapping hands and almost falling from their desk seats.

Munro held his tongue and was ready to burst. But he knew a meltdown in the middle of class would not go over well. Only he, his alienated friend, Ethan, and the killer foursome knew about the dead Mr. Wiggles. Under the cover of his desk, he clenched down on a pencil and snapped it in half. "Yes. As a matter of fact, I really do love dogs," he said nonchalantly, his body beginning to quiver as he felt a rush of tears swell behind his eyes. But it was too much. Ahh, fuck it! He was ready to explode when his classroom door swung open without a knock and in marched the principal.

"Mr. Munro," said Dent. His tone of voice showed zero of his usual jollity that seemed to never leave him. Until now. "May I have a word with you? Out here if you will please."

It was every set of eyes on him as Munro ached to lunge himself to a standing position. But it wasn't the gawking students who had him agitated, all their faces looking fairly enthusiastic to see someone besides themselves or a classmate getting in trouble. It was the eccentric and identical looks pasted to the four hoodlums at the back. It was as if they were saying in silence: You're so done now.

"Hey. What's up, Charlie boy?" Munro coolly asked, closing the door gently behind his back.

Dent's face dropped like he had just sat through a movie with a terrible anti-climax. "How are you feeling today? Right this minute?" he sternly asked.

"Fine." And that was the absolute truth. For once.

"Good," Dent said, rocking on the heels of his cheap dress shoes. "Good," he repeated, right away saying, "Been drinking lately?"

Munro was taken aback. No one had dared to question his life of alcoholism so long as he always showed up to work on time and never let it get in the way of his competence in teaching. "As of lately—no. Not that it's anyone's business, but I actually went the whole weekend without touching a drop. I'm still in mourning over a sudden loss, you see."

Dent seemed to overlook the mourning remark, jumping right to what he was initially there to disclose. "Someone, who will remain nameless, found this in the refrigerator of the teacher's lounge." He brandished a bottle from behind his back, cracked it open and brought the fragrant liqueur to Munro's face.

Munro got a whiff of it and recoiled. "What the hell is that stuff?" he asked.

"I was hoping you would tell me." Dent rotated the label-free bottle in his hands. The words 'Property of Randall Munro' appeared, written in the same cursive style as the messages scrawled on the kitchen wall and the textbook.

"May I?" Munro asked, reaching for the bottle.

Dent retracted the bottle, a look of vibrant disgust forming under his demanding eyes. "May you what—have a shot? I think not, good sir."

Munro let his arms drop to his sides, his own disgusted look to match emerging. "I was going to have a smell of the stuff. It smells awful strong and fruity for something I would ever drink."

Dent wasn't having any part of it. He capped the bottle and stuffed it into his thick blazer pouch. "There's another thing we must chat about. Come, follow me. Why don't we both head down to my office, shall we?"

• • • •

Four minds are better than one. Even if none of them is even close enough to post-secondary edification status. The four little bastards had him, back to the wall, and there was absolutely nothing he could do about it. Nothing at all. They outsmarted Munro without reverting to violence, beating him to the rocket-powered punch by planting a mixed spirit—something he didn't even drink—in the teacher's lounge, and the worst of all; a fabricated story of Munro making a sexual advancement toward Josh Roddick while he reeked of the previous night's booze.

"Take the rest of the week off, with pay, while we conduct our own little investigation, we'll call it," Dent said, his secretary, Ms. Cooke standing above their heads with her hands resting on her oddly shaped hips. "No need to get the cops in on this right away. I want to believe you, Randy, I really do." And of course, he had to end his scolding by reciting the school guidelines are school guidelines decree.

And as he drove, white knuckling the cold steering wheel, there was that reasoning again, seizing his brain like a loathsome virus. Reasoning that hadn't been by his side since he was just a few years older than the Quarrelled Quartet's age range. But it had left him for good, an eternity ago, because if it didn't, then it would only mean a lifelong stint of prison and the likes. Or worse yet. But today it didn't matter. His career and a roof over his head were on the line. Munro needed to be parallel to the ground with their ways of thinking. They may have won the first battle. And without reverting to old habits, there was no other way he would win the war.

But at least he made another stopover to the permanent and student files room before storming out of the school. All their home addresses were written down, except for the Flores kid. His home address was bound to be somewhere amid all that Spanish. But Munro would deal with that later.

First a beer or three followed by a shot or two. Something rather fancy came to mind. Lemon drops. Munro decided on a place he hadn't been in well over twenty years. A bar. He didn't want to be totally alone while he brooded over the ways in which he would kill the boys. Snub-nosed .38 included.

• • • •

It was show time. And it was a bitterly cold Wednesday, so Munro figured the hoodlums would be hanging out at the Quartet's home address closest to the school. And how right he was. Roddick, Stanton, and Heller strolled on in even before the school's end-of-day bells tolled out, all of them oblivious to the man parked not a hundred feet away. The falling flakes of snow acted as the teacher's concealing friend.

The plan was to wait patiently for the visiting twosome to go home, and then he would sneak in and get the job done. And by the looks of things, there was no parents or siblings' home. Superb.

Sitting in his far from eye-catching car, Munro waited down the street with no idling motor. But he came prepared. A thick buffalo robe and extra blanket were enough to keep him from shivering his bones to dust. Every few moments he found himself reaching for the paper with Stanton's address, studying it just to be extra sure.

He wished he had extra drink to keep his blood flowing, but he decided against it. He wanted to be most of the way sober when he was to skulk onto Stanton's property and plant the perfect gift.

The lampposts had long since flickered to life, the bright orange glow adding in more of a smokescreen. Munro's buzz began to wane, and he was ready to call it a night and reschedule the ultimate plan when the merriment of young men erupted into the hollow, breeze-free air. He snapped himself back to full alertness, his old eyes catching sight of the two young men strolling beneath the lamppost nearest to the Stanton residence. They were chatting boisterously, probably to fight against the biting cold, enacting crude gestures as they vanished out of sight and into the snowstorm.

It was now or never.

Munro exited his vehicle, slowly and prudently. Present hidden in his jacket pocket; he made his way to the side facing yard of Terrence Stanton.

Two weeks went by. It was as though no one really cared that Terrence Stanton was picked up by the police and charged for drug possession. But he did live in a sub-standard part of town. Drug addicts ran rampant there.

In due time Mr. Munro was allowed back to teaching at Iverson High. Mutually, Principal Charles Dent and the superintendent reasoned that his virtually unblemished record, minus the occasion he smelled of booze, surpassed the detail of them finding his one-time stash of alcohol. The fact that he was never actually busted being drunk while in class was the answer to withdrawing his woes. And he never had a documented case of sexual misconduct towards a student. Ever. So, no evidence spelled no reason to punish him. The strong speculation that Josh Roddick was a sociopath also played a major role in Randall Munro's ultimate acquittal.

A few faces in the crowd of students looked at their teacher differently following the news that he may have tried something against one of their peers. But Munro didn't care at all about what they thought. He knew the truth. But what he did care about was desk bound at the back row of the room.

The Quarrelled Quartet was back to the Terrible Trio. And Munro was happy to see that their young faces did not convey the former looks of problematic youth in revolt. They looked worried. Scared. They had lost a valuable member of their troupe and they had no idea why or by whom.

Maybe I don't have to worry about them after all, he said to himself, smiling as he turned and began jotting down notes on the chalkboard. The calming notion was indeed a relief. He swung back around and said to the class, "Before I begin to explore further into the story. Can anyone tell me who or what the main protagonist is in *White Fang?*"

One hand went up. Followed by three more. Then another, the students each glancing at one another and giggling timidly like it was a race to win.

Munro smiled. Things were getting back to normal.

• • • •

The broad smile wouldn't leave his lips. He was happy and content with the way life was going. He hadn't had a drink in over two weeks, and he was even contemplating heading down to the pound and rescuing a new dog. New to him at least. But the best part: he had gotten off squeaky clean, the perfect framing he committed. And who even missed the kid anyways? No one. Except for his remaining three homeboys who sat at the back of the class like caged dogs, beaten silly.

Munro eyed his rear-view mirror and flashed a capricious smile at his aged reflection. "Who's the man? You're the man. The fucking man who didn't even have to fire a single shot."

But the righteousness that had been himself for a few weeks was not to last. His taste buds craved a beer. And maybe a shot or two to chase.

Nevertheless, the man's good conscience came into play. His good guy mentality fought against his thirsty taste buds and yearning liver, although the liver probably detested alcohol the most, and pulled into the nearest A&W. A root beer would have to suffice.

He parked in a spot he'd never consider under ordinary circumstances, except for the newfound courage coursing through him. It happened to be the first stall, right in front of the restaurant's illuminated row of observation windows. As he entered the establishment, he couldn't help but second-guess his newfound audacity. It seemed as though all nine diners in the restaurant were fixated on him, silently challenging his newfound boldness. Of course, in reality, they were completely oblivious to his inner turmoil; it was all a figment of his imagination.

He ordered his tall root beer and food to go.

Another early February flurry had moved overhead while Munro was inside, ordering his double teen with cheese and root beer to wash it back. He waddled to his car, fumbled with the sticky lock and then felt it. Eyes. Staring at him from somewhere beyond the downpour of snowflakes and early evening darkness. He yanked open the whining door and shoved himself inside the car. Safer than being caught out in the snowy starkness. His key went for the ignition when an ice ball slammed into his windshield, leaving a small fissure. That would surely turn into a full-on split once the interior heat touched it.

"Sons a bitches," Munro swore out loudly. He reached under his seat and fumbled for the knife he always had on his person, ready to defend himself at all costs.

"Where the hell are you, you little pricks?" he screamed to the breezy air, his eyes carefully scanning around the flurries of white in the light.

"Heeeey, Mister Muneeeeee!" screeched one of the boys in a falsetto tone. It seemed to be coming from every direction amidst the falling snow lit up by four different lampposts.

"We knooow you did it," crooned another of the teenage voices. This one seemed to be coming from the sloped roof of the fast-food joint. Munro yanked his hand out of the car's interior, aiming a shaking snub nose at the roof. Naturally, there was nothing.

Somewhere in the snow-covered streets was a sharp stomp, followed by an outburst of obnoxious giggles which reverberated through the night air. Then back to silence.

A bang.

Munro was ready. Like a skilled warrior in the heat of battle, he trained the combat knife on the two people who came casually strolling out of the A&W. Both instantly had their hands in the air, silent mouths agape.

"Whoa, buddy. Be cool," said the taller male, taking a step back into the closing door. The husband or boyfriend.

"S-s-sorry," Munro stuttered out, lowering the knife, and tossing it onto the passenger seat. "Thought you were someone else." He lowered himself back in the driver's seat, started the ignition and peeled out backwards.

Munro rushed inside his house as though the trio was hard on his heels. He did a brisk once-over of the entire main level landing. Twice. He then stopped dead in the middle of the large kitchen to have a listen. He heard nothing. No bangs or cracks on the old wooden flooring caused by the weight supplemented by a few teenage bodies.

He was ready to give up and crack open a rainy-day bottle when his telephone screamed out, making his soul nearly abandon his body. The ringing phone was a dormant snake as his hand went for the blaring earpiece.

"Hello," he said as he brought the receiver to his reddened ear. Too guardedly.

He received no informal greeting. All that announced, bringing gooseflesh to his iced over skin, was heavy, raspy breathing.

"Fuck you!" he belted into the circular outgoing speaker and slammed the phone into the cradle.

His eyes felt as though the very force of gravity itself was orbiting inside his skull, the heaviness of his bloodshot eyeballs an extravagant weight for his spent eye sockets. He had stayed up most of the night, US Marine issued Kabar combat knife at his side, wobbly sleep not coming until the early skies of grey and pink began to emanate on the eastern horizon.

In a daze, as if hearing himself while standing within the deepest recesses of his inner skull, he heard his own voice, tired and discreet, ordering the class to read on in their books for the remainder of the class. Then he sat down, the swiftness in which he dropped to his chair enough to thrust the air from his lungs. He eyed the back of the classroom through the vacant aisle between the desk arrangements.

At least the Terrible Trio had decided to skip class for that day. Hopefully until the end of time. Or at least Munro's time. It was too unlikely that they were playing hooky due to a sudden illness. Nope. They were almost certainly somewhere close, plotting the ultimate retribution.

The in-between period bell chimed out, throwing Munro to reluctantly gravitate off his padded seat. "Okay, class. That's it," he heard himself say in a ricochet of a voice that sounded strange even to himself. "There will be no homework today. Just read on two chapters ahead. Have a nice rest of your day. I'll see you tomorrow."

A wave of pleased whispers washed through the room, the chattering voices like a cavern full of people praying in eerie undertones. Cold gooseflesh popped up all over Munro's body until the sounds all drowned out through his open classroom door.

"Oh god," he breathed out, "I thought that would never end." He glanced at the clock. 9:57 a.m. He had just over an hour until his next class. He wanted to get up, imagined it, but his body seemed to be on shutdown. Sleep mode.

The lights. He wanted to turn out the lights and maybe catch up on some much-needed shuteye. But a sinister thought, of being alone in a place which wasn't his realm, overtook his sleepy brain.

"But I need the damn sleep," he said to himself. He rose from his slumped position and gathered up some scattered papers, readying to put them away in one of the bureau's four sliding drawers when he imagined a loud creak, like a cat being gradually squeezed to death.

Only he didn't imagine it.

His sleepiness drained as the teacher looked up and saw the tall, muscular teen take a leaping step inside the classroom, nicking the light switch off as he noiselessly scuttled into the darkness. "Yes, I agree. You do need the sleep. Hell, why not just sleep. Forever," growled Roddick. In the near-dark of the room Munro watched him seat his backside on the top of the nearest desk, his gaze switching to the rectangle of hallway illumination where the others waited.

Then came Heller followed by the newest member of their clique, Frankie Flores.

"Hey there, Teach," said Flores. "Long time no see." He snickered like a demented sprite from hell as he moved to his right and kicked the door closed.

Heller was the last to speak up as he stood in the space between Frankie and Roddick. "Ready to die, old man?" He whipped out a long steel pipe, the tip ground to a faultless dagger of a point.

The knife, Munro thought in hungered desperation at the trusty weapon hidden in his pull-out drawer. Only it wasn't where it should have been. It was snuggly wrapped up within the under-seat confines of his beat-up old sedan.

"You guys are just going to kill me? Right here in the middle of my classroom, during school hours?" Munro scoffed. "Pathetic."

"You got my best friend thrown in the slammer. I know you did!" spoke Roddick. Without turning his body, he reached a shaking hand to his right, Heller placing the hollow cylinder of death in his grip.

Munro watched the gleam of the steel pipe switch hands. "Yeah. So, what if I did? Don't you want to at least know how I accomplished such a feat?"

"You motherfucker!" Roddick lunged forward and brought the blunt end of the pipe down on Munro's desk, hard, the metal on wood smash enough to drive a muffled ringing though the teacher's ears.

"W-w-w-wait. Just wait!" With the gathered energy of a young adult, Munro sprung from his chair and buckled backwards until his lower back was caught by the chalkboard's eraser track. Wheezing for dear life's breath he cried out: "Not now. Not here. Not like this."

"But you have to die," said Heller. "For fuck sakes, it's because of you that my life is so fucked up. It's because of you that my dad never went pro. And it's all because of you that—"

"Tonight then. Here in my classroom. But for Heaven's sake, yes, do it—end me. But can you please at least wait until my good students go home for the day? Do them that honour, at least," Munro huffed out, his right hand cupping his heaving chest.

Silence crept into the room.

"Fine," said Roddick, backing away a few paces. "But if you run, we'll make sure you take a long time to die. And if you stay, we'll get it done nice and quick—just like we did to that whore teacher's pet of yours; Lucinda Baxter." He handed the steel rod back to Heller, who took it in his hand and stuffed it down the leg of his pants. Without saying more, he followed Roddick out of the room.

And then there was one. "You will be here tonight," demanded Flores, his tanned face looking like hooded death in the room's dimness. He turned on his feet and wandered out of the room, leaving Munro with only the sounds of a racing heart and stuttering breaths.

• • • •

Munro waited alone in his classroom until the late evening, faking as if he was sitting in his desk catching up on the usual grading. Once the conclusive sounds of youthful laughter and pelting footfalls of lingering students left the school, he took one stroll around the maze of halls to make sure the custodian had gone home—if he even had a home. By that time, the sun had fully settled over the mountainous horizon, leaving an eternal gloom to submerge the whole of the midland valley like one big cave from hell. He stayed in complete silence, no lights or radio to drown out the delayed hush of the empty school.

Age was just another number, and at 75 he realized now was the time.

He was ready to die. The time had come. Steady footfalls rebounded through the lower-level corridor. Munro kept his ears on watch, reclining in his chair, as the sounds of footsteps picked up pace, storming up the bricked staircase just down the hall from his classroom. The stomps lessened once they reached the top of the staircase and continued by way of sneaky tiptoeing.

"Hooody-hoooo," said one of the teens. Frankie Flores.

"We're coming for youuuuu," carolled another. Wilton Heller.

"Shut the fuck up, you guys," snapped Josh Roddick in a harsh whisper.

The trio went quiet, but their unmistakable shadows loomed and appeared like the veil of death standing on the opposite side of the closed door fitted with a square observation glass. They stopped right in front of the closed door, the tallest of the bunch, Roddick, practice swinging the sharpened conduit in his hands. And then two more silhouettes of weapons appeared in the other boys' hands.

Then a loud smash broke the uncanny stillness as the observation window shattered to a thousand pieces.

"Yo, Munny Man, you ready to die?" hollered Roddick as he reached in and fumbled with the doorknob.

"It's already unlocked, my boys," said Munro, his voice as calm as ever.

"Cool," said Heller. "All the easier to kill your old ass." With that said, he booted the door open, a loud crack spilling into the roomy, box-shaped classroom as the door smashed into the doorstop. Then the lights flicked on.

Roddick waved his crew in and using silent hand signals, ordered them to fan out. Flores took up his previous lookout spot near the closed door, while Roddick and Heller converged on Munro's desk like two hungry hyenas. Malicious intentions were smothered in their beady eyes.

"You got our six?" said Heller to Flores, keeping his evil eyed regard levelled on the inaudible old man before him.

Flores glanced out the broken window. "Yeah, bro. We're in the clear." He did a last double check in the empty halls and the rushed to his standing comrade's sides. "We gonna do this now?" he asked, the same appetite for death reeling in his brown eyes.

"Fuckin' rights," said Roddick.

As if an unanswered query popped into his head, Heller hopped and turned to face his friends. "Wait. Who gets to do it?" he asked like a little kid on his first excursion to a carnival.

"Whose life has been more worked over by this old asshole?" said Roddick, pointing the stick of death at the still speechless teacher.

Heller started, "Well, it's all because of him—"

"Fuck it. I get to do the honors," declared Flores, pushing aside his friends, and taking a snappy step up to Munro's desk. He brought the old-fashioned baseball above his head and smiled defiantly.

"Don't you at least want to know how I framed him?"

Munro at last spoke up, keeping a composed voice within his shaken wits.

Roddick and Heller shot each other uneasy glances.

"I don't care. You made me lose my best friend!" screeched Roddick from behind Flores.

"And that I did," confirmed Munro with a giggle. A sinful giggle to match the three boys' current temperament.

"And that's why you will die this very night." Flores raised the bat high above and over his head until his arms could no longer reach. His eyes gleamed with animosity as he was about to bring the bat down—when BOOM! The bat gradually slipped from his fingers, an awful look of undeniable defeat sinking his facial expression. No more bat in his hand, he two-hand clutched the charred, smoldering hole in the chest of his camouflage jacket, stumbling drunkenly backwards as he brushed shoulders with his two unharmed buddies, and collapsed into the nearest set of desks. Lying motionless, he stared up at the ceiling with dead, glossy eyes, his face frozen in a state of bewildered dismay.

Munro rose from his seat, smoking snub-nosed revolver aimed at the two remaining boys, and chuckled obnoxiously. "That I did. Only need to use my own smarts. That I did."

"You son of a—" Roddick was about to pounce but was brought to a dead halt by the demoralizing force between himself and the locked and loaded pistol. He yearned not to be next.

"But how?" asked Heller, his voice sad and vanquished as he tried not to stare at his dead friend lying behind him. His homemade weapon slipped from his grasp and fell to the floor with a dull thud.

"I would say something like this," Munro growled. With the small handgun's taunting barrel trained on the two wobbly young men, he pinpointed on the closer of the two.

Wilton Heller. He closed his eyes and was ready to squeeze the trigger when Heller was bowled into an arched back posture, blood spurting from his skyward mouth. Munro shot anyway, out of stunned disbelief, the careening bullet just a nick in the skin compared to the gruesome incision slicing up the entirety of Heller's back.

Heller dropped to the floor, his blood-dripping lips warped to show final feelings of suffering an ungodly death.

And then Flores showed himself, grinning; a malevolent madman with his blood-spattered face looking like a ruthless warrior's war paint.

"What the f—" And just like that, as if a flash of black lightning blazed across the room, Josh Roddick was stumbling backwards, his useless hands fighting bleakly to stem the surge of blood rushing from the horrific gash in his throat. And like his dead friend, he didn't last long. He fell to his knees, closed his eyes forever, and fell on his face into a pool of his own blood.

"Well, that's that," snarled Flores, still grinning an evil smirk, while eyeing his fresh kills like game-winning trophies.

Munro still held the barely smoking pistol in his trembling grip. "But I just killed you," he uttered in disbelief, raising the pistol to his eye-level sights.

Flores wiped blood-spattered hands on his camo jacket and stepped over Roddick's gore-spilling corpse. "Go ahead, shoot. You can't kill me twice, you old prick. I thought a smart man like you would have known something like that. Come now, don't be silly." He winked and flashed a menacing smile of extraordinarily white teeth.

"Who the fuck are you?" Munro whimpered, slurping back his onrush of runny snot and salty tears.

"Has it really been that long?" Flores tittered. "Or could it really be that you killed so many of us that you can't even remember our faces—let alone our names?"

Munro's mouth dropped. An eerie memory came flooding back like a parade in fast motion. The kid. The teenage Indian kid who tried to flee the residential school where Munro worked as a young orderly. Back in 1946. Iverson High's 'forgotten' ancestral past.

"That's right, Mr. Dark Prince," the teen, so-called Flores, sneered. "I have returned."

"But how?" Munro was now shaking like a sopping wet man in a blizzard.

"You did kill me in this very building—or at least just outside of it, did you not? Because of you these are now my eternal stomping grounds, old friend. Welcome to my home."

"Oh god," Munro cried out. "Oh god. I—I—I knew I recognized you. But it can't be. No. It's—it's just not possible."

The mysterious teen calling himself Flores took a few short steps and sprung with inhuman vigour, up onto the dazed teacher's desk, and right back off landing without so much as grunt on the teacher's corner of the room. "Well. Do you at least recognize this mug!?" he shrieked and brought his everlasting youthful face—which had suddenly warped to a sickly grey-green like the emaciated, undead, oil black eyes dripping—right up to Munro's nose.

Munro screamed.

Then something happened within the darkened confines of the uncluttered classroom. It wasn't exactly possible to know what it really was, but the air turned dense and ancient, like stepping into an old tomb for the first time in centuries. There was also a rank stench that boiled the stomach and congested the throat. Munro's peaceful classroom hummed and bulged with a different feeling.

Death.

All around the petrified teacher, the black, child-sized shadows seemed to grow as if sprouting impossibly from the floor. Inhuman screeches erupted into the black of the room, knocking down anything that wasn't fastened in place.

Munro screamed again as the mist of shadows hemmed in on him. His last scream ever.

And then he was penetrated. A jagged knife. A large knife that sucked out his breath and made it a guaranteed impossibility for him to regain his steady gulps of fresh air. Munro was stabbed by the mystery teen turned suddenly familiar. And the teen laughed cold and ominously as it happened.

He couldn't scream again. All Munro could do was exhale and let his ripened essence of life escape his leased body while his lungs and heart fought overtime to keep him alive. They failed.

• • • •

The news crews just began to gather their cameras and tripods and wires and microphones. It was one of the biggest stories of the year to break the nation's airwaves. The remains of numerous children buried in a mass, unmarked gravesite in the paved-over back lot of an old residential school turned modernistic high school. All the children's names, ages and causes of death were undocumented by the residential school staff. The mass grave was accidentally stumbled upon by some plumbers who were contracted to expand the school by adding a new gymnasium fitted with a modern, full-sized swimming pool.

"Well, it's getting pretty late. I'm about damn ready to call it a day," said the cameraman to the on-site correspondent. But she seemed to be detached from the declining situation settled around the ground-level parking lot littered in upturned dirt and gravel. "Hey, Monica. Whatcha looking at?" he asked, stepping closer until he was shoulder to shoulder with her.

"Up there, the second floor. That row of classroom windows," she said, keeping her squinting eyes pinned to the string of murky looking windows.

"What? I don't see nothing," snickered the cameraman. "What, are you seeing ghosts now?"

"No. I would really doubt that." The reporter set her head down and smiled at her loyal cameraman of five years. "Just some old guy. Probably the night-time custodian or something."

AN EXCLUSIVE EXCERPT

THUNDER AMIDST
THE STARS

"The year is 2055, hordes of desperate people rush
up North to mine for the new, cutting-edge mineral:
Puranium. Despite desperate warnings from Inuit People,
they excavate deeper and deeper, until at last they awaken
what should have remained dormant
until the end of time."

—*From the Preface*

AN EXCLUSIVE EXCERPT
OF ALEX SOOP'S
UPCOMING NOVEL

THUNDER AMIDST THE STARS

∼ *PREFACE* ∼

T HERE IS A LOST LEGEND about the first inhabitants of
Turtle Island that has been forgotten on purpose; a
story of a Terrible War that raged in the North, millennia
ago. Had this war not been resolved, then all of life on
Turtle Island, perhaps even the whole of the world, faced
extermination.

A dreadful disease had arisen among the First Peoples of
Turtle Island. The longest winter in history had struck, and
famine was widespread. It wasn't long after that the Peoples
of the first tribes began turning on each another. Hunger
caused by the unrest turned to violence, and then the violence turned to cannibalism. Before long a new race of cannibalistic beasts evolved .

The tribes of the Great Plains put their differences aside
and planned a strategy together, sending their fastest path-
finders as scouting parties to the farthest reaches of the
settled land, for aid. Within months, the First Peoples had

amassed an army of warriors strong enough to repel the legion of cannibalistic beasts, fighting many brutal battles with many great warriors lost. But the warriors did not give up, persevering and eventually pushing the beasts to the farthest reaches of the frigid north. At last, the Terrible War was won. What was left of the beasts iced over where they stood in the sub-zero temperatures. The noble Inuit, with their bodies acclimatized to the wintry cold, volunteered to remain up north to watch over the icy tombs of the cannibalistic beasts until the end of time

For thousands of years following the Terrible War of Turtle Island, the People lived in harmony, each Nation respecting one another's territories. The story of the Terrible War was deliberately forgotten, except by the Inuit Elders. For the safety of the land and People, tales of the Terrible War fell into nothing but dust in the wind.

Inevitably, another threat was looming. The Medicine Men and Shamans of the most plentiful tribes had foreseen the coming of the White Man, who brought with them deadly diseases, and a new, dreadful attribute: greed. Once again, the Elders dispatched warriors throughout the land, but it was too late. The White Man had already stepped aground of Turtle Island, starting with the outlying islands of the warmer southern seas, and then moving inward, spreading out like wildfire. These White Men also carried with them a new facet of war unparalleled to all the land's warriors, indestructible armour and fire-propelled arrowheads.

Within a few centuries, all of Turtle Island's unbroken peace and prosperity was thwarted by the newcomers. The first tribes to encounter the newcomers were nearly destroyed by their filth and disease. The survivors were infected with the destructive power of greed, and therefore turning on neighbouring tribes. The millennia of harmony was completely undone in a matter of a few decades.

Surviving descendants of the First Peoples fell into a state of despair caused by the White Man's government-forced assimilation and the attempt to eradicate their traditional ways of life.

It wasn't until 560 years into colonization that the entirety of Turtle Island, (which was henceforth known as "the Americas") along with the rest of the world, was barely more than an overheated rock caused by pollution and a lengthy Third World War, which stretched into the second half of the twenty-first century. Bludgeoned by global warming effects, endless famine, and overpopulation, the inhabitants of the Americas and Europe decided to explore the Northern reaches of Mother Earth in search of a newly discovered source of fuel for their newly developed space exploration ships.

The year is 2055, hordes of desperate people rush up North to mine for the new, cutting-edge mineral: Puranium. Despite the desperate warnings from the Inuit People, they excavate deeper and deeper, until at last they awaken what should have remained dormant until the end of time.

EXCLUSIVE EXCERPT

CHAPTERS FROM

THUNDER AMIDST THE STARS

~ *CH 1* ~

2055 AD: A NEW BEGINNING TO AN END ALREADY UNDERWAY

AFTER COMING TO from a dreamless sleep, lying awkwardly on a sack of rotting potatoes, face up, with no blanket to keep him warm, the persistent, loitering smell at last became too much for Sam. He sat up, his pensive heart beating, his blur-spotted eyes cast to the nearest exit. His mouth watered with a sour, tangy taste as he felt a spell of squelchy spews churning in his stomach. In the blink of one eye, he was up on his feet and at full tilt, vaulting over sleeping people and conked-out wooden containers in his stumbling haste for the watertight exit hatch.

Sam burst out of the stale, piss-stinking corridor, slammed the whiny, watertight door shut, and inhaled a lungful of the icy Arctic air. It felt fantastic but only until it morphed into tickling fingers of permafrost, attacking the linings of his febrile throat and lungs. For nearly three weeks he had been forced to endure the foul aromas of unwashed human bodies, along with the supplementary odours one might expect in steerage class, beneath the decks of a rusted out voyaging ship. Musty piss, soured wine, turning food, bad breath, and stale cigarette smoke wafted through the entirety of the below-decks accommodations.

A thick curtain of icy water crashed over the ship's bow as Sam stumbled towards the weathered, chipped railing. He leaned over, gazing down at the turbulent waters below, his bewildered thoughts drifting to daydreams of clouds drifting at 30,000 feet. He badly missed his private jet plane. Over ten years had passed since his last flight, but he remembered that last airborne voyage like it was not two days past.

Dizziness struck him hard as he stared at the whooshing water, taking shapes of formless ghosts clawing for the surface. The eventual outcome of going hard for two nights of drinking the cook's homemade wine at last arose; the dreaded moment he had been sullenly anticipating had come. The very reasoning to his quick departure from the smelly, but warm inner bowels of the ship. He gripped the railing hard and heaved his upper body over the top rung, his stomach expelling a sickly mess of yellow discharge which immediately became one with the bubbling breakers below.

A raspy laugh from behind, followed by the rigid slam of a cupped hand landed Sam hard on the back. "Sir Colin's cheap wine got the best of ya, huh?" said Lester, the man with whom Sam had become fast friends only a few hours into the turbulent, three-week sea voyage. Lester had managed to stay drunk for at least a third of the coming-to-a-close sea crossing.

"I'm rather surprised, actually," he said, leaning against the inner wall of rusted steel and lighting up a cigarette, his grinning teeth suppressing a spell of shivers. "I figured the ocean's rock and sway motion woulda got the best of ya within the first few days, but nope. That cook's engine sludge-tasting wine gone and done it."

Sam kept quiet, his upper body dangling off the side of the ship, until the pit of his throbbing stomach was only sending up tremours of dry heaves. Wiping off his mouth with a used napkin and turning around to face his only real friend aboard the ship, he said, "This isn't my first rodeo, man." His voice was deeply saturated in cragginess. "My family owned a—"

"—yacht or two," breathed out Lester, a screen of smoke spraying from his nostrils and immediately crystallizing upon impact with the frosty air. "Yeah, yeah. I get it. You used to be rich. Weren't we all, though?" he said in a teasing manner, although he had never been rich. The unpleasant, three-week ship voyage was his third time aboard this vessel, powered by burning coal or wind in canvas sails. His family hailed from a small farm settled within the heartland of the Canadian prairies, thousands of miles from the nearest ocean. Their farm had gone; ruined along with the countless millions of others around the agricultural world.

"Damn it. I'm so fucking sick. What the hell did that guy put in his wine?" complained Sam, nicking back his gaze from the dizzying view of waves crisscrossing one another in the distance. A cold hoarfrost, like he had never felt before, leached into the pores of his uncovered face, the wind unhindered by the endless miles of oscillating emptiness.

"Not anything you, nor I for that matter, wouldn't drink." Lester inhaled a long drag from his hand-rolled cigarette and stepped to the ocean-rusted banister, holding in the smoke for an additional second as he assessed the grey horizon. The misty waft that he finally blew out looked like a mini storm cloud erupting from his lungs.

He tossed his still-burning cigarette into the black and white waves, watching it vanish from sight. "Well at least the water around here isn't flammable," he said, his vision falling on a massive accumulation of plastic bobbing past the ship. "Those damn scientists and their philosophy of the world's oceans becoming flammable from all the pollution and oil spills? What they overlooked were the millions upon millions of tons of plastic and trash floating around, just floating there, jamming up our beautiful seas."

Sam snickered, although what he was hearing from Lester wasn't at all humorous. "Breakfast ready, yet? I'm ready to eat now." Fish. He craved fish. But there had hardly been any sources of edible seafood in the oceans for over ten years.

Lester kept his eyes fixed on the lapping waves for a silent moment, finally turning to his friend to say, "Yes sir, it's ready. You ain't going to like it though. I know I sure ain't."

"I dunno, man. What can possibly be worse than non-stop cream of wheat and government-sanctioned powdered milk?" Lester kept his unbroken gaze fixed on Sam, his left eye twitching slightly, an old wound from the World Oil Wars, from which he'd never recovered. "Moldy toast with no butter, and purified sea water. You surely look like you can use some fresh water right about now."

Sam scoffed, half jovially, like his new best friend had disclosed a funny tall tale. But it was no joke. Food was never a joke in the newfound era following the most recent worldwide conflicts. Rumbles of hunger replaced the scorching acid sloshes in his stomach, Sam gathered up his jangled willpower, took another glance at the grey and pink horizon, and followed his spirited friend back into the bowels of the coal-powered ship.

• • • •

He wanted to read the letter., but he didn't want to read the letter. So, he took it upon himself to read the letter. Of course. And now, as he stood atop the ice-glazed deck waiting for the ship to dock, he really wished he hadn't read the letter sent from his wife, still back in Corpus Christi, Texas, who he hadn't seen in over four months—the longest he had been separated from her throughout their fifteen-year marriage. At least he had no children to worry about, only his trusty Rottweiler dogs that he felt better about leaving under his wife's care. Postal snail mail was the standard form of long-distance communication, as cellular and internet transmissions were solely reserved for the standing governments and remaining militaries. Like always within the last four months, there was absolutely no good news in the letter. Melanie stated that she just had to tell him of the latest update: his cherished Ferrari was stolen by one of the several factions of drug cartels 'safeguarding' the Gulf of Mexico. The world was at an end, or at least damn near close to it, yet people still sought after their daily fix of prized, mind-altering remedies provided by the ruthless cartels. To get as high as the sky. Perhaps being spaced-out of their minds all day had a positive impact on living a hazardous existence in a broken-down world.

What the fuck would they even do with a car? Sam griped within his inner conscience. There's no goddamn gas for it.

Or maybe there was.

After the near exhaustion of the world's supply of oil—most of it used up for the 18 years of World War battles, all-out nuclear war diverted—followed by gasoline shortages, it seemed like no one, not even government officials, were equipped to run their fancy gas-powered machines. Horseback cavalry was once again the soldierly norm after over a hundred years of impracticality. A far cry from what the world's elite militaries had been accustomed to. But the Mexican and North Venezuelan cartels, the real monarchs of the recently formed Centro Americano Confederación, still thrived by using powerboats (almost certainly owing to their near-endless supply of home-grown corn fuel), their only real adversaries being the few nuclear-powered submarines of the leftover navy fleets. America managed to retain just three of their state-of-the-art submarines; the rest had sunken, fallen into disrepair, or left abandoned in the merciless seas following the war.

Grinning with an infusion of anger and coldness, Sam's exasperation was torn away from his mind-nulling thoughts by another one of the floating plastic islands tottering a few hundred metres from the ice and rock shoreline. The plastic island's multiple colours, which mingled sickly into one another, made them unmistakably distinctive from the plain white icebergs which were on short supply in the northern seas. This sight of the plastic island slammed Sam with a sense of dread. He was well aware of the innumerable ships that were abandoned in the middle of the oceans when the gas was all gone, but he didn't think for a second that he would happen upon just one of the eerie aftermaths so up close and personal. The pale, multicolored island was huge, about the same size as his dearly departed yacht now sleeping eternally at the bottom of the Caribbean. An improvised shanty town was established aboard the uneven landing of the sky-facing surface. Red and neon tattered rags fluttered in the frigid wind, hanging from poles stabbed into the plastic mound. Flapping, makeshift tents sat empty and unused.

A chilling shudder, colder than the air enveloping him, sent a sharp chill through Sam's bones as he beheld the deserted settlement. With no other ships in sight, the individuals who were once on (or abandoned on) the plastic island might have already been rescued, or worse, swept away by a Beaufort Sea tidal wave."

"Well, that's a pretty one, ain't it?" said Lester, pulling up beside Sam with his one duffel bag slung over his shoulder, his squinting regard aimed at the lonely body of artificial landscape. He removed his crisp, paperboy cap to gaze out at the open water. "Looks like someone, or some people, had already claimed it. Hell, I would have. Look at the size of that thing. Looks Texas-sized to me," he joked. Death and destruction were nothing new to Lester, having survived eight years of brutal, hand-to-hand combat shortly following his draft into the global conflict by the Canadian Marines.

"Dead," said Sam. A whisper, barely perceivable in the whistling wind.

"I may not have the best eyesight, new friend. But I do have killer hearing. And yes, I can only imagine that they're all dead," Lester articulated with a hoarse chuckle.

Sam turned to his friend, teeth still clenched, looking more like he was grinning insolently. "And you don't give a shit or two?"

Lester scoffed, "Why would I? Hell, why would you? You're a rich boy—or at least you once were. So why the shit would you even care if a band of down-and-out strangers keel over or not? All I have to say is better them than me." He inhaled a throat-rasping snort and spit in the direction of the fleeting island of built-up human litter, then used the rail to guide him towards the portside rear of the ice-riddled deck. "That compassion's gonna getchu killed, boy. Let me tell you," he hollered, his back turned to Sam.

Sam exhaled heavily, his peripheral vision catching sight of a vast, secluded wall of ice-coated concrete looming closer to the bow of the rocking ship. "Yeah, I guess," he said. "Better them than us." He picked up the two duffels at his feet and began following the same path as his friend, using the corroded rail as support. An assembly of men started streaming out from a small watertight hatch in the centre of the rusted ship.

Spine-tingling curiosity made Sam throw a glance over his shoulder at the now bench-sized island, fading slowly into the seaborne nothingness of grey and black. He paused, mouth agape. A shudder ran through him as he thought he'd seen a lone head pop out from one of the emptied tents. Shaking off the psychedelic notion and blaming it on his extreme hangover, and maybe being too long at sea, he jumped in line with the rest of the slowly shuffling men and prepared to disembark from the ship.

• • • •

A light snow began to fall like miniaturized fluffs of air-borne cotton. Stern-faced sentries outfitted in all-white fatigues patrolled the worn-out planks utilized as the train station's promenades and boardwalks. All the roving guards were armed with crossbows and ancient Roman-style Gladius swords, while the officers carried old pistols tucked into leather holsters, or bolt-action hunting rifles slung over their shoulders. As he strolled politely past, Sam nodded appreciatively at one of the rifle-toting officers, the man replying with a rude sneer and agitated shake of his Sherpa cap-covered head.

Seeing his friend's sociable gesture rejected, Lester leaned in and preached to Sam's right ear, "Welcome to the new and improved Sachs Harbour, eh? And don't worry about the guards. They're just peeved because we're gonna be the ones raking in the real dough and, in the end, making the worthwhile headway to advance the people of Earth. And to be honest, I'd still much rather have an axe-pick in my hand over that rusted-out rifle any day."

Sam suppressed a snicker at his friend's sly remark—for sheer concern for his own life from the disturbed-looking sentries—and slammed his head back down as he kept in sync with Lester's quick-footed paces. He was acquainted with the fact that many of these watchmen fought in some of the most vicious of battles between the Chinese and their allies against the Americans and their northern allies— Canada being the top participant. When the dependable machines of war were retired, it was all small-scale bombs, bullets and bayonets right up until the bitter end. Both sides had no choice but to eventually sign an armistice, or continue on fighting with sticks, stones and shabbily constructed bow-and-arrows.

In contrast to the desolation of the rough and ready ship dock coated in sheer ice, the train stations and pedestrian precincts were teeming like shopping malls back in Sam's prime teenage years of spending sprees, his father's Black MasterCard at the ready. How the heck could such a northern and desolate place be so packed? he asked himself. He was reminded of scenes from the age-old Western flicks, the shabby towns chock-full of burlesque houses, saloons and six-shooter toting men. Few women, and mostly men, sauntered about the broken boardwalks. They had either arrived from, were taking an R&R breather, or heading on one-way trips to their primary destinations, which were one of the four Puranium mines owned by their respective country of origin. Natives from the local populace had set up vendors along the sidelines, selling everything from hand-carved totem poles to ancient Inuit survival weapons and clothing.

Sam and Lester shadowed closely behind a troupe of men from their ship, all heading to the same destination: Track 3 en route to Beta Mine A-2, governed by a joint federation between the remnants of the Canadian and American governments.

"Keep your bags close to your body at all times, fella. You don't wanna get aboard the train only to realize that you've been pickpocketed by one of the locals. And trust me when I say they sure as hell know what to grab," said Lester, stopping to toss a panhandling child, sitting alone beside an overflowing dumpster, a badly worn coin.

Sam watched in reverence as the dishevelled kid grinned a mouthful of remarkably white teeth before propelling off to what he could only assume was his father and brothers, themselves pleading silently while jutting out overturned hats. "What the . . . I didn't think there would be any Asian folks living so far up north. Especially in this cold," he said, his tone of voice full of skepticism.

"Man, you Texas boys sure are as ignorant racists as they say you are, aren't ya?" teased Lester, doing a quick spin around on his feet as he kept ambling ahead of Sam.

"What—what the hell do you mean by that?" snapped Sam, pulling his luggage bags tighter as he partially sidestepped past a group of thuggish-looking young men stumbling drunkenly out of an open doorway, all of them wearing warm, Inuit parkas.

"Those ain't no Asian folk you speak of," he haughtily confirmed. "Those folk are the local Inuit people. Inuktitut. The First Peoples of this exotic land. In the beginning they sternly detested us coming here, but then they heard about the good fortune this very special mineral would bring to themselves and the rest of the world. And now . . . well let's just say they're more than happy to have us over for dinner in their house." He halted just as another group of ragtag men, wearing overly worn coveralls, stumbled out from one of the many taverns lining the provisional train track line.

Giving the new age roughnecks reasonable space to pass without instigating a confrontation, Lester hunched over to whisper spookily, "But not all are fond of us being here."

Sam stopped dead in his tracks. His mind began flickering with images of his Native American wife narrating stories of an ancient land—a northern land covered in ice. Although his wife, Leanne, was a direct descendant of the Comanche Nation, the 'Lords of the Plains', she knew many of the age-old stories of Turtle island's northern inhabitants that her grandmother had learned from generations of oral history.

Staring past the looming boundaries of the shoddily constructed train station, a swirling waft of illuminated ice and mist caught his attention, his wandering imagination pitting him against an eerie depiction of ice giants emerging from the whiteout, their massive, clawed hands balled up into fists ready to kill.

"You okay there, buddy? Come on, we're gonna get left behind," said Lester, tugging on Sam's duffel bag.

"I—I know this land," Sam stuttered. "Or at least, I know of it. Stories. I know stories about this place. And trust me, these stories ain't no happy fairy tales." He turned to face his friend directly, his expression stern. "Are we still in northern Alaska, or have we now crossed into northern Canada?" he asked, his voice trembling slightly.

Lester remained immobile, his eyes flaring as he leaned in, whispering at an almost inaudible range, "Dude, you can't be asking questions like that around here. You know this. We're way the hell up north, and that's all that matters. Now come on, let's pick up the pace before you get us both iced—and I'm not talking about the frosty kind."

Sam held his ground, deliberately slowing his pace to keep his steady gaze fixed on the swirling snow beyond the bright illumination of the last station's towering lampposts. A greyish-blue sun was setting somewhere beyond the blanket of cloudy white wilderness. An unnerving sensation coursed through him as he tried to envision his wife with the warm and crackling fire berth at her back. She used to share tall tales of a horrible beast, the name of which was strictly taboo to discuss among the Northern Plains tribes.

While he stood pondering, the loud whistle of an approaching steam train made him jump. The view directly ahead of him was once again nothing more than another endless expanse of lackluster tundra and air-borne snow.

• • • •

The narrow, corridor-like interior of the antiquated steam engine locomotive car reminded Sam once again of his lost private jet, a reminder of a life of luxury now gone for good. At least, for his lifetime it was gone. The relaxed seating arrangement of his twin-engine jet wasn't as cramped and stiff as this early 1900s passenger car where he, his newfound bestie, and about a hundred other men sat. He exhaled a puff of frosty breath, watching as it mingled with the arctic air.

"Bet ya wish we were back in the warm bowels of that piss-smelling, ship undercarriage, now, eh?" joked Lester, gritting his teeth and shivering as he fought against the bitter cold of the unheated train.

Sam wiped away his observation window's buildup of frost, his fuzzy view landing on a group of warmly dressed locals shovelling away at the backlog of snow and ice bottlenecking the steel tracks on both sides of the train. "I wish I was piloting my plane, that's what I truthfully wish for right about now. And you, I bet you miss your good ol' John Deere, huh?"

Lester puckered his lips, forced a clever smile and shook his head. "Pipe dreams now, my good sir. Nothing but good ol' pipe dreams. I'd have never thought it, though. Never thought it once," he barked, his hands making an ear-splitting clap that seemed to rattle the frozen window perched a few inches from Sam's temple.

"Thought about what?"

Lester trained his eyes on Sam. "You."

"What do you mean, me?" *What the fuck are you trying to say?* Sam thought angrily, keeping his plain-spoken, thinking words to himself.

"Not once in my whole existence of being a petty little farm boy did I ever think I would be sitting on an ancient train with none other than the likes of a man who lived the life I only ever saw when I peered up at the skies on a cloudless night. Or in my case, a blackened, sloped gable of a roof. And there's a shit ton of stars in the skies I used to stare at, I'll tell ya what." He beamed heavily and laid down another one of his hard smacks to Sam's frozen kneecap.

"I'm truly flattered," Sam teased, tuning his absentminded stare toward the train car's open seating arrangement. He wished there was at least some kind of eye candy to take glances at amongst the bunch of grungy looking men headed to work. As a married man, his lifelong philosophy: he could look, but never touch.

"So, a pilot you once were, eh? Dammit man, what haven't you been, Mister Yacht Captain? But I would like to hear about life in the skies, though. I would reckon there ain't too many of you flyboys hanging about these days. But these,"— he performed a two finger salutation—"secret spacecraft that they're working on. You think you'd be able to pilot one of them ginormous bastards?"

Sam didn't have to cook up a concoction of a story. His father was one of the lead designers of the first top-secret prototype spacecraft devised to search the galaxy for planets suitable to sustain life. The newly found conception was put on ultimate hold when World War III was instigated. "Yes," he replied smugly, "my father was a skilled flight instructor. At first, he trained the world's top commercial pilots. But then the war broke out and he used his expertise to train the tactical precision bomber pilots. Long story short: my pops lost his life during a sneak attack on the Texas situated air-base, by the Nicaraguans. I—"

"So sorry to hear that, brother. I guess we all lost some-one or something in that lengthy, good-for-nothing war."

"Thank you," Sam said with a nod of appreciation. Continuing with his story, he said, "By the time my father was killed, he had already passed down his knowledge to me. You see—" he patted Lester's kneecap, "—under my father's watchful eye, I was trained to fly anything from the classic single engine bi-plane to fighter jets, and last but not least: the mighty 797. You name it, I can most likely fly it."

"Even spacecraft?"

"Even spacecraft," Sam echoed. "I would reckon the controls oughta be the same." The talk of flight made him yearn for his long-lost jet plane for a third time, like a man addicted to pepprin. His cherished, private aircraft was now just a hunk of mixed metals laid to waste in some Texas junk-yard. The jet plane was peppered into disrepair by Mexican anti-aircraft bullets after an emergency rescue mission to recover stranded American and Canadian special forces beyond the walled off US/Mexico border.

"Ah, who knows?" yawned Lester. "If we survive this work expedition, then maybe you can take to the skies again. I was a foot soldier during the war, but I'm way too sure that we lost most of the pilots who could fly those colossal space-ships. And by the sounds of it, you're more than qualified."

"Perhaps," said Sam, feeling buoyed by his newfound

friend's deliverance of hope. Absorbing Lester's conta-
gious action set into him, he yawned with a wide stretch
of his arms, zipped his jacket up to his throat and let the
thumping commencement of the train's clacking against
the tracks coast him into the restful land of Shangri-La.

Deep sleep was next to impossible, Sam dozing in and
out of a fragmented slumber. The train ride was anything
but smooth sailing, the unheated and crowded passenger car feeling as though it was going to jump track at any
given moment. Threatening sounds of a constant hammer
drill sounded from below the undercarriage. Following
an unspecified number of tedious hours, Sam awoke and
decided to sit silently with his head leaning up against the
frigid window. His eyes strained to discover any sort of
natural life amongst the endless flat of snow and ice terrain—trees and flourishing vegetation nothing but a long-
lost memory. A bright, almost impossibly sized moon had
taken watch, trading places in the sky with the sleeping sun.

Sam was reminded of the high plains of Texas in the
way the craggy, white and grey terrain fumbled into the
mountainous horizon. Snow wasn't completely unheard of
in his hometown of Lubbock, but the endless fields of ice
looking like the surface of mirror-polished shoes under a
white flamed candle was a brand-new phenomenon.

"Where the hell are we?" he muttered to himself, huffing
his breath on the window and then sketching an unhappy
face in the condensation.

"Don't beat yourself up so much, my brother," said
Lester. "You'll get used to camp life. Just think of it as a
minimum-security prison—a workcamp—and then you
oughta start to feel better right away."

Sam faced his comedic friend humorlessly. He knew for
a fact that there were a sizeable number of convicts, direct
from the overflowing prisons in the south, who were forced

to work in the Puranium mines with next to nothing for pay. A sharp poke to an already infuriated bear. "That does not make me feel better. Not at all. We are indeed going to be working right next to these rapists and murderers, you know."

Lester chuckled and took a giant sip from his silver flask, keeping a straight face as he gulped back another one of the ship cook's homemade spirits. "Hey. They're not all murderers and rapists. Some are also drug dealers and petty thieves. Maybe even a few pepheads too. You know how much that drug took the world by storm ever since those disgraced air force scientists released it to the world-wide public."

"Yeah but—" Sam was cut off by the sudden lurch of the train, followed immediately by the ear-splitting whine of an aged braking system working overdrive.

"Hold that thought," said Lester, upping himself and rushing for the nearest set of closed exit doors. He politely brushed past a group of drunken men struggling to get off their own seats, stopping at the wide set of glass encased doors. He spun around, his face reeling in amusement. "Come on over here, Brother Sam. You just have to see this, my man."

Sam's eyes were tightly shut, his heart was sprinting at Mach 1, thinking the train was about derail and plunder into an embankment of bottomless snow. He exhaled a long breath—breathing techniques instilled into him by his strict father—waiting for the slowdown of his galloping heart to shift into pace with his slow respire.

"You're gonna miss—"

"Coming," Sam barked, opening his eyes just as a large group of disorderly men began stumbling toward the partially opened doors. An unfriendly breeze slapped them in the face. "What's so important," he hollered, hopping out of his seat and rushing ahead of the oncoming group, "that I have to come and face the—" He stopped abruptly, his jaw dropping open at the breathtaking spectacle unfolding just 40 feet beyond the train tracks.

Lester stayed mute and smiling, his eyes twinkling from the unintentional lightshow glowing up at them. Hundreds upon hundreds of LED lights sparkled like a mini city, each one placed meticulously in the massive hole, and along the endless spirals of roadways and steel parquets lining the near-vertical slopes. The enormous manmade pit looked like a perfectly chiselled mountain had turned upside down, pointy tip down, then carefully drawn back up, leaving nothing but a flawlessly funnelled hollow in its wake.

"Holy shit," said Sam, his enlarged glittering eyes saying more than his words alone. "That's—that's where we're going to be working?"

• • • •

On especially foggy nights while out on a seaborne yacht excursion with his now deceased mother and father, young Sam used to enjoy hitting the open decks to shine his brightest LED spotlight to the blackened skies. His young imagination portrayed him as a one-man, naval search team, the shaft of glowing particles reminding him of the war movies he was so hooked on. This was the reasoning to his desire to becoming a pilot.

Slogging alongside this immense manmade crater, his childhood wonder was amplified by ten thousand by the intense stars of light from inside the Puranium mines radiating upward and carving through the fog with colossal vivacity. It was as if the gods in the heavens were reaching down into Mother Earth, the single arm sheathed by the vivid whiteness of the glowing mist particles.

A lone, coyote howl of a wind shrieked through the open emptiness, the thunderous metal on metal smashes and knocks from inside the grand chasm.

"Can you even believe it?" said one of the many men trudging in sequence through the knee-deep snow. Sam whirled around to see who it was that was speaking in such a happy-go-lucky manner. A tall, stout man dressed like a 20th century Russian infantrymen tramped next to a shorter fellow dressed almost identically to him, his face being the only animated one amongst at least a hundred or so empty expressions in the extensive, snow crunching formation.

Sam wished he had packed one duffel instead of two as he watched Lester coast through the snow with ease, his puckered lips whistling a happy tune as he walked effortlessly, taking intervals to switch his heavy duffel from shoulder to shoulder. "Is it always like this? Having to trudge through this infinite snow for the last mile or so?" he complained, feeling the uncomfortable sensation of stress sweat beginning to accumulate under his bundled-up neckline.

"No sir. This is the first of my two ingoing trips," Lester casually answered. "But hey, what do ya figure, right? With an old ass train and no more gas to power up the fancy airplanes or snowmobiles, it would be expected to have the occasional breakdown. But look at the bright side of things: our train could have broken down in the middle of butt fuck nowhere." He slowed his roll and turned half around to face his decelerating friend, the white light to their left flank animating his charismatic presence like a heatless bonfire. He stared hard at Sam until his shoulder was unintentionally struck by a passing man, the shoulder clash making him turn back around to resume trailing the horde around the curved, mile-long crest of the manmade cliff.

Sam took another glance over his shoulder to say good-bye to the motionless train, which was just another serrated silhouette against the ghostly moonlight. A large and bright spotlight was settled on the group of men scuttling frantically aboard the lead locomotive trying to get the 150-year-old engine going, looking like little worker ants from the distance. The slave-driven workers looked cold, as cold as Sam felt. As he watched, a smile creased his lips at the thought of being over a thousand feet deep in no time, the natural balminess of Mother Earth's cradle warming him up just from the notion. At least I'm not them, he thought, turning away from the stalled locomotive.

At least I'm not them.

∼ CH 2 ∼

SHAFTS AND MAMMOTHS

S AM HAD TO COAX his numbed legs to carry his thousand pounds of bags and bodyweight past the snow-meets-concrete threshold. He fell to his stomach, embracing the warmth of the massive trailer. The remaining men from the long line of snow trampers rushed inside, with some taking their time to sit on their backpacks and duffels, while others remained standing, engaged in quiet conversation. A low hum of a mechanical motor filled the air as the enormous sliding door sealed shut behind the last man to stumble inside the building.

"Let's not get too comfortable," persisted Lester, tossing his bag over his back while he stooped over to snatch up Sam by the shoulder lapels. "If they see you collapsing to the floor like that, you'll be on the first train back to nowheres-ville. And we don't want that now, do we?"

"Maybe," answered the floored Sam, pushing himself to his elbows to stare through his iced-over eyelashes. "Can't I just lay here for a minute ... maybe ten?"

"There'll be time for that when they assign us our living quarters. Now come on, upsy-daisy." For a second time, Lester hunched over to grasp onto Sam, this time adding more force to his clenched-up fingers around his friend's furry-rimmed hood. He pulled hard until Sam was sitting on his backside, huffing and puffing as he smeared away the mini-icicles dangling from his eyelashes.

"Wow. This place is huge. Is it safe to ask where we are?" queried Sam, slumping into a comfortable position and letting his shouldered duffel straps slide to the floor. Overcome by awe, he stared up at the massive trailer with a industrial plant in the centre, a ceaseless network of twisting, polychrome pipes and conduits interweaving into and over one another. Men and women adorned in shiny red hardhats scampered about the mathematical grid of steel planks, some reading one of the several gauges, checklist in hand, while others turned wheel valves. Hissing steam evaporated from the very centre of the plant, the blue smoke twisting upwards into a large, coned vent.

Lester took a knee and watched with a smile as an extensive, girder-secured crane arm, clinching a rather large army tank-looking apparatus, zipped by overhead. "This, my friend, is the main fabrication hangar. This is where all the real magic happens. From servicing of the mighty Mammoth excavators to refinement of the freshly unearthed Puranium bullion." He pointed toward an area situated further down the complex, where armed sentries guarded a towering set of fortress-like doors. "All that and then some."

"So, this is where we start?"

"No, my friend," Lester began with a chuckle, placing a firm grip on Sam's shoulder, while still beaming brightly. "This place is for VIPs only. You and I—we're nothing but two foot soldiers in Napoleon's grand old empire. If ya catch my drift?"

A feeling of thwarted joy overcame Sam at the disheartening news of not being able to procure work inside the somewhat comfortable boundaries of the colossal warehouse. At least the place was warm. "Well I guess—"

"Good evening, men," yelled a short, scrawny man, skating to a rubber-hissing stop in a Polaris ATV. This guy didn't appear at all like a genuine labourer of the mines. He looked as though he would either hit the dirt or make a break for the nearest exit if someone was to so much as flog a wad of spit his way. His rare and expensive-looking work attire spelled out his boss status, with a shiny steel hardhat and creaseless hi-visibility vest worn over the lavish business garb. A gold-trimmed letter M, scripted in old English, was stamped onto the hardhat and the chest of his hi-visibility vest.

Shutting off the side-by-side vehicle, the jobsite superior scrambled from the driver's seat, stood up in the back of the ATV's cargo box and picked up an electronic bullhorn. Clearing his throat, he continued in his high-pitched, rasping voice, "I want to welcome you all to Beta Mine A-2. First things first; I apologize about the train breakdown and the treacherous walk through the snow. The damn war left us with next to nothing, so we make do with what we have. My name is Ivan Orlofsky. I am one of the senior lead hands of this Metacom-owned Puranium mine. Secondly, are there any old hands amongst the bunch of you?"

Sam craned his neck to have a curious look around. A dozen or so men standing about raised their hands in sync, including his best friend, standing next to him, still retaining a bright, beaming face.

"Good," said Ivan, raising the volume of his voice to counteract the area's loud hisses and knocks. "Now, if I may ask that you gentlemen follow that man." He heaved a bony finger to another man on approach, also wearing bright and crisp PPE, stopping to lean casually against a large blue c-can. This man's work coveralls were covered in months' worth of hard labour tarnishes. Ivan carried on, "He is one of the field lead hands, and he will guide you to the abridged orientation."

Stopping once more to clear his throat and wait for Lester and the others to follow the secondary lead hand, he began once more: "As for the rest of you. I am sorry, I know you are tired from the arduous journey, but at this current time, we are pressed for time. Now if you will all follow me, I will lead you to the new admit orientation hall."

• • • •

A screaming headache drummed on Sam's temples from the inside whilst he occupied a seat at the farthest corner of the desk tables. For the first time in months, he truly felt alone. Even though he knew his good friend, Lester Morrissey, was only a stone's throw away in an adjacent orientation chamber, the dreadful feeling of abandonment consumed him. Being half a continent away from his home played a vital role in his newfound sense of bitter nostalgia.

Propping his chin up with his left hand, he kept his scouring gaze moving back and forth between the glass-interrupted view of a few hundred people at work in the main fabrication hangar, and the creases on the inside of his palm. While an old man up front addressed the group of novices, Sam envisioned the crisscross of his wrinkles as the Puranium mine tunnels, the visible green veins under the skin acting as the deeper recesses like a twisting maze of insect burrows.

"Now," half yelled the old man decked out in a pristine set of work coveralls. "This here ain't no coal mine, gentlemen. Ain't nothin' like that at all. We're well over a thousand feet deep. But now, here's the real tickler." He paused and flaunted a smile of crooked teeth, his crown of grey hair looking like a mini snow fortress guarding the shiny bald centre. "In any other regular mine, the deeper ya go, the warmer it usually gets. But not this here Beta mine. It seems the deeper we get, the colder too. Ain't that funny somethin', you might be sayin'. But no sir it ain't nothin' funny," he chuckled. "Nothin' funny at all. Somethin' to do with the natural cooling process for the Puranium, we ain't too sure. Anyhoo, you dare take off yer inhalation apparatus, and the sub-zero oxygen will burst the blood vessels in yer lungs in a matter of seconds—not minutes, fellers. So no matter how uncomfortable it gets, dontchu never take off that regulator. Now. Any questions?" Just over half of the assembly of newbies raised their hands in sync.

The first taste of life in the tunnels was the long walk to the barracks section of the partially underground centre of operations. The entire complex was built girdling a portion of the massive hole in the icy ground. Due to the extremities of the northern weather, Metacom—the company's name came from the Wampanoag warrior and leader of the 1600s—selected to build their military-style installation just below the ground, and keep all sectors connected through a heated tunnel system. Sam again trudged in line with the rest of the inexperienced workers, his slow-footed pace presenting no problems, as most of the men tramped along like they were back from their first 10-hour shift.

"Where's the rest of the fellas?" asked a young kid standing a few men aft of Sam. Too tired to twist his aching neck around, Sam could only picture a scrawny kid with horn-rimmed eyeglasses and a face speckled in acne, squeaky undertones breaking through his croaked speech like a mouse was caught in his throat.

"I unno mane, I think they done gone and jumped a head start of us. Since they was the onliest ones that already been worked here yet," replied another chap. Southern, Sam assumed silently. But not Texas, much too asinine and backroadish in the way he spoke, like his mother had let him drop out of homeschooling at the age of eight.

"Well I sure hope they come back to us. My good friend, Peter, is among the bunch, and he was the one who was going to show me the ropes," complained the teenage one. Sam agreed with the kid. Having someone like Lester working at his side was definitely a good thing. It was without a doubt that working deep underground was a dangerous occupation, especially if someone such as an untried kid, was to trigger an erroneous cave-in or worse yet.

"Don't getcher pannies in a wad, there young'un. Heck, if ya don't see your good friend no more, than y'always got me to look after ya. I done me some time in the old coal shafts of North Carolina. Ya seen one mine, ya seen em all," asserted the southern bloke. This brought a comical smile to Sam's face. The experienced mine worker hailed from the Appalachians, most likely. Deliverance country.

As the smooth, square-shaped hallway came to a reduced, narrowing point, a T-intersection branched off to the left and right, the perceivable endings impeded by the curve in the elongated corridor enshrouded in mirrored steel. One slat of crystal glass decorated the inner, mine-facing perimeter of the corridor, a shiny sign, pasted above the gash of window facing the junction reading: "Pit

Employee Dorms 100 – 200," with two arrow markers pointing to the left side of the crossroads. Sam stopped in the middle of the junction to partially observe the slit of window extending down the entirety of the curved wall, ignoring the few elbows that inadvertently brushed against his shoulder-slung duffels. Other men of the group seeing his nosy action, stopped too, and gawked out the thick window, some with their dirty hands smearing the immaculate stainless-steel lip.

Shielding his eyes from the onslaught of intense LED brilliance, Sam inched forward until the tender skin of his forehead was grazing the coldness of the window well's blunted rim. Squinting past the intense illumination, an unblemished view of the Puranium mineshaft came into full visibility. The work being performed inside the huge synthetic hole made the fabrication hangar look like a peaceful library. Massive trucks, most likely ethanol powered, with tires the size of a two-story house, travelled up and down on one of the many engineered roads carved into the steep sloped precipice. All roads were coated in a silvery substance. State of the art anti-slip varnish without a doubt. Concentrated inside the central chamber of the mile-wide hole, thick ropes of interwoven chains were connected to the Mammoth excavators, slowly lowering them down into the ceaseless abyss stretching out of Sam's direct field of view. Elevators and metal stairways, fused to one large central column, teemed with workers going up and down. A hum, like a thousand wasps trying to break their way through, jangled gently against the solid paned glass, the vibration from the outside work just a quiver in the water compared to what it must really sound like up close and personal.

Staring on at the infinite tendrils of steam and brown walls iced to a mirrored finish, a recurring, dreadful thought choked Sam's inner conscience. He wasn't home. He was far from home. His elegant home with views out to the golden horizon was replaced by an endless expanse of merciless ice, flesh-anaesthetizing air, and eternally grey skies, far from Texas warmth and luxury.

"If we can keep on moving, please, gentleman. Your rooms and hot showers await you," hollered yet another one of the company's supervisors that seemed in no short of supply.

At the mention of hot showers, a drum of pleased whispers set in motion through the now harmonized assembly of men, until the voices were torn apart and echoed by the steel walls no warmer than the frost from which they defended the interior corridors.

The blurry edges of Sam's exhausted attention was stolen like a jolt of vaporized caffeine had been pumped into his veins. Complete exhaustion was now just a suggestion of drowsiness as his eyes snapped open. Hot and shower were the keywords to this alleviation. For the past three weeks he had endured only bird baths aboard the cramped ship innards; exclusive privacy a completely disregarded characteristic of his new life.

Picking up his pace like the rest of the outlines of swaying men, Sam fished into his pockets and took out the key card with three numbers stamped into it. 188. The first door in sight read 100. He still had a way to go to find his room.

Besieged by an eclipse of blindness caused by the interior shaft's artificial stars, Sam's weary eyes surveyed his living quarters, the space-age door sliding automatically shut behind him. To his surprise, the manual workers' dormitory rooms were small, but comfortable. Prison-cell small with racked beds stacked up against the wall. A window with a privacy curtain was positioned above the tallest beds of the rack. Floors, as cold and glossy as a sheet of ice, rested below a lone throw rug. Two miniature desks were plastered to the opposite wall, with the chairs being the only objects that were movable.

Sam waddled to the bunks and tossed his two duffels to the bottom bed, seeing that both beds were still crisp and pressed like no one had ever slept in either of them.

"Oh, well, look who finally made it," said Lester, looking cleaned up, slinging a towel over his shoulder as he stepped out from a small door that blended into the metallic wall.

Sam jumped, nearly smacking his head into the stationary frame of the top bunk. "Shit, man. Where the hell did you come from?" he snapped, whirling around to face his friend.

"Finished up early so had a shower," Lester replied nonchalantly, rubbing his wet hair. He craned his neck to scan over Sam's head. "Oh, so I see you get the bottom bunk, huh? No worries, I prefer the top, window bed anyways."

• • • •

The innermost sectors of the mine shafts were cramped and murky. Their tangle of asymmetrical, jagged walls were dangerous enough to punch a devastating hole in the thermal suits if anyone was to accidentally swipe an uncaring shoulder across the surface—or perhaps trip and stumble. The manual labouring of a miner was nothing at all like Stan initially imagined. Instead of hot steam and warmth emanating from slits in the floors and walls, it was ice cold mists of crass green and sub-zero temperatures unbearable to any living being on Earth. Sam clung to a childhood fantasy to cope with his unfamiliar work environment. He repeated to himself, without words, that he was an astronaut on a distant moon, sent to discover a new substance to save Earth's people. However, as hard as he tried to rationalize, it offered little comfort. As he swung his ice-pick, a persistent gloominess hung over his thoughts like an everlasting storm cloud. Gloom rained over his conscience. He was nowhere close to being on a remote moon orbiting a grand planet formed of green gas, but he might as well have been. And he wasn't used to the work being performed, especially since he was inflexibly suited up like a spaceman from the age-old Sci-Fi books and magazines he was used to reading, not living. The safety suit was as stiff as a plastic. Nevertheless, the helmets were equipped with attached LED headlamps.

He took a moment from swinging away his government issued, diamond-tipped axe-pick to glance around him. The distant sight of the jagged wormhole was obscured by the accumulation of carbon dioxide condensation building up on the inside of his gasmask-like apparatus. A never-ending line of men toiled away at the frozen underground tundra, looking like seven hundred dwarfs labouring away in unison. Strings of bright, temporary lighting hung from the rigid ceiling of the pithead.

The jagged, oval-shaped tunnels, with barely enough room to set a full swinging strike in motion, were meant purely for the legions of hard labourers, while the Mammoth operators sat around in the grander tunnels or in the pit, reading books while waiting for their time of utility to come into play. The inner excavations, nearing the Puranium deposits, were deemed too fragile and unstable for the mighty Mammoth excavators.

Shortly after the primary find at the mine, a massive explosion was caused by the first Puranium prospectors burrowing carelessly with Chinese knockoff Mammoth machines. Luckily for the company at fault, they had only suffered a hundred or so casualties, a milestone back then compared to how many workers were now situated under and around each mineshaft. Since then, only Canadian-made Mammoths were in service.

Even with the ultramodern thermal suit worn tightly around his body, Sam still felt the sub-zero temperatures. Just barely. "Negative 70 degrees Celsius," said Lester in his Canadian farm boy accent, burning with an overgenerous smile before slipping into his thermal suit's inner comfort layers. "This be the kind of weather I used to go out and feed the cows in—wearing nothing but my slippers and housecoat." The ever-present, undying coldness beneath the ground, not like the heat a regular deep-rooted mine would impose, was a scientific anomaly directly connected to the Puranium and the layers of ground that kept it in its crystallized state for millions of undiscovered years.

An abnormal feeling, somehow connected to faint whispers drifting through the corridor along with the perpetual mist, captured Sam's wandering thoughts. He instinctively reached for the back of his helmet and foolishly began to undo the safety fastener, hoping for a clearer listen. But then he abruptly regained his senses. A shiver of recollection coursed through him, evoking memories of the old man who had conducted the safety orientation. "You dare remove your inhalation apparatus, and the sub-zero oxygen will rupture the blood vessels in your lungs within seconds, not minutes, fellas. So, no matter how uncomfortable it gets, never take off that regulator." The old man's words were like bible verses. Lifesaving bible verses.

Sam re-secured his helmet and was about to get back to work, feeling as though he had wasted enough time in daydream land. And then nature called. An ill-timed event by all means. It wasn't the worst that could happen, but it was something that didn't sit too well with Sam.

The latrine chamber was exactly what it sounded like. A hand-carved dugout positioned just past the primary entrance tunnel, isolated by thick, pewter-infused cloth strips with a state-of-the-art electric heater situated in the centre. Past the halfway point to the twenty-second century, and the only bathroom facilities in the deep mines oper-ated more like a medieval dungeon setting—with a mod-ernized heater. The smell of frozen death and raw sewage greeted every man who marched by the latrine chamber, let alone having to use the facility, en route to their predes-tined section of the mines, the smell filtering right through their cold-air sieves.

"What's up, guy?" asked Lester, his headlamp radiance popping out between two men down the line, his own face shield slightly fogged up. His voice came out crackly and distorted like he was speaking through a hoary telephone with a frayed line.

"I gotta piss, man," said Sam, his own mask of conden-sation concealing his sour-faced expression. More than just the bathroom was on his mind. Everything from the hate of his new life to the despair of being away from his wife and home had him badgered.

A mocking laugh, and then, "Well you know where the latrine level is. Don't get lost now."

Behind his fogged-up face shield, Sam flashed a sneer at his friend before scuttling up the stone-cold dirt surface.

Overworked arms already feeling like frozen rub-ber, Sam swayed up the jagged flooring of the squared-off cave, taking extra caution not to roll his ankle on the diamond-hard bristles of the spacious passageway. He scoffed at the lack of safety measures put in place around the prickly flooring, such as zero hand railings. What about wooden planking? he wondered.

At last, after what seemed like twenty minutes of trot-ting up a spiky, uphill gradient, he knew he was in close proximity to the latrine by the sickly, yellow hovering mists.

He was more than thankful for his breathing apparatus knocking out most of the potential smell before it had a chance to clout his nose. A sickly gold stream, thick with slivers of putrid ice, trickled down the deliberately notched sideline trenches of the manmade burrow as he stumbled like a drunk down the scarcely lit gangway. In contrast to the rough terrain found in the rest of the network of underpasses, this particular section of flooring stood out for its unusual smoothness. It was possible that this smoothness had been intentionally designed for safety or had simply resulted from the countless footsteps of workers who had hurriedly traversed this path on their way to the latrine chamber.

Sam pushed aside the second set of safety curtains, ducked inside, and immediately peeled off his sweaty helmet. Even amidst the putrid stench of decomposing fester, shit, and piss, the high humidity felt relatively good. Sam tweezered his nose closed while relieving himself, closing his eyes and putting himself somewhere warm and humid, such as his home in southeast Texas. Memories, of the cavern he and his chums had found while cliff diving on Galveston Island before the war, swarmed his weather-beaten brain. For a split second, he was back home.

The fantasy ran short, just as another man stumbled into the corrugated chamber, tossed off his helmet and stripped down, not caring that he had a small audience of one. Sam knew what was next. He did not want to witness a fellow worker go number 2, caveman style. He finished pissing and picked up his helmet, ambling his way out of the brightly lit, fetid bathroom hollow constructed to resemble a Stone Age dwelling.

A well-crafted sign hung directly above the initial set of exit curtains, firmly secured into the tundra. It read: "Do Not Forget: Your Helmet and Breathing Apparatus Mean The

Difference Between Life and Death." Just like that, Sam had almost forgotten to replace his helmet in his quick haste to leave the men's room. A slow, wheezing death would have been in store for him as the minus 70 degree Celsius air, just past the safety curtains, transformed the fleshy air pockets in his lungs into pouches of instant ice.

Sam took one last clearing step past the secondary set of curtains dangling like frozen strips of meat and stopped to have a listen before securing his helmet. The hints of coolness seeping into the mini atrium had a sound. A peculiar sound, like nothing he had ever heard. It was like holding his breath, and swimming to the bottom of a deep pool, then floating there, letting his ears try to catch onto any distant sounds. Almost.

Helmet secured, he was ready to get back to work, stepping through the primary curtains, when he felt the smallest sliver of a shake rumble beneath his feet. He stopped dead, his partly restricted ears straining to hear over his ragged breathing. What the hell was that? he wondered. The air seemed to become quiet, the constant buzz of an unseen mining mechanism stalling and leaving nothing but the hollow ambiance like a long, circular tube running through a frozen lake.

"It's nothing," he reassured to himself, his crackly, electronic voice rebounding eerily off the frozen walls. "Nothing but my imagination acting up in this faraway land." He inhaled a lungful of the apparatus-made air, right away noticing the spike in warmth as beads of sweat began to drizzle down his forehead, the Plexiglas face shield fogging up as he exhaled.

"What the f—"

KABOOOOM!

Sam's jabbering was cut off, as the faint rumbling escalated into a full-blown volcanic earthquake. The powerful tremors dislodged frozen soil, causing it to crumble from the walls and ceiling. In a matter of seconds, the temperature skyrocketed by at least 40 degrees Celsius, rising with each breath he took. Realizing it was safe to do so, thanks to the sudden surge in heat, Sam unfastened his helmet and removed it. Beads of sweat now formed a steady stream down his face.

Finally, his terror was unmistakable. An intense inferno, of yellow, red, orange, and, in the end, a brilliant green fireball engulfed the tunnels directly in front of him. He was swept off his feet and hurled into the unyielding wall.

END
EXCLUSIVE EXCERPT
FROM
THUNDER AMIDST THE STARS

To read the rest of the book,
stay tuned for its release...

OTHER TITLES IN THE DURVILE
SPIRIT OF NATURE SERIES
SERIES EDITORS: RAYMOND YAKELEYA & LORENE SHYBA

PUBLISHING AUTHORS WHO HAVE THE FORESIGHT TO BRING NEW KNOWLEDGE TO THE WORLD

THE TREE BY THE WOODPILE
By Raymond Yakeleya
ISBN: 9781988824031

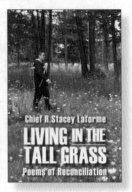

LIVING IN THE TALL GRASS
By Chief R. Stacey Laforme
ISBN: 9781988824055

LILLIAN & KOKOMIS THE SPIRIT OF DANCE
By Lynda Partridge
ISBN: 9781988824277

WE REMEMBER THE COMING OF THE WHITE MAN
Eds. Stewart & Yakeleya
ISBN: 9781988824246

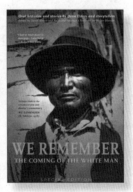

WE REMEMBER SPECIAL EDITION
Eds. Stewart & Yakeleya
ISBN: 9781988824635

STORIES OF METIS WOMEN
Eds. Oster & Lizee
ISBN: 9781988824215

ⓕ FOLLOW US ON FACEBOOK "DURVILEANDUPROUTE"

DURVILE IS A PROUD CANADIAN INDIE PUBLISHER.
DISTRIBUTED BY UNIVERSITY OF TORONTO PRESS (UTP) IN CANADA
AND NATIONAL BOOK NETWORK (NBN) IN THE US AND THE UK.

OTHER TITLES IN THE DURVILE
SPIRIT OF NATURE SERIES

VISIT DURVILE.COM
OR CLICK THE QR CODE FOR
MORE INFO ON THESE TITLES

SIKSIKAITSITAPI: STORIES
OF THE **BLACKFOOT PEOPLE**
By Payne Many Guns *et al*
ISBN: 9781988824833

WHY ARE YOU STILL
HERE?: A LILLIAN MYSTERY
By Lynda Partridge
ISBN: 9781988824826

NAHGANNE TALES OF THE
NORTHERN SASQUATCH
By Red Grossinger
ISBN 9781988824598

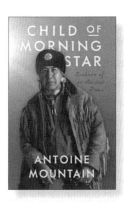
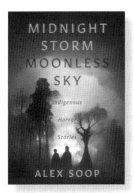

CHILD OF MORNING STAR
EMBERS OF AN **ANCIENT DAWN**
By Antoine Mountain
ISBN: 9781990735103

MIDNIGHT STORM
MOONLESS SKY
By Alex Soop
ISBN: 9781990735127

THE RAINBOW, THE
SONGBIRD & THE MIDWIFE
By Raymond Yakeleya
ISBN: 9781988824574

A percentage of publisher's proceeds and author royalties have been donated to: The Food Bank, Calgary and Bracebridge; Oldman Watershed Council, Stargate Women's Group; Esquao Institute for the Advancement of Aboriginal Women: CFWEP Clark Fork Watershed Environment Project; Chytomo: Support for Ukrainian Literature and Book Publishers; "Home In Our Hearts" for Ukrainian Evacuees; The Canada Ukraine Foundation; Doctors Without Borders; The Elizabeth Yakeleya Fund; Calgary Communities Against Sexual Abuse; The Canadian Women's Foundation; The Salvation Army; (MMIWG) Missing and Murdered Indigenous Women and Girls; Days for Girls International; Red Door Family Shelter, Toronto; Ikwe-Widdjiitiwin Family Shelter, Winnipeg; The Schizophrenia Society of Canada; and the Elizabeth Fry Society.

ABOUT THE AUTHOR

ALEX SOOP

Alex Soop of the Niisitapi Blackfoot Confederacy
authentically voices his stories from First Nations
Peoples' perspective. While striving to entertain with
his bloodcurdling tales, Alex also integrates issues that
plague Indigenous Peoples of North America. These
specific issues include alcohol abuse, systemic racism,
missing and murdered Indigenous women and girls,
and residential school after-effects. He also incorporates
stories from Indigenous traditional knowledge, such as
folklore, ghostly spirits, and the afterlife. Alex's urban
home is Calgary and his ancestral home is the Kainai
(Blood) Nation of southern Alberta, Canada.